S

Storm over Land and Sea

a thriller

Book 2

Legends of the Winged Scarab

INGE H. BORG

Author of

KHAMSIN, The Devil Wind of The Nile

(Book 1)

Cover

This is a Work of Fiction.

* * *

* * *

With gratitude to my friend Jo Cryder,

who would not let me quit.

* * *

CONTENTS

Cover Painting

Rembrandt's *The Storm on the Sea of Galilee* (1633), with an alternate title of *Christ in the Storm on the Lake of Galilee*, was purchased by Isabella Stewart Gardner in 1898. Mrs. Gardner left her art collection to Boston's Isabella Stewart Gardner Museum.

On March 18, 1990, audacious thieves disguised as museum guards broke into the museum and cut several paintings from their frames. To date, not one of these irreplaceable works of art has been recovered.

If you have any knowledge of the whereabouts of the Rembrandt or any of the other stolen paintings, please call the authorities or the Museum. A reward has been issued for the successful recovery of this and the other works of art stolen from the Isabella Stewart Gardner Museum in Boston, Massachusetts.

* * *

Prologue

Trexa! Sorokos!"

Barely, the fishermen pull their boats onto shore when the storm arrives all in a rush, malevolent and laden with Libyan Desert sand.

"Run! *Sirocco!*" Again, the men cry the warning against the feared wind that had spawned over the Sahara. After giving birth to its unbridled son Khamsin, the Devil Wind of the Nile, it froths the waters of the Mediterranean and mercilessly claws at the islands in its path, scything the coastal shrub into stubble.

The old women of Crete call it The Big Tongue. Innocent-looking at first, a lazy yellow haze comes drifting north. It grows larger, turning the air into choking ochre mist. Its hot breath churns the sea and drives salt spray deep into the island's interior. As if on cue, tempers turn sour and people suddenly find fault with friend and neighbor. Fights erupt over nothing. Secretly harbored thoughts of suicide and murder attack the mind as voraciously as wild goats strip young plane trees bare. All things bad can now be blamed on the *Sirocco*.

It is only when the cool steady *meltemia* breezes blow again out of the northwest that the island breathes a sigh of relief, and much is forgiven.

* * *

Naunet listens to the little bird chirp so sweetly, and a half-forgotten poem momentarily calms her racing heart. It reminds her of the *Ba-bird* which, in Ancient Egypt, was believed to be a sinner's soul returning to earth to find atonement for its transgressions against *Ma'at*.

The sudden breeze tugs fiercely at her dark flowing hair, and at her tears. Its enervating whistle relentless now, the *Sirocco* drowns out the little bird's valiant efforts. With her mind in utter turmoil, she wonders if her own *Ba* was destined to lose itself on this windswept island.

Robbed of all reasonable thought, Naunet sobs the High Priest's words into the fierce wind. The *Sirocco* rears up and tears them from her lips, and flings them out over the roiling waters. The steep cliff eerily echoes her despair. Yet, with a last ray of hope, she clings to the ancient wisdom that *the end is but a new beginning for the eternal soul.*

* * *

Part I - The Challenge

Chapter One

For you, my Nefertiti." With a boyish grin, the young scientist handed his exotic colleague a bouquet of fragrant tea roses. He was like that, always doing something nice for her. She really did like Jonathan.

The murmur around the Institute was that Jonathan was rather fond of the striking Egyptologist. The two of them laughed at the good-natured insinuations. They were friends. They had a supportive professional relationship. They were comfortable together. And they respected each other.

On occasional weekends, Jonathan might invite her up to Marblehead where she stayed as a guest at his parents' home. The two spent those carefree days mostly sailing. Jonathan never suspected that Naunet returned home to Boston invigorated, but also very grateful for dry stable land.

"Hurry up," he laughed while she pushed her laptop aside to make room for the vase. "We don't want to be late."

Dr. Naunet Klein, Senior Institute Research Fellow and well-respected Egyptologist, and Jonathan Wilkins, Institute Fellow for Research and a doctoral candidate in Materials Science at MIT, hurried along the sun-lit corridor for the ten o'clock meeting with their boss.

If there was one thing Dr. Bruno von der Heide insisted on, it was punctuality. The sixty-four-year-old Director of The Cambridge

Research Institute for Antiquities, located around the corner from Harvard University, insisted on other things as well, such as excellence and dedication. 'He's German,' new hires were forewarned even though Dr. von der Heide, a naturalized US citizen, referred to himself as an American.

The weekly Monday morning updates also included Dr. William Jefferson Browning, the Institute's sixty-year-old Head of Research, who was never on time. 'Occupational hazard,' the Einstein-maned scientist decreed when someone suggested that he might think about installing an alarm clock in his lab.

As Naunet and Jonathan entered the Institute's inner sanctum, their boss was pacing behind his massive desk restrained only by the long cord of the old-fashioned instrument. The receiver was pressed to his ear as if it had been super-glued there. The two hesitated but he urged them in with his free hand.

"Oh, God! You didn't," he cried into the receiver and then added quietly, "Yes, I will take care of it. Of course. Consider it done." After listening to the party on the other end, he added, "Have a good evening," and, clamping the receiver back onto its black cradle, he sat down heavily.

Naunet and Jonathan looked at each other, and Jonathan shrugged his shoulders and mouthed to her *good evening*?

"Unbelievable," their boss cried and slapped the burgundy leather inlay of his desk so hard that a pair of scissors clattered to the floor.

Naunet feared something might have happened on her boss's home front. Luisa von der Heide had a bit of a reputation of being difficult. Or perhaps he had received bad news from relatives in Germany, now that she remembered his *good evening*.

"What's wrong, Dr. Bruno?" she asked.

Bill Browning was the only one to call the elegant man solely by his first name, and then it was mostly in private. For those who had earned the privilege, *Dr. Bruno* was permitted. The Director's imperturbable calm was as much admired as his knowledge was revered in and outside the Institute. Therefore, the unaccustomed outburst was startling. Nothing short of a severely damaged piece of antiquity would rattle the Prussian-born aristocrat, who had spent his previous twenty-four years as the much respected Curator of the Egyptian Department at the Museum of Fine Arts in Boston.

His wife, the former Luisa Klammer, had been a minor actress in East Germany. When numerous film makers and actors fled the GDR as a result of restrictions on their work, she was one of them. After his own harrowing escape from East Berlin, Bruno von der Heide met and married her in West Berlin. In 1975, Bruno and Luisa decided to move to the United States when he was offered the curatorial position in Boston.

After several years, the couple managed to purchase a demure brownstone house on Marlborough Street where Luisa became known as an engaging hostess who happily held court telling anyone willing to listen about her former life as a celebrated German film star. Now, due to Dr. Bruno's more exalted yet academically less fulfilling directorship at the Institute, they were looking to move to a house on Brattle Street in Cambridge across the Charles River—not exactly a shabby address either. Luisa was not easily pleased and the search took longer than her busy husband had hoped it would. The intriguing phone call from overseas, he feared, had just cut his spare time in half.

Jonathan pulled two chairs up to the mahogany desk. He left the third chair where it was and wondered what was keeping Bill Browning this time.

Finally, Jonathan could not stand it any longer. He had to ask. "Did we hear you say *have a good evening?*"

"Dinner time in Cairo," Bruno von der Heide smirked. "You won't believe who that was."

"God?" Jonathan ventured, always fast on the uptake. "Or, may we at least hope Moses? We could use a miracle right now from either one. With their escalating unrest, Cairo might have second thoughts about shipping the Narmer pieces. And there go all the hours of our hard negotiations. Down the drain."

Jonathan's diction was pure upper class New England without sounding affected. His family was rather well-to-do, Boston-speak for coming-from-old-money. Ensconced on a multi-chimney estate overlooking the Atlantic, the parents could have easily supported their handsome heir to do nothing but show off his moxie in and out of Marblehead Harbor where he skippered his father's forty-two-foot black-hulled classic Hinckley sloop. They were true New Englanders though, and Jonathan had been taught thriftiness and respect. His father had turned him into an excellent sailor, and the son became sought-after crew on the annual Newport-to-Bermuda races. He also accompanied his mother often enough to social gatherings for the boy to grow into an engaging young man. Any Junior League mother would have gladly propelled her daughter toward the altar with this husband-worthy prize. Naturally, he was expected to follow in his father's footsteps. The venerable Boston State Street law firm's letterhead had intentionally left space to add the names of well-groomed junior partners from good families.

Jonathan's own plans had lain elsewhere. Harvard Law School, his father's alma mater, was not for him. His interests lay in science. He was good at it. To his parents' surprise, he chose Georgia Tech and their excellent School of Materials Science and Engineering, where he specialized in nanotechnology. After a few years around archaeological sites, he finally enrolled at MIT, and now hoped to complete his doctorate by year's end. While he had several women friends there was no steady girl that anyone knew of.

The Director looked at his lanky assistant with a rare mischievous grin. "You are almost spot-on, Jonathan. While it was not God or Moses," he glanced from Naunet back to Jonathan, "it was someone almost as powerful. That, my dears, was *The Pharaoh* himself."

"Jabari El-Masri?" Naunet mouthed.

Jonathan moaned, "I knew it. They are canceling."

"Nothing of the kind." Dr. Bruno grinned again. He enjoyed their eager young faces.

"You two better pack your bags. I hope your passports are in order. Especially yours, Naunet. You really should apply for citizenship, you know. You've been here, what, twelve years now. I assume you want to stay in this country."

"Uh-oh." Jonathan rolled his eyes. "Here comes the citizenship talk."

It was a frequent topic between the two. As he wanted them back on the main issue, he quickly added, "Oh, now Cairo is putting the pieces on some decrepit old freighter. Do they want us to baby-sit the shipment?"

"Just hope they'll stuff us in a crate full of tennis balls as well. In case the old tub sinks."

Naunet recalled her early museum days when artifacts were sent overseas packed in tennis balls. Of course, there was a Spanish fresco that had arrived smeared with green cheese. Amazingly, the gift of the goat had sealed in vital moisture and the museum lab was able to restore the beautiful artwork almost to its original splendor. To this very day, she refused green-marbled cheesy condiments sprinkled on her salads.

Seeing Egypt again was exciting news for Naunet. It was her maternal homeland where her soul and her passion lay deeply buried in the sand. At the same time, she felt apprehensive to being close to the Red Sea.

Naunet had inherited her height and blue eyes from her Austrian father, Leopold. Her voluptuous mouth and exotic features came from her Egyptian mother, Akila. Leopold still made the professional papers as an archeologist, mostly in Turkey now. Years ago, he had led Crete's initial excavation for Minoan artifacts on Mount Ida at Zominthos which lay nestled in a plateau at four thousand feet, close to the sacred Ideon Cave. The legends insisted that it was the birthplace of Zeus.

Akila had gained respect as a marine biologist even before she met and married Leopold. From an early age, she was inspired by the pioneering ichthyologist Dr. Eugenie Clark, and strove to follow in the footsteps of that diminutive scientist who had not let a man's world stand in her way, nor the failure of her five short-lived marriages. Red Sea reefs were a favorite dive site where she dove with Jacques Cousteau and swam with sharks. Well in her eighties now, Dr. Clark was still on the lecture circuit around American universities and aquariums.

Because of Akila Klein's love of the water, she had named her only daughter after a mythical goddess of the sea. Unappeased by the gesture, the Red Sea nevertheless had claimed Akila's life. During a cave dive near Safaga, she had become separated from her dive partner. They never found her body.

After Naunet's undergraduate work at Vienna's Institute for Egyptology, she studied for her doctorate at Humbolt University in Berlin.

It was during that time that she acquired the nickname 'Nefertiti.' Secretly, she preferred a queen's name to that of the vengeful sea goddess, especially when more than one wise guy had wagged his finger at her, grinning sheepishly: 'No, no, Nanette.' Some fool or other had even added a suggestive wink.

Specializing in the translation of hieratic scripts from the Old Kingdom, the cursive writing developed alongside the more formal hieroglyphic system, Naunet spent several months in Egypt. She had briefly met Dr. Jabari El-Masri on a Saqqara dig of First Kingdom *mastabas*. Then Director of the Giza Plateau, the animated man lectured hordes of eager interns hanging on his every proclamation. Naunet doubted that he would remember her after all these years. Quite possibly, he had not even noticed her then, surrounded as he constantly was by young followers all vying to attract his attention. Some had, of course, though not necessarily by their academic brilliance.

At thirty-seven, Naunet was a striking woman who might have been called intriguingly exotic had it not been for her almost innocent blue eyes. Her brilliant smile should have brought more than one suitor down on his knee. After a few love affairs and other brief interludes though, Naunet's professional passion was winning out. Over the years, finding love or marriage inched further from her mind, as well as her heart. She prized her comfortable life and the privacy of her brownstone apartment in the middle of Boston's humming Kenmore Square. Decorated with items from Austria, several excellent small Persian rugs and New England antiques, it somehow retained a distinct Viennese flavor. Curiously, there were no Egyptian artifacts, nor their beautiful museum copies. Only rows of books on hieroglyphic research. And, always, there were fresh flowers.

"All right, you two, listen up." Dr. von der Heide tapped his index finger against his desk.

His two assistants sat up straight. He had that effect on his staff.

"It's still on then?" Jonathan just wanted to make sure.

It had taken the Institute over a year to get the provisional Egyptian military rulers to permit the loan exhibit to travel to the States. More importantly, the illustrious and on-and-off powerful Minister of Antiquities, the very same Dr. Jabari El-Masri, had at last agreed to a shipment of newly-discovered pieces that supposedly came from the First Dynasty king Narmer—minus the priceless Palette, of course. There were also several pieces, El-Masri's office had hinted, from the second Horus-king, Aha.

The Institute was to conduct in-depth dating and materials analysis with their new laser. After that, the pieces were to go on display during an already much-publicized loan exhibit at the Boston MFA. Neither Dr. Bruno, nor Jonathan or Naunet would have been eager to break bad news about a cancelled shipment to Bingham Adams, the Museum's illustrious director, and their former boss.

Bruno von der Heide nodded distractedly. "Yes, yes, it's on. They are shipping."

"So, why did *The Pharaoh* call himself? He always had us deal with his minions." Naunet, just like Jonathan, was still apprehensive about the unusual call.

"Because they want more money," Jonathan declared flat out.

Loans to other museums, while wrought with headaches and worries, were nevertheless lucrative for the lending institution; unless something went awry during transit or while on display. Insuring these objects had become prohibitive if not impossible. Lending them out was therefore a risk many institutions were no longer willing to take.

Dr. Bruno smirked. "His call had nothing to do with the Narmer pieces. You see, Jabari and I met at Penn in eighty-three. I was there to have my German doctorate recertified, and Jabari was getting his M.A." He paused and nodded to Naunet. "That's where I met your father too. Of course, he had already left when Jabari got there."

"His M.A.? I thought El-Masri got his doctorate at U-Penn," Naunet said.

"He did. But that was some years later. In eighty-seven, I believe."

"So, what about Dr. El-Masri's call?" Jonathan could not care less who got what doctorate when. He wanted to know what the call was all about. *Really, there are times when the boss can be infuriatingly obtuse.*

"The great man just admitted to me, if you please, that I run the best research lab in the world." Dr. Bruno sat back in his chair, hand crossed over his chest, as if ready to accept their accolades.

"And so you do," Jonathan agreed and bowed toward his boss. Then he added, "Of course, that's in no small part due to the PELL."

His boss forgave him with a benign smile. It was true. A British facility had come up with the Portable Extreme Light Laser—the

PELL, among physicists. It produced an intense light beam equivalent to the power received by the earth from the sun. Focused onto a speck smaller than the tip of a pin, it was capable of nano-millimeter precision. It could cut into any material without destroying even the smallest particle of what was underneath by creating a 'vacuum fabric,' which it then pulled apart. Most importantly, it was portable. The Institute had been given a prototype to analyze priceless antiquities. Harvard's Peabody Museum as well as the Boston Museum had agreed to provide trial materials from their stored items. It had been infinitely more difficult to persuade the Egyptians to let them test some of the newly unearthed Narmer pieces.

"Let's get back to what you just said about Naunet and me to pack our bags," Jonathan reminded his boss.

Naunet simply asked, "When?"

"He said he needs you ASAP. Would Wednesday be too early?" Which meant, Wednesday it was.

"Do we need visas? I have no idea what their current policies are," Jonathan, the ever-practical one, wondered.

"You'll get your ninety-day visas upon arrival. Anyway, Jabari is smoothing the entry formalities for you."

"I trust that we won't be there for the whole three months. Precisely, what are we supposed to do for him?" Jonathan was still far from jumping onto some nebulous bandwagon.

"You are literally, and I mean physically, to uncover whatever it is they dug up. Actually, they retrieved the objects from their storage rooms. Apparently, they are encased in some kind of insoluble unguent. He is afraid they will damage the writing underneath the black pitch. That's where you come in, Naunet. To decipher possibly pre-dynastic writing etched into the gold. It is all quite secretive."

Naunet was perplexed. "How do they know there is writing underneath if these objects are covered up?"

"And how do they know it's carved on gold?" Jonathan added.

Dr. Bruno's face turned red again. "They broke a large corner off one of the pieces."

"Ah, that explains why you were somewhat perturbed when we came in." Jonathan stretched his long legs and slouched lower in his seat.

"How does one break a corner off a slab of gold?" Naunet could just imagine Dr. El-Masri's wrath swooping down like a vengeful Seth on the unfortunate researcher who had committed the unspeakable. "I can't believe Dr. El-Masri and his assistants can't do the job themselves, especially if it's to be kept quiet? The Cairo Museum has a great lab. I know. I've been in it."

"They already tried everything, Jabari told me. The stuff won't come off. Also, it is too big a job. He no longer has enough trustworthy people around. He prefers that we take this one on." Bruno von der Heide noticed the lingering doubt in their faces. He quickly added, "There will be bonuses..." He could see that his last statement did nothing to make them jump at the opportunity. So he added, "Jabari really needs our help. He has some bigger problems to deal with at the moment."

"Such as having been too closely associated with his ousted president? I'd like to know how the interim military guys feel about *The Pharaoh* and his autocratic rule over all of Egypt's antiquities." Jonathan did not expect an answer. His focus was back on his own priorities. "What about our own research here on the exhibit pieces?"

Jonathan's expertise was the composition of unknown ancient materials. Gold no longer held any challenge for the thirty-two year old. Prior to his doctoral studies at MIT, he had spent a couple of months as a research fellow at the Department of History and Archaeology of the University of Cyprus. Never one to miss an opportunity, he had then sailed over to Crete where he had met Naunet's father, although he never ran into the eminent archaeologist's striking daughter even though she had been on the island. If he had, he doubted that the sophisticated twenty-five-year-old daughter of the prominent Dr. Leopold Klein would have noticed a twenty-year-old student just having dropped in for a look-around. Then, both Naunet and her father had suddenly left Crete due to her mother's diving accident near Safaga, Egypt. Jonathan liked the Mediterranean and planned to go back one day on another bareboat charter, perhaps to sail from the Turkish coast directly to Crete, an island of great interest to him.

"The exhibit doesn't open until December, Jonathan. That is a long way off. Jabari needs you there now. For a couple of weeks, max. He wants Bill to come too."

"Oh, darn! We'll have a chaperone." Jonathan patted the back of Naunet's hand resting on her thigh.

Bruno von der Heide sighed. This travel request might not be well received by his independent Head of Research. The crusty old bachelor was a proud and at times stubborn man. Over the last twenty-odd years, he had built up the Boston Museum's laboratory into a widely renowned research and restoration center. As one of the last descendants of a Founding Father, he was rumored still to be eating off the original Jefferson silver. Now completely immersed in his work at the Institute, he could be a bit touchy when someone meddled with his timetable—even if it was his boss. However, what an excited Jabari El-Masri had just told his old college friend was too important to consider Bill's aversion to foreign travel. Besides, tourists should be far and few between, because of the current political upheaval and because Cairo, right now, was an oven.

The story went that after a vacation trip to Europe, Bill was overheard to complain at a museum board meeting, that 'Florence would have been great, except for all those tourists.' At which point another member of the old Boston establishment, one of the illustrious Cabots, had supposedly remarked, 'And what the hell did you think you were, Bill!' It had provided a rare snicker for the thirty-plus trustees. Over time, their meetings had become more terse than academic, and they welcomed any morsel of good humor thrown their way.

What a relief, Bruno von der Heide thought, *that those days of endless curatorial and administrative meetings are behind me.* Being the curator of a museum department used to be a pleasant and rewarding job, if one knew one's stuff. Then things had changed.

Bingham Adams, the seemingly forever museum director, was affable and well liked. An artist himself, he was an excellent judge of a good brushstroke. There was a saying among the crusty old Bostonians. 'Before you invite Bingham to dinner, lock up all of your Singer Sargents.'

More often than not, Adams would walk out of one of those patrician brownstone homes encircling Louisburg Square on Beacon Hill with a host's unplanned contribution of a stern forefather gazing from his gilded frame.

While this was great for the collections and the museum's

standing in the art world, it became painfully clear that Adams sorely lacked in administrative talents. The venerable institution's cash flow was in dire straights. The board elected a new president. George Searing, the business-savvy fifty-six-year-old CEO of a fertilizer company, was thick-set, demanding and utterly impervious to the tender psyches of the art world. He scythed and bullied the Grande Old Dame back into the black. Bingham Adams and his curators hated him.

The financial upheaval had not immediately affected Bruno von der Heide, or his department. Still, like many of his colleagues, he saw the writing on the wall; and it was not in hieroglyphics. When he was offered greater professional and financial freedom at the new Research Institute, he accepted. He also persuaded Bill Browning to join him; as did Naunet and Jonathan. They had liked working with Dr. Bruno at the Museum. And they liked working with him now as they had always appreciated his mostly low-interference style. However, if someone were to cause damage to a precious art object, Dr. Bruno—usually a calm and civil gentleman—had no qualms to slam into the unfortunate perpetrator like a German wrecking ball.

After an initial coolness about perceived disloyalty, the shunned Museum soon cooperated with the Institute on projects which required specialized research and the expenditure of significant sums of money.

The new Institute's main funding came from one of Silicon Valley's new billionaire whiz kids, Richard *Hobo* Percy. A long-haired California surfer turned collector, *Hobo* had developed a keen interest in the research and dating of antiquities and chose Cambridge, Massachusetts, over California laboratories to sprinkle some spare millions. He had made it clear to a naturally delighted Dr. Bruno that exciting new projects would unquestionably find his ear and his deep pockets.

Bruno von der Heide smiled. That phone call from his old friend certainly fit into the 'exciting and new' categories.

"We need to admire Jabari's zeal to keep research and treasures within his own country," he told his assistants.

"That endeavor," Naunet said, "has unfortunately resulted in making him some enemies in the international art community. To his credit though, he managed almost single-handedly to have many of

Egypt's national treasures returned by their former looters, his preferred view of most of the world. At present, he is working on Berlin to hand over their famous Nefertiti; so far without success."

Jonathan almost added that it was never going to happen. The Germans were an obstinate people. Given his boss's origins, he thought better of it. Naturalized citizenship went only so far with the born aristocrat.

Dr. Bruno's thoughts had already jumped to the future. For a non-Egyptian facility to be invited to work on a new discovery was a great honor. It could also be a financial asset. No matter how comfortable things were at present, the Institute's Director needed to think ahead. Fortunes came and went, especially in California's dot-com environment. Should the Institute ever need funding from another source, every research success was an additional bargaining chip with potential new investors.

"Naunet, can you make sure we have the necessary paperwork for all the research pieces? Adams needs to present the completed indexes to the upcoming meeting of their Committee of the Collections. His board still has to authorize the loan exhibit formally." Bruno von der Heide stood up and shook his head. "I hope he doesn't get the axe before then."

"Why? I thought things were going great right now."

"Searing is like an elephant."

"Elephant is right. And by that I mean as in china-shop." Jonathan remembered the massive lay-offs and budget cuts that had affected several of his former colleagues at the MFA. Who knew what would have happened to him if he had not quit and joined the Institute.

"Well, I rather meant that he does not forget past infractions," Dr. Bruno explained. "He has it in for Adams as he still blames him for almost running the Museum into the ground, financially. It has become personal between the two. We all need this exhibit to come off without a hitch. Anyway, I think you two better get packing."

"Yes sir, right away," Jonathan saluted and sauntered out the door.

Naunet stayed behind, hesitating. "I was thinking, Dr. Bruno. My father is back on a dig in southern Crete. I'd love to take a couple of days afterwards to stop over and see him. It's practically on the way."

"Really? And what is my old friend Leopold up to now?"

"He is visiting an interesting Neolithic site in Kommos, where the McPeals are working on a dig."

"By Jove! Josef McPeal? He got his doctorate at U-Penn as well."

"You know him?"

"Yes, of course. Not very well, mind you. Still, I have met both Josef and his charming wife Mary. Interesting couple, those two. Completely dedicated to their work on Crete. If memory serves me right, they have been there since the mid-seventies. Do give them my very best, when you see them."

So it was settled. She could go. It might not be very professional, but she gave her boss a quick hug. The virile man did not object at all.

Dr. Bruno really did not want to see his delightful and capable assistant gone longer than necessary. Of course, he realized that she had not asked for vacation time since starting work at the Institute. Who had, he thought. Perhaps after the work for the MFA, he should take a couple of weeks off himself. He and Luisa might go back to Germany and visit relatives.

He smiled. "I am sending you on vacation with two men and you want to add another?"

Naunet knew he was just giving her a hard time. As coquettish as she could, she smiled at him. "You are sending the sacrificial—ah—lamb to the offering basin with a boy and an old man." She was glad she had stopped herself from saying 'sacrificial virgin.' You never knew with Dr. Bruno whether he was in the mood for supercilious jokes or not. Still, his sharp reaction surprised her.

"Naunet, the *boy* is thirty-two years old. Don't toy with him. And don't underestimate him either. I assume it hasn't completely escaped your attention that he is infatuated with you." After a brief pause, he smiled and added, "Not that I blame him."

Naunet opened her mouth a second too late to protest. The agile sixty-four-year-old was already out the door, on his way to break the news to the Institute's Head of Research. The request for Bill's precious laser should be one of the main reasons to persuade the crusty *old* man to make the trip. Bruno von der Heide only hoped that the *boy* and the exotic Naunet would concentrate their energies on their exciting tasks ahead.

For a brief moment, he felt a twinge of conscience. He had not told his two assistants what else El-Masri had confided in him. Jabari had seethed over the telephone that he had been given to understand that the gold from the tablets would come in handy to finance the interim military government's outlays. This apparently included funds for the upcoming presidential elections. Listening between the lines, so to speak, Bruno realized that most likely, given Egypt's current political climate, Jabari had been ordered not to sell the tablets off as well-documented art treasure to high bidding museums; but to have them melted down into untraceable nuggets to be sold to dubious buyers. His only hope of saving them was to have them cleaned and translated. Then he could approach *National Geographic* to make a film about them. Jabari then counted on the world's art community to unify behind him and his efforts to preserve them.

Bruno decided not to tell Bill either. Why complicate matters. The three would be in and out of Cairo within a week, two at the most.

* * *

Chapter Two

The following Thursday, Naunet Klein, William Jefferson Browning, and Jonathan Wilkins were quickly processed at Cairo International Airport. The official assigned to them stamped their passports, and with great flourish validated their visas for them. Without so much as a question or closer examination, the special laser was issued a temporary import certificate. No doubt, some baksheesh had been pressed into the appropriate palms. A summons by a pharaoh had its advantages.

Dead tired, the trio checked into their small hotel in the residential district of Gezira Island, an oasis of expatriates and upper class Egyptian families. On shaded streets embassies, schools, art galleries and nineteenth century villas hid demurely behind hedges. The shopping was supposed to be exquisite. Not that the new arrivals would find time for any of the Zamalek district's exotic and undoubtedly overpriced wares.

The Hotel Longchamps was especially popular with visiting archeologists, due to its proximity to the Ministry of Antiquities— and thus to the omnipotent Dr. Jabari El-Masri, reigning member of the Supreme Council.

On Friday morning, still somewhat jet-lagged, the three scientists presented themselves at Dr. El-Masri's offices at the Ministry. They where met by a very apologetic young man who seemed to be floating toward them clad in a white *galabya*, obviously of fine Egyptian cotton as they could see the outlines of a sleeveless undershirt. Naunet was sure to keep her eyes above the waist. They were told that, so very sorry, but Dr. El-Masri had flown to Luxor to check on a new find. Any further questions were deflected with shoulder-shrugging and expansive arm-waving.

Bill Browning seethed. They had just rushed halfway around the world on the prominent Egyptian's urgent request only to be now stonewalled by an assistant. All those pressing projects they had abandoned! And for what?

Naunet on the other hand remembered the frustrating machinations of the Egyptian bureaucracy well. There was nothing to be done, she told her colleagues, but to wait.

"Perhaps tomorrow," the assistant said, "Amsu Abusir will show you the research laboratory at the museum."

"Abusir?" Naunet asked. There had been many telephonic arguments over the loan exhibit with a stubbornly obstinate representative of Dr. El-Masri's office. Abusir was not a name she recalled.

"Yes, Mr. Abusir. Dr. El-Masri's executive assistant," the young Egyptian emphasized as if speaking to someone hard of hearing. Naunet's hearing was perfect but she was thinking of the *Abusir Papyri*. Most likely, that assistant was from Abusir Village and had adopted its name as his own. It was common practice, especially among Egyptians dealing with foreigners who found the complexity of Arabic surnames utterly confusing.

On the short drive back to the hotel, their taxi took a circuitous route driving them off and then back onto the island via its two main bridges. When Naunet questioned the driver, he told them in fairly good English that there was much unrest in the streets nowadays and that they should not leave their hotel at night.

Saturday came and went. So did Sunday and, still, they had not heard from Dr. El-Masri, his executive assistant or anyone else from the Ministry or the Museum.

Jabari El-Masri saw himself as the undisputed ruler over his country's past, present and future archeological treasures. It was a passion to which he, *The Pharaoh*, felt predestined. Considering that his name translated into *Brave Egyptian*, he assumed he was at great liberty to exercise his calling. He was known to be an extremely volatile and self-promoting man who did not tolerate foreign archeologists well, especially when they openly contradicted his own unshakable opinions.

The three scientists rightly suspected that they might not receive due credit for whatever they were asked to uncover for the glory of Egypt. Despite this, their professional commitment and curiosity easily overruled any hope of public recognition. They impatiently anticipated *the call* while sipping small cups of thick, sweet coffee on their hotel's beautiful rooftop terrace. At least some productive hours were spent on their laptops since the hotel provided Internet access. As there was not much to report, only a brief e-mail informed their boss that they had arrived safely and that, alas, they where still waiting for an audience with the elusive Dr. El-Masri.

True to himself, Bill inserted a small barb that Dr. Bruno had sent them off to Cairo on such an 'extreme rush-job' when nobody seemed particularly interested in their arrival.

Naunet pretended that she wanted to add a personal message for Dr. Bruno about her proposed detour to Crete. After that she would send the e-mail. Before she did so, however, she deleted Bill's sardonic sentence. Her conscience should have prevented her from doing so, but her regard for both Bill and Dr. Bruno told her she was doing the right thing. Why antagonize either one over something they could do nothing about.

The call came at six in the morning on Monday, May Fourteen, their fourth day in Cairo. Having been sound asleep, Naunet managed to fumble for the telephone.

"Dr. Klein here."

"Ah. Yes. Good." Clipped voice. Accented English.

Naunet sat up with a jolt. There was no mistaking that tone. It was him!

"Please! Be at the Ministry at eight o'clock sharp. You have much work to do."

Before she could open her mouth, the telephone went dead.

"That's him all right," she mumbled and jumped out of bed. After calling Bill and Jonathan, rousing them from sleep as well, she carefully chose a mid-calf tan sleeveless sheath. Linen would have been cooler but Naunet disliked the way it wrinkled. The thin jersey-knit was a lot more practical, though slightly more clingy. Over it, as a jacket, she wore a sheer cream-colored chiffon blouse. Lastly, she slipped on a pair of neutral wedge-heeled sandals. Surveying herself in the bathroom mirror, she was satisfied that the full sleeves sufficiently covered her arms yet still conveyed enough femininity to soften her dark hair, twisted into a loose bun at the neck. There would be plenty of time for lab coats and khakis, as well as heavy socks and boots should they ever be able to venture out onto a dig. Rummaging in her flight bag, she pulled out a filmy leopard print scarf and draped it loosely around her neck. Better, she nodded at her mirror image.

Naunet went down to the hotel's small dining room. It was deserted except for a distinguished-looking man at a corner table with another who wore a black *thobe*, the traditional long shirt usually seen in Dubai. What further drew Naunet's attention was that this man also had on a black Turkish *fez*. It was more like a skullcap than the popular red-tasseled headgear most people recognized from Hollywood movies. She noticed how the European shamelessly sized her up and down, and up again. *Impertinent sod. Handsome though.* Around fifty, if she had to guess. Seemingly self-assured, he was perfectly turned out without appearing the least bit overdressed. Naunet smiled but was instantly annoyed with herself. Why did her cheeks suddenly feel hot? Perhaps the air-conditioning was off. Or was it that she appreciated the unexpected attention from the attractive man? To cover her embarrassment for staring at him a second too long, she nodded briefly in his direction. The stranger's return smile was guileless and open while the other man turned away and faced the wall. When she passed their table, the European rose from his chair and inclined his head. "Good morning, Mademoiselle."

Mademoiselle? If that's not fishing! But she had to say something in return or she would be considered rude or, worse, arrogant. "Good morning." It came out as arrogant anyway. *How original*, she fumed at herself and went quickly past them.

Then she heard him say to her back, "May I tell you what a pleasure it is to see such an attractive fellow-traveler."

She turned and blushed some more. He stood there, easy and elegant, and very tall. Nothing in his demeanor suggested anything other than genuine pleasure of running into someone pleasant in a foreign country. Suddenly pleased by the unexpected compliment, she smiled and mumbled what she hoped was a demure "Why, thank you." Her face flushed, she rushed to join her colleagues.

Compared to her—and to the elegant stranger—her two colleagues had not taken much care in selecting their wardrobe for the important meeting. Bill's outmoded sear-sucker jacket attested to long hours in a suitcase, and the white-collared button-down shirt and brown wing-tipped shoes screamed 'Boston Brahmin, sightseeing.' Naunet had often wondered why Bill's barber never trimmed his rampant eyebrows. Neither, to all appearances, did the man apparently trim Bill's white mane enough to earn his money. Thankfully, strands of his lush white hair lay swept over Bill's ears and Naunet was spared further judgment of the dear man's grooming habits. At least Jonathan wore neat khakis with a finely striped polo shirt. His lightweight jacket was slung over the back of the fourth chair and, of course, he wore his inevitable Sperry Top-Sider boat shoes. Naunet smiled at the two and sat down, grateful for their easy-going company.

"You look nice," Jonathan said and raised himself halfway up from his chair to acknowledge her.

Bill smiled up from under his brows and pushed a menu in front of her. "And none of this eating like a bird," he said. Back in Cambridge, he had often chided her for eating plain yoghurt from a small container and calling it lunch.

That's the Bill Browning I know. Naunet felt much better now for having forestalled a caustic e-mail reply from their boss who did not take well to other people's temper tantrums.

"Who is that guy?" Jonathan kept his eyes on the menu.

"What guy?"

"You know exactly who. The dandy back there. Anybody you know?"

"Oh, him. Nope." Naunet quickly turned to Bill. "What are you going to have, Bill?" She could feel that Jonathan was not happy about her brief encounter with the European. "And you, Jonathan," she said and looked directly at him. "See anything that strikes your fancy?" Whenever Naunet smiled, it was something to behold.

"I definitely do," Jonathan winked and they all laughed.

They ordered a simple European style breakfast, which would leave them plenty of time for another possible detour on the way to the Ministry. Naunet and Jonathan could not help but feel a bit like students being summoned to the headmaster's office, while Bill put up a stoic façade drumming is fingers on the white table cloth between bites of toast and sips of sweet coffee. He still resented the outrageous waste of his time.

"He did say Ministry, not Museum, right?"

Naunet missed her mouth and a small piece of melon dropped from her fork back onto the plate. Self-conscious and embarrassed, she glanced over at the other table. Hopefully, her mishap had not been observed by the elegant man.

"Jeez, Jon! Don't try to confuse me. Yes, he said Ministry." After spearing the elusive melon slice a second time, she winked at Bill and mumbled loud enough for Jonathan to hear, "I think."

A man in pressed slacks and a tight-fitting black tee-shirt met them outside the Ministry. After several anxious glances up and down the street, he ushered them hastily inside the building before introducing himself.

"I am Amsu Abusir. I am special assistant to Dr. El-Masri." He looked bright, and appeared fit and young, though close-up his cropped hair showed signs of gray.

"Monsieur Abusir," Naunet greeted him and introduced her two companions.

The Egyptian bowed. "Please. For you," his comment seemed to be directed solely at Naunet, "I am proud to be just Amsu."

Sure you are, Naunet smiled to herself. While her Arabic was not perfect, she understood more than she often wanted to be privy to, especially around men. His name meant *procreation*.

Two armed guards emerged from a niche and barred their way. They apologetically asked the American men to lift their arms. They ignored Naunet. Then they roughly pummeled Amsu, grinning widely. Apparently satisfied with their body-search, they waved the small group into the Ministry's hallowed interior.

Startled at the rough treatment their guide had received, Bill asked, "Amsu, don't these guards know you by now?"

"Of course," the undoubtedly lusty Amsu nodded, "The tall one is my cousin. But they must do their job, otherwise ..." He slid a finger across his throat.

They hastened after him along several intersecting hallways until they reached an impressive double-door. The exotic wood was carved into exaggerated hieroglyphs. *It's like the entrance to a royal tomb.* A scene from Aida flashed before her inner eye. For some reason, New York's Metropolitan Opera always used dim and haunting scenery. Still, she was grateful that she was able to afford herself a season ticket with the occasional weekend in The Big Apple. Without knocking but with great flourish, Amsu swung both panels open. They were entering *The Pharaoh's* inner sanctum.

Mahogany-paneled, with sumptuous silk curtains pooling on the marble floor, the huge space could have been a museum in its own right. Showy objects from late dynasties stood among colorful art books, and carved stone beetles inlaid with semi-precious stones seemed to crawl across glass shelves pushing invisible balls of dung.

* * *

Chapter Three

Dr. Jabari El-Masri strode toward them all smiles, hands outstretched.

"This is quite extraordinary," he greeted them effusively.

His guests correctly assumed that the impeccably dressed Egyptian did not refer to their having traveled to Cairo on extremely short notice.

"Yes. Quite extraordinary." *The Pharaoh* stared intently at Naunet. He shook his head as if to dispel an errant thought. "Please, do sit down. Coffee?"

Acquainted with the heart-racing syrupy concoction, they politely declined.

"Good. Now, before I tell you about my revolutionary find, let me impress upon you that this is to be kept strictly *entre nous*. I must have your word on this. Do not telephone or e-mail anyone about what I am going to tell you." He looked at Bill and Jonathan and waited for their nods. When he looked fully at Naunet again, he drew in his breath for a second time.

Perhaps he remembers me after all, she wondered.

Shaking his white mane that rivaled Bill's in thickness but not in carefree styling, the Minister continued, "I am certain you know that, at the present time, my government has to deal with a few miscreants. These elements will do anything to bring discredit to my efforts."

Bill sat quietly, and Naunet found herself strangely drawn into the eminent Egyptian's hypnotic eyes, while Jonathan admired the man's

English.

"Excellent." Jabari El-Masri was pleased to find his audience appropriately attentive.

"A month ago, the Upper Region was hit by a rare late-season Khamsin. Sand covered everything. Well, we are used to that," he shrugged. "However, at the same time, the fierce wind laid bare more of the pre-and early dynastic capital of Nekhen. Kom el-Ahmar, as we call it now. The old Hierakonpolis, you know."

Naunet bit her tongue as undoubtedly did Bill and Jonathan. *Yes, we know*, she wanted to fling at the condescending man. Glancing at Jonathan, she twitched an eyebrow which caused her younger colleague to feign a coughing-fit. Jonathan never missed a sly glance or hidden meaning; she promised herself to be more careful.

Undeterred by his young visitor's gasps for air, their host continued. "I found some tablets in a depression a ways from the ancient remains of the Temple of Horus, possibly in the old Sacred-Lake bed. So far, there are twenty-five. There could be more. Of course, I flew up there at once to secure the site. Another interesting point is that these slates, or tablets, are seemingly of the same origin as two that were unearthed in Saqqara some years ago. All are covered with the same kind of resin or pitch. It has proven impervious to everything we have used so far in trying to remove the bonded material. But underneath, we know, they are pure gold."

Now we are getting somewhere. As innocently as he could, Bill asked, "How do you know they are the same?"

El-Masri pointed a finger at them. "Right before the War, we discovered a group of royal First Dynasty tombs in Saqqara."

A British Egyptologist, as I recall. Naunet grimaced but was careful not to glance at Jonathan this time. An approving nod from El-Masri told her that he was obviously pleased. He must think that she was duly impressed by his revelations.

"One tomb contained the sarcophagi of the Scribe of The Temple of Ptah and we assume his family. Hidden in a secret compartment in the scribe's sarcophagus was a scroll. Unfortunately, due to the impending threat of war, these sarcophagi were hastily relegated to our museum's storage area. Only years later, after I became the museum director and took inventory, did I find and translate the scribe's writings. They pointed to the tomb of three important high priests. Later, after I had those excavated, I found two blackened tablets. They did not look appealing at the time."

Again, the Egyptian directed his liquid gaze at Naunet. "One of the mummies had an extraordinarily beautiful death mask of a girl or young woman wrapped into his chest." He fell silent and then sighed as if to banish his inner-eye's image.

"I have to admit, Dr. Klein. Your appearance startled me."

Naunet felt the heat rise from her neck into her cheeks. Had he thought she would be a man? Did he disapprove of her wardrobe? She had dressed so carefully so as not to offend anyone's sensibilities. Even if she had come in her khakis he, of all people, should be used to women archaeologists dressed in practical attire.

"I am sorry," she mumbled automatically. "I did not mean to offend you."

The Pharaoh stood up and raised his hands like an ancient priest sending supplications to the gods. "No, no, Dr. Klein. I did not say you offended me. I said I was startled by your appearance. By the resemblance. Yes, that would be a better word. It is uncanny."

Naunet looked at him, confused. "Yes, people sometimes think they see a resemblance between me and my father. But I was under the impression, Dr. El-Masri, that you had never met him."

"Not to your father, Dr. Klein. To Nefret." El-Masri stared at her some more.

Naunet was again mesmerized by his black eyes. She was also still confused. *Nefret? Surely he means Nefertiti.* The annoying heat in her cheeks did not go away.

"Did you know that the Egyptians believed that a sinner's *Ba* must return to earth many times before it can find atonement?" Clearly, El-Masri was not referring to his present-day compatriots. "Perhaps it is by a higher design that you have come back to us," he smiled disarmingly. "I mean, to Egypt."

Was the great man implying that she had an ancient sinner's soul? Naunet sat stock-still, not quite knowing what to say. The room fell away. There was an eerie silence. She was alone; hypnotized by this mesmeric man.

A great bellow of laughter jarred her from her thoughts. El-Masri waived his hand at her. "Of course, we don't believe in all that nonsense now." He practically sputtered with amusement before he continued in his normal, matter-of-fact lecture-voice. "Nevertheless, there is a certain resemblance. You will see it shortly for yourself." He seemed to speak only to Naunet. "It is pure gold, you know. Given the dull, unpromising state of the tablets, however, only this astoundingly exquisite mask became part of our Old Kingdom exhibit."

At least, Naunet thought relieved, *he compares me to someone astoundingly exquisite.* She brushed a loose strand of hair from her forehead and hoped her colleagues had not noticed her momentary lapse into another world. How could she have been so gullible? It was clear to her now that the jesting Dr. El-Masri was having a good laugh at her expense.

"What about the other two mummies?" Jonathan glanced at Naunet, glad to see her regain her composure.

"Well, one mummy was King Aha's High Priest of Ptah, an important and powerful man for his time. We found out later that his name was Ramose. His mummy was practically covered with *khepri*, the sacred winged scarab. Perhaps a personal seal. Possibly a family crest. We don't know yet."

El-Masri paused, his thoughts miles away once more. When Bill discretely cleared his throat, he jerked his head up. "Ah, where was I? Right. In two-o-five, when I turned some basement rooms into exhibition galleries, I rediscovered the tablets. I further discovered a scroll signed by Ramose in the high priest's tomb in which he names the other two. Badar and Tasar. All three had successively been High Priest of Ptah. Curiously, that scroll warned that the populace of the Two Lands should 'take heed' and 'alter their ways'," El-Masri grinned. "I guess, even in ancient times, people feared things would go from bad to worse if nothing was done about it."

Again, El-Masri paused to let his story sink in. "And this is where it gets interesting. This scroll makes specific reference to the two Saqqara tablets."

"You rediscovered all this only a few years ago?"

"Well, yes. As I mentioned, these items were placed aside at the time for future examination. With all the other important research and cataloguing going on, they were again, ah, overlooked. After the recent find, I remembered the similarity between the two sets of tablets. Saqqara and Nekhen. They attempted to clean one here in

Cairo. Without much success. Except that I found there was gold underneath."

The use of *I* when success was described and *they* when things hadn't gone so well, was not lost on the director's increasingly captivated audience. Naunet forced herself not to look at Jonathan who re-crossed his long legs kicking her ankle apparently by accident.

"So sorry," he mumbled and this time Bill caught on. He shifted in his chair so as not to have to look at his colleagues for fear that he, too, might be caught up in their silent jest.

"How significant is the damage," he asked bluntly.

Naunet was appalled. *Oh, God! They've already destroyed whatever was under the ancient pitch!*

"There was some to one edge." *The Pharaoh* turned the corners of his mouth down. "Only to one tablet, you understand. At least, I learned that the gold underneath is inscribed with a geometric design on one side. And, it looks as if there is cursive writing on the other. I hope that you, Dr. Browning, can peel the coating back with your new laser equipment without etching into the gold. And with your excellent reputation, Dr. Klein, I know you will decipher the symbols in no time at all. With the help of Mister Wilkins here. Naturally."

"Naturally." Jonathan lowered his eyes. The man had done his research as he did not refer to him as 'doctor.'

"Then I suggest we start with the damaged tablet." Bill was his scientific self again. "I have the laser with me." He patted his briefcase.

"Excellent. By the way, only the two Saqqara tablets are in Cairo. I couldn't very well stuff the Nekhen ones into a rucksack and carry them down with me, could I now. Besides, they may dig up more."

"So, how then are we going to work on the ones from up there?" Jonathan looked squarely at the eminent Egyptologist. He had an inkling of a detour into a broiling Upper Egypt which had never been discussed, much less agreed to.

"You fly up there, of course," El-Masri smiled amiably and stood up. "A friend's private plane is at your disposal."

They wondered who the good doctor's friend might be, now that his really, really good friend had been ousted by the people. However, the previous regime's military—with a prominent general from the air force in the fore—still held the reigns on Egypt's provisional government. At least a private plane would be a lot more comfortable than the local milk run.

"My esteemed colleague, Mr. Mahmoud Zawwam, the Head of Luxor's Antiquities, has arranged for private quarters near Luxor. The house is air-conditioned. There is also a fully equipped laboratory. You'll have your own driver, of course," El-Masri assured them. "The new excavation site is not too far from Luxor. There will be no need for you to visit it. It is not air-conditioned." Jonathan wondered if El-Masri's remark was a dig at soft American living or some obtuse attempt at Egyptian humor.

Naunet had to ask. "Forgive me, Dr. El-Masri. What about the Saqqara tablets?"

"I suggest that you examine them right away to get a head-start."

And then? Naunet silently prompted Dr. El-Masri to elaborate. Instead, their host smiled contentedly and rose from his chair. "I know you are going to do an excellent job. Amsu will meet you at the museum."

Their audience with *The Pharaoh* was over.

"He can be quite charming when he wants something," Naunet said after they found their way back outside. There was no car waiting for them. Apparently 'having your own driver' did not extend to Cairo. They would have to catch a taxi.

"Charming, my foot," Bill growled. "He was downright insulting. I assume you noticed that, Naunet. And furthermore, he seems to think that this is going to be as easy as peeling a banana. Which brings me to the question, why does he really want us here?"

"To get a head-start," Jonathan mimicked the Egyptian perfectly, adding an apparently favorite, "Of course."

"He gave me the creeps with this reawakened *Ba* nonsense," Naunet said.

"Yeah, what was all that about. When we all know that you are Nefertiti-reincarnated," Jonathan smiled. She swiped lightly at him and they all laughed, relieved to be outside again.

Their taxi squealed to an abrupt halt in front of a massive building. The museum's official name was 'The Egyptian Museum in Cairo.' Practically the whole world referred to it simply as 'The Cairo

Museum' or more recently, 'The Egyptian Museum.' As soon as they stepped into the rising heat, Amsu appeared from behind a thick pillar on top of the wide steps and motioned to them to follow him. There was another tactile security check.

"More cousins?" Jonathan asked and Amsu nodded happily as he ushered them into a roomy elevator which floated them to the lower floor. Naunet remembered the dank basement laboratories and dusty store rooms littered with forgotten treasures. The elevator doors opened and they found themselves spilling out to a brilliantly lit gallery.

"My word," Naunet breathed.

"Ah," Amsu laughed. "You remember how it was?"

"What a change!" She turned to Bill and Jonathan. "When I was here in two-thousand, this was a maze of dusty crates and boxes."

"Dr. El-Masri did all this," Amsu beamed. "He selected many splendid treasures from all over. With the museum's centennial only months away in the summer of two-thousand-and-five, he transformed our basement into this exhibition space."

"It's beautiful." Naunet said. By habit, she wandered off to look at the displays and suddenly found herself in front of a tall glass case: 'Death Mask of the Princess Nefret, First Dynasty, Ineb-hedj, ca. 3080 BC.' Without warning, her cheeks started to burn again. She stared into the hollow eyes.

"That must be the mask Dr. El-Masri meant." Jonathan had come up behind her and was bent over the description. When he straightened up to look at the display itself, Naunet heard him gasp.

Good grief. Will he ever stop joking? She turned to him. "Yes, Jonathan. It is pure gold."

"That's not it," her stunned colleague whispered. "Look! He was right."

"About what?"

"This *is* you!"

Now she really meant to box him on the arm and scold him to be serious; but he was not joking. She stared back through the glass. Did she really bear such likeness to the serene mask? A shiver crawled up her spine. 'A sinner's soul,' the Egyptian had said. Naunet straightened herself up and pulled Jonathan away from the haunting image.

They hastened to catch up with Bill and Amsu. The laboratories were at the end of a long corridor. After they entered, Amsu explained a few things and then left with a promise to return later with some refreshments and sandwiches. Apparently, they were to spend the rest of the day working.

Taking stock, the three looked for the tablets. Suddenly, a ghost—or was it a mummy—appeared in their midst.

"Jeez," Jonathan jumped.

The apparition wore a flapping white lab coat over blue jeans. A white sheet covered his outstretched arms in ghostly fashion, trembling slightly as if holding up a great weight.

"Hidden entrance," the man grinned, having played his little trick before on unsuspecting archaeologists. He removed the sheet with his teeth and let it drift to the floor. *"Voilá!"* Left in his hands was a rectangle which he dropped quickly onto a table shaking out his wrists from the effort. It was all black except for a gleaming diagonal seam from a missing corner.

"This you need," the man said. "Now, you work."

"Where is the corner-piece," Bill asked.

"Lost." The wide sweep of the hand could mean somewhere in the lab, or somewhere in the museum, or somewhere in the sand. If they had expected the dour man to vanish into thin air again, they were disappointed, or perhaps relieved. He walked straight out the door. They heard a distinct click.

"He just locked us in," Jonathan confirmed the obvious. "I trust there's a head around here somewhere."

Naunet ignored Jonathan's practical comment. The avid sailor's speech was often peppered with nautical terms. She hoped he was right, though.

"I have seen that guy before," she said.

"Another Amsu-cousin?" Bill mumbled, already focused on the tablet. He took a metric precision ruler and the laser from his briefcase.

"No. I am sure I saw him at breakfast."

"Oh yes, now I remember. He was the scowling native sitting at that table with the dandy you flirted with," Jonathan teased.

"I did not."

"Well, then he flirted with you. Same thing," Jonathan insisted.

"Be serious." Naunet knew it came out too emphatic. "Besides, he was not a 'native,' as you put it. He wore a Turkish *fez*."

"Oh, that explains a lot."

Naunet ignored him and went over to join Bill who had started to measure the tablet. He began to call out its dimensions and asked Jonathan to punch them into his computer, "Twenty-five by eighteen by two centimeters."

There was a large scale and he and Jonathan heaved the tablet onto it. "Twenty-point-forty-five kilos. That would speak well for gold," Bill nodded happily.

"Or lead," Jonathan added hoping he was wrong. One never knew what fakes lurked in museum basements.

Then Bill swore softly, "Damn. Look at this! These idiots simply took a chisel to knock off the corner."

* * *

Chapter Four

They mixed combinations of acid liquids and alkaline pastes. Like true scientists, they forgot about the time and the place, and focused only on the task in front of them. Naunet's bun had come undone and her hair fell about her face like a curtain of dark silk which she swept back with a free hand from time to time, barely aware of the gesture.

After several hours of back-bent toiling, Bill jumped up, let out a cry and jigged around the lab. The last solution Naunet and Jonathan had concocted following his instructions had again not dissolved the unguent. However, once absorbed, it had softened the ancient pitch into something akin to sun-baked asphalt. While it still bonded tenaciously to the gold underneath, at least it had become more workable. Bill's 'crazy jig' was well known at the Institute, as was his legendary war cry 'I struck gold.' This time, it meant not only that he had solved a scientific puzzle. This time, it meant that he had literally done exactly that.

"We've struck gold," he sang out again as he slowly, carefully pried a minute fleck of black unguent away from an edge. "This'll work," he muttered to himself. Taking up his laser, he carefully guided it in a crisscross pattern over a small portion of the tablet missing its corner. If his millimeter-deep precision cuts proved too shallow, it would not work. If too deep, he would etch into the precious metal underneath and possibly damage or worse obliterate whatever had been stamped on it.

"I need some help here," Bill urged.

Naunet and Jonathan left the vials and joined their intense colleague. Once Bill finished his cuts, they each chose a strip of the scored squares and gingerly started to pry one minuscule square off at a time. Jonathan scooped some of the flakes into small vials and carefully stored them in a divider in his briefcase. He could hardly wait to analyze a material which had so far supposedly defied every solution, according to Dr. El-Masri.

They had uncovered just half of one minute strip when they heard the door being unlocked from the outside. Amsu stepped in, looking rather anxious. His hair was plastered to his forehead and he wiped his face with a perfectly white kerchief, obviously thankful for the cooler laboratory air. Bill looked at his watch. Four-thirty, local time. No wonder, his stomach growled. To his dismay, *The Pharaoh's* efficient assistant did not appear to have brought any food for them. Worse, neither was there any sign of cool refreshments. They surely could have used some at this time. Bill's tongue was starting to stick to the roof of his mouth just thinking about a long sip of something cold.

"I drive you back to your hotel right now," Amsu said. He was clearly agitated and had lost his pleasant smile.

"Right now?" The three asked in unison.

"Why," Jonathan added.

And Naunet protested that they were just about to make some progress. She was in her element and this sudden interruption disappointed her to no end. She wanted to photograph as much of uncovered writing as she could before they left the lab. That way, she could continue her examination in peace during the evening after dinner and check the hieratic symbols against her computer files.

"Yes, right now. There is much unrest in the streets and a general curfew has been issued by the provisional military government. You must leave immediately. It is for your own safety."

"Great timing," Bill sighed and gathered up the laser. Then he lifted the weighty tablet and held it in both arms as if to carry it with him.

Amsu placed a firm hand around his wrist. "No, Dr. Browning. The tablet stays."

"Of course." Bill's gesture had been automatic rather than rational. He immediately realized that a hotel room was no place for an ancient treasure, especially one that could easily be melted down into a handy bowling ball of pure gold.

They gathered up their laptops and briefcases. Amsu led them through the basement and out the loading dock entrance where he herded them into what seemed to be his own car. The white Fiat was unobtrusive, dented, and very small. Instead of taking the Nile Corniche Road onto Twenty-Six July Bridge that led directly into the Zamalek district of the island, Amsu drove south to El Tahrir Bridge. While it was the closer bridge linking the museum with the island, it took them across to the lower end of it.

They did not encounter any demonstrations driving back up the length of the island and began to wonder what the fuss was all about, until Amsu stopped in front of their hotel. Two men in fatigues stood broad-legged at its entrance, glaring at passers-by and checking others entering the building. It was not clear whether they belonged to the provisional military government or were sympathizers of the demonstrators. Their guns left no doubt, however, that they meant business, whatever that was. Amsu flashed some sort of pass and thankfully the guards stepped aside to let them in. When Amsu tried to follow, they barred his way.

"Please," Amsu called after the three and Bill went back to see what he wanted.

Amsu stepped very close to the older man and quickly whispered, "Be ready at four o'clock tomorrow morning for your flight to Luxor."

"What about the tablets?" Bill asked as quietly as he could manage, given his naturally booming voice. "Will they be on the plane?"

Amsu shrugged, "I will be here in the morning." His mien was stern and he nodded several times for emphasis. Bill assured him that they would be ready.

As important as science was to the three, their stomachs rumbled clamoring for nourishment. They decided to have a bite to eat before returning to their rooms to pack. In this heat, no one was up for a heavy meal anyway. One thing was for sure. They had to let their boss back in Boston know about these unforeseen events, and assumed that Bruno was not included in El-Masri's request for secrecy. They went to the dining room where a handful of guests were finishing an early dinner. With the large room relatively quiet, they were quickly served before a late crowd would undoubtedly storm the buffet usually set up after nine o'clock.

The Longchamps, a comfortable three-star hotel, had first opened in 1953. After a career as an airline stewardess, the owners' daughter had come back to Egypt to take over the family business from her aging parents. Hebba Bakri approached their table, all smiles. She was a slim, tall woman in her mid-fifties perhaps. Guests immediately became aware of her long-practiced charm and ease to deal with the public, no matter how demanding or difficult. After her pleasant greeting she inquired how the three visitors from Boston liked Cairo. Then, after a few more pleasantries, she told them to their surprise that their hotel bill had been paid. Someone was planning ahead.

They lingered over coffee and discussed what might be their best option. They briefly considered quitting right then and there and getting out of Egypt while they still could. The conclusion of the half-hearted conversation was that if *The Pharaoh* wanted them in Luxor, trying to fly back to the safety of the States on their own would undoubtedly be met with certain obstacles at the airport. The man was too powerful to be crossed. Besides, always the consummate scientists, they had to admit that they were hooked by the mystery of the golden tablets. They simply had to know what lay written underneath the pitch.

During a lull in their conversation, they became aware that the European from breakfast was approaching their table with his purposeful stride. Jonathan thought the man zeroed in particularly on Naunet, an impertinent grin on his face as if he knew her well. He had shed his jacket and the sleeves of his blue silk shirt were rolled up to the elbows—casual, yet somehow still elegant. He oozed continental laissez-faire, but his French greeting of "Madame, Messieurs" carried a decidedly British inflection. With a slight bow, and without anyone encouraging him to do so, he now introduced himself.

"Edward Guernsey-Crock. May I join you for a moment? I have some useful information for you." He pulled his calling card from a gold case and placed it nonchalantly on the table.

"Ah, Mr. Crook, we are just about to leave," Jonathan said at once, not giving Naunet a chance to extend an invitation. Normally, he would of course have deferred to her as the lady in their group, but he had taken a dislike to the man from the first moment he had set eyes on him that morning when he shamelessly flirted with Naunet. If his antenna was on target, he had better find out what this guy was really up to.

The man's 'It is Crock, actually,' was accompanied by a tight-lipped smile toward Jonathan which only intensified the younger man's dislike for the interloper. There was really no particular reason. Jonathan glanced at the attractive woman on his left and noticed that she flashed one of those brilliant smiles of hers up at the tall intruder.

"Oh, please do join us, Mr. Guernsey-Crock," she said graciously and motioned to the empty fourth chair standing pushed a ways back from their table. With lightening speed, the man swiveled it into the narrow space between Jonathan and Naunet which brought him practically shoulder to shoulder with her. Jonathan noticed that their thighs almost touched.

Bill held his demitasse in mid-air. "Guernsey? Is that as in island?"

"Or," Jonathan was quick to add, "as in cows."

The very British Edward Guernsey-Crock sniffed dismissively. "An ancestral home," as if embarrassed by implied bovine fortune. Then, pulling his chair closer to the table and with it leaning even closer to Naunet, he bent over and whispered in a conspiratorial tone, as if he were alone with her. "I just wanted to caution you about certain developments. I gather that you just arrived and therefore you may not have heard that the presidential campaigns are not going smoothly by any means. Too many splinter groups, you see. Also, there is this young woman, an Egyptian archaeologist, who is extremely active in the counter-protests. You might know her. No? Anyhow, any adverse outcome of this revolution will reflect badly on the ex-president's Minister of Antiquities, and consequentially on any of his protégés. Do you get my meaning?"

Jonathan was going to say, first, that it was a bit inflammatory to call these protests a full-blown revolution. And, second, yes, they somehow had managed not to forget their mother tongue after their few days in Egypt. Indeed, they did get his meaning. Before he could relieve the pressure that kept mounting inside his chest by a snide remark aimed to put the man in his place, Naunet had turned toward the know-it-all. She was fairly aglow and her attention was completely directed at the unbidden bringer of political doom. Had it not been for Jonathan's upbringing, he would have exploded in a torrent of smutty remarks. As it was, good breeding prevailed and he bit his tongue.

Through the red fog of rising anger, he heard Naunet ask, "Are you telling us the situation has become that serious?"

He also noticed how she inclined her head the way she often did when doubting someone's statement, but was too polite to say so outright. Despite this, she looked into the pale blue eyes way too long. Then she smiled! Asking if something was serious did not warrant a smile like that! Jonathan's jaw tightened to the point where he ground his teeth.

"From what I have been told, it very well could be." The apparently well-informed Mr. Guernsey-Crock shrugged and leaned even closer to Naunet. "I assure you, as of tomorrow, Cairo will be completely unsafe for us."

Us? To Jonathan it sounded as if he was referring to the two of them. He pushed his chair back so abruptly that it caught in the rug and he almost tipped over backward.

"Oh, we won't have that problem," Naunet said without thinking. "We are off to Luxor tomorrow morning." She bit her tongue. It was so unlike her to divulge information to a stranger. What was she doing? At the same time she wondered if the promised plane ride would still be available. One could never tell with the quick sands of a fluid political climate. To prevent further slip-ups, she added quickly, "Interesting thing. We ran into your friend from this morning."

"Karakurt? You saw him at the museum, I imagine. But he is no friend of mine. A mere acquaintance, I assure you."

"His name," Naunet said sensing that she should not ask further questions. "Karakurt. I wonder, does it fit his personality?

"What do you mean?"

"It's Turkish for 'black wolf.'"

The elegant Mr. Crock's face froze for just an instant. And then, Jonathan felt, the man pulled back with a trace of caution. "You speak Turkish?" he asked Naunet. She shrugged.

Bill, who had sat by and watched bemused as Jonathan got more agitated by the minute, asked without really being interested, "What brings you to Cairo, Mr. Guernsey-Crock?"

"Business, mostly." The evasive answer did little for Jonathan to be more civil. To his relief, Naunet stood up and looked around the table. At last, she smiled at all of them. "I am going to my room." Then, as if by accident, her eyes rested on the self-proclaimed business man. "Are you coming?"

It seemed, at least to Jonathan, that her question could easily be misconstrued. As if being shot out of a canon, Jonathan jumped up, and almost overturned his chair. He wanted to make it clear to this Guernsey-cow-man that Naunet's remark was intended only for her colleagues. "Yes, Bill and I are going up with you." He turned toward his adversary, "Obliged for the warning, Mr. Crook."

For a second time, the two men sized each other up until, with a lopsided sardonic smile, the Brit broke his stare. He bowed and before Naunet knew what was happening, he had taken her hand, raised it to his mouth and then brushed the back of it lightly with his lips. Naunet seemed completely at ease with the sudden gesture, unlike American women who fluster and stammer, thereby voiding the compliment. Jonathan felt like voiding something as well. But the pesky Brit had stepped away and, wishing them a pleasant evening, waved back one more time. As he walked the length of the dining room, his stride was purposeful, almost jaunty. Somehow, it would not have surprised anyone if he started to whistle a little tune.

"The balls," Jonathan muttered under his breath. Bill grinned and shook his white mane, thankful that he was no longer young.

Half hidden under Naunet's discarded napkin lay the calling card. Jonathan reached out and quietly pocketed it.

"Jonathan? Oh, I am glad I reached you. I can't get on the Internet."

"Neither can I." Just to hear her voice on the house telephone brightened his mood and he told her that he had just hung up with Bill. "He complained about the same thing. Plus, he said he tried his cell, as well as the hotel phone. He couldn't get an outside line."

"We have to let Bruno know what is happening. We simply cannot leave without telling him that we are about to traipse off to Luxor tomorrow, don't you think?"

"Of course, I do. But right now it seems that we are incommunicado. Period," Jonathan said. "Let's just hope the good Dr. El-Masri can still get us that ride to Luxor. Things should be calmer up there."

"Does Bill agree with this new development? Do you know? We haven't really had time to discuss it among ourselves."

"Why don't we have an after-dinner drink on the rooftop terrace? It's a nice evening, and some relaxation will do us good. I'll let Bill know. Half an hour okay with you?"

Naunet agreed, hoping that their level headed older colleague would be able to alleviate her foreboding that all might not go so well with this new unplanned Egyptian venture of theirs.

"I'll see you up there." Jonathan hung up, his mood much improved. As he reflected on their predicament, he remembered the stranger's card and pulled the now somewhat crumpled cream-colored parchment from his pocket. He ran a finger over the raised maroon imprint, and read it out loud, "Edward Guernsey-Crock, Esquire. Fine Arts and Antiquities." He turned the card over. "That's it? No Import/Export? No cell? No fax?" On impulse, Jonathan re-dialed Naunet's room number. "Just wanted to tell you. Bring a wrap. It might get cool up there." Without knowing why, he added, "Are you okay?"

"As long as you are," Naunet quipped. Her young friend's unease over the handsome stranger's charm and attention had not escaped her notice. 'Poor Jonathan,' she smiled to herself. She was so lucky to have a friend like him.

This took her thoughts back to the tall stranger and she was sorry that she would not have a chance to get to know the enigmatic Edward better. It was very rare for a stranger to evoke such delicious thoughts in her. *I have the worst timing*, she sighed inwardly, sorry for the missed opportunity. To console herself, she imagined that he was likely married with five kids; probably had grandkids as well.

A few rooms away, Jonathan was relieved. He had imagined her smile as they talked on the phone and rightly suspected that she had resented his uncharitable attitude toward the *crook*. He slapped himself on the cheek. *Must stop calling him that.*

Her tone and ease on the phone had reaffirmed the camaraderie between them which had always made their working relationship so enjoyable. That the appearance of a stranger could suddenly drive a wedge between them was distressing. It was his fault. He promised himself to be more open with Naunet and to make her realize his true feelings for her. It was unimaginable to him that someone could appear and within minutes sweep her off her feet. Not a suspicious character like that guy. He knew she was much too level headed for that. Not that he expected any of them to run into the annoying *ancestral-home-my-foot-Brit* ever again.

The three lounged with their after-dinner drinks on the hotel's pleasant rooftop terrace. Jonathan had been right to suggest it. The evening was beautiful with a clear sky which was unusual for the teeming city. A cool breeze swept up from the Nile. The last few riverboats stirred toward their docks to disgorge themselves of hot and hungry tourists. Eager to experience Cairo at night, they would soon crowd every hotel dining room and casino. The three were glad to have found this little haven atop their own hotel. Surprising for the relatively early hour, there was no traffic noise from the road below and only intermittent crackling from across the river shattered the peaceful setting.

"Fireworks? This early?" Naunet wondered aloud, taking another sip from her glass.

"Gunfire," Bill and Jonathan said in unison.

* * *

Chapter Five

Early the next morning, on the fifteenth, Naunet and Bill were in the hotel lobby at a quarter to four waiting for Jonathan. Despite his penchant toward tardiness, Bill was a detail-oriented man. He was double-checking with a sleepy desk clerk to make sure that their bills had indeed been settled, when Jonathan and Amsu approached from opposite directions. It was way too early for the dining room to be open, so they picked up their luggage and followed Amsu outside.

Jonathan grinned when Amsu steered them toward a green Hummer, its motor snorting like an angry rhino. "Now that's what I call safe transport."

"Bulletproof," Amsu grinned back.

After he had pushed Naunet up into the monster and slammed the door behind Bill, Jonathan took the seat in the front while Amsu took care of the luggage. They sped off in the direction of Cairo International Airport. The streets were devoid of traffic and protesters. Even demonstrators require a good night's sleep.

Two miles from the airport, Amsu swerved off the main road and drove toward what looked like part of the vast airport compound except that it was surrounded by heavily enforced barbed wire.

Jonathan jolted awake. "Where are we going?"

As if someone was listening, Amsu turned his head left and right and then, very quietly said, "Almaza Air Force Base."

When their entry was barred by two heavily armed guards, Amsu flashed a red pass and after he was quickly waived on, he sped down a feeder road, screeching to a halt in front of a jet.

His three passengers gasped. For some reason, they had expected something like a small Cessna. Instead, they stared up at an impressive Gulfstream-IV, its yellowish paint-job dissected by burgundy stripes. In English and Arabic, the lettering read 'Arab Republic of Egypt.'

Jonathan turned to Amsu, "Republic of Egypt? Dr. El-Masri said it was a friend's private plane."

"Same thing." The Egyptian suddenly sounded bitter. "We wanted a change. But now, things may not get better, after all," he added in a rare admission from which he quickly recovered. He pointed to the jet. Its engines started to whine and the plane strained against its chocks like a racehorse chomping at its bits.

The point of no return. For an insane instant Jonathan felt like turning back, jumping into the car and roaring off into the night. No one had ever accused him of being cowardly. He just had a bad feeling about all this cloak-and-dagger playing. Were they not here on an official visit, requested by the Ministry of Antiquities? *What is Jabari El-Masri really up to?* Jonathan looked over at Naunet who watched Amsu pull their luggage from the Hummer. The jet's gangway came down and two armed men in fatigues descended, taking up stations at the lowest rung touching the tarmac, guns at the ready.

"You must go now," Amsu urged them. "Dr. El-Masri will be in touch." Then he stepped so close to Bill that the older man arched back for fear of being kissed on the cheek, Arab style. He may be in Egypt, and he usually abided by local custom, but this was one he did not fancy.

"The tablets are on board. They are safe with you now. Please, guard them for Egypt." And in his normal voice, Amsu added, "Allah be with you."

"I hope so," Jonathan said out of the corner of his mouth, having caught Amsu's last remark only because the engines had changed their pitch. Before they could tell their likeable guide good-bye, Amsu was back behind the wheel of the Hummer. He slammed the bucking monster into gear and roared off without looking back.

Because of her upbringing, and despite years of independent living in the States, Naunet still expected a certain 'charge to the rescue,' if not from her two colleagues busy with their own luggage, then at least from the two idle guards. When she finally concluded that none of the men had any intention of lending her a helping hand, she sighed and slung her laptop-bag over one shoulder, her shoe-bag over the other, and grabbing the handle of her carry-on, she followed them up the narrow stairs which clearly had not been designed for people having to wrestle with their own luggage.

"So much for chivalry," she muttered, amazed that Jonathan at least had not jumped into the breach.

The main cabin was luxurious but surprisingly small. The back of the plane was partitioned off by a bulkhead with a substantial-looking door and intimidating hardware.

"Good morning." Pleasant, slightly nasal voice. British Eton-tinged accent. Vaguely familiar. The back-facing leather chair spun around.

The new arrivals stared in disbelief.

"We must have the same friends," Edward Guernsey-Crock smiled affably.

"So it seems." Jonathan was the first to recover. "You know Dr. El-Masri?"

A second of wide-eyed silence, then "Of course. Who doesn't know the good Dr. Al," the Brit replied amiably and pushed his pith helmet toward the back of the table.

Jonathan was about to say something really sarcastic when the back bulkhead-door opened. There stood the Turk, comfortably dressed in a white Egyptian *galabya* complete with turban.

"Planning to rob a few tombs?" Jonathan asked, looking from one man to the other.

"You have met Karakurt Tiryaki, of course," Edward said as easy as if he were the host on the trip.

Jonathan's mental antenna grew another few inches.

Bill, huffing—whether from the stairs or the on-board surprises—handed Jonathan his bag, who in turn passed it on to Karakurt. When every bit of their luggage was secured in the aft compartment, Karakurt closed the division firmly from the other side.

Bill settled himself at the table and asked as casually as he could, "So, Edward, if I may call you that, what takes you to Luxor?"

He, Naunet and Jonathan looked expectantly at their fellow-passenger. The ensuing stare from their traveling companion stretched into an awkward silence. It was as if the man's mind had gone completely blank. To everyone's relief, the cockpit door opened.

"Good morning. I am your pilot, Colonel Rahman. My co-pilot, Lieutenant-Colonel al-Husri, and I welcome you on board."

"Another Al," Jonathan whispered to Edward. His sarcasm was lost as everyone's attention stayed on the pilot.

"Our flight to Luxor should take about an hour. We expect no heavy weather along the way."

"Just like home," Bill whispered and said louder, directed at the pilot. "We are glad to be in your capable hands, Colonel."

"He sounds like someone from Ohio. No accent," Naunet whispered.

"Compliments of the American taxpayer," Jonathan whispered back. "His training was undoubtedly footed by us. As I am sure was the entire presidential fleet." *Or*, Jonathan added to himself, *whoever claims to own it now.*

Four luxurious leather chairs were grouped around a square table, with two singles bolted down across the aisle. Edward and his pith helmet were comfortably ensconced in the forward-facing window-seat so that Bill and Naunet had to take the two chairs facing backward.

Jonathan had had enough. He was not going to squeeze in next to the Brit. "I am sure you won't mind," he said as innocently as he could, "we have work to do. You'll be just as happy sitting on the other side. You understand."

"I understand," Edward said pleasantly and moved across the aisle.

Bill smiled to himself. *Two bucks in rut.* Not that he blamed them. He just hoped it wouldn't become a problem.

Naunet pretended to check her special program for Egyptian hieroglyphs. As it ran on her much older, heavier laptop, that was the one she had brought with her. Unfortunately, it did not have Outlook and she had to use her Yahoo e-mail account. Also, it handled involved Internet searches badly.

From under half-closed lids, she glanced over at Edward.

Fascinating man. Definitely older than she was, yet there was a youthfulness about him that she found very attractive. A mite overly confident, perhaps. She had always liked a man who was sure of himself. A worldly man, who knew how to treat a lady. *Such beautiful hands.* She briefly imagined being caressed by the long fingers.

"Are you booted up?"

Naunet was startled as Jonathan intruded on her daydreams. Poor kid, he was either all business or playing the sailing jock. They had worked together a long time yet he had no idea what she was really like inside. Of course, she had never let him close enough or, *God forbid*, told him of the longings that haunted her empty nights. It wasn't fair. As a child, she had imagined her life would turn out completely different.

One summer, Naunet's parents had rented a home southeast of Vienna. The sturdy brick house had the traditional red-steepled roof and had formerly been part of a magnificent Baroque Schloss. Though modest and mostly ignored now by the throng of visitors to the Schloss itself, a small bronze plaque affixed to its peeling imperial-yellow plaster walls afforded it national monument status. Supposedly, Franz Liszt had slept there.

Naunet spent long afternoons roaming the ripe fields and fragrant meadows that surrounded the estate, bare-footed and mud-caked, indistinguishable from the caretaker's children. It was a happy time for an only child left alone often by caring but internationally in-demand parents.

She must have been barely six when her father, one evening, asked the age-old question parents throw out without much thought, sometimes simply to keep a waning after-dinner conversation alive, "So, what do you want to be when you grow up?"

"A matriarch."

Leopold half choked on his espresso and Akila pressed her napkin to her lips, giggling into the starched damask.

"Do you know what a matriarch does?" Leopold had given up on his demitasse and reached for his pipe.

"I do." Naunet sat up, her chin only centimeters above the rim of their massive dining room table. "She has lots of babies and rides a beautiful horse around her estate." Missing the wink that passed between her parents, she continued earnestly, "And when she is old everyone calls her grand-mama." Vaguely, she remembered her father saying something about all that possibly requiring a husband.

Instead, the passage of time had turned her into one of those sure-footed independent women; charming and well-liked—most of the time—and still looking for someone to love. It just had not happened yet.

*

Edward Guernsey-Crock, Esquire: Tall, urbane and pleasingly buff at fifty-four, adored women. Not the juicy twenty-year olds with their smooth thighs, uncontrolled appetites, and scheming mothers. No, it was a seasoned woman whose company he cultivated. The one bored with her workaholic, albeit wealthy, husband. The recent widow, overwhelmed by pushy stockbrokers and patronizing tax attorneys. The tummy-tucked single, over-forty-something, real estate agent with an expense account and keys to unoccupied mansions. Invariably, the ladies believed they'd died and gone to heaven as he lavished his noble breeding upon them.

Without fail, their sympathy and generosity knew no bounds when he let tidbits of recent bad luck slip through his wooing. As if reluctant to admit his present lack of funds, he would mention the burglary of a storage unit having contained valuable paintings, priceless antiques, and Grade-A investment diamonds. Alas, all uninsured. Gone forever. The story varied according to his audience and audacity.

Edward—he never changed his first name—leaned back in the luxurious leather seat, closed his eyes and smiled. The last couple of months in San Diego and, in particular, well-shod La Jolla, had been close to perfect for a gentleman of his discerning taste.

La Jolla, California: Topographically breathtaking and financially bountiful. Edward parked free on Silverado and strolled down to the Museum of Modern Art, where he zeroed in on a short, sixty-something matron. He doggedly followed the plump, Shape-Wear-squeezed docent reciting memorized details of bizarre paintings and angular sculptures to sun-seeking Canadians and corn-fed Mid-Westerners, secretly longing for lunch and a cold beer on the outdoor patio. At the end of the tour, Edward smiled his thanks and went out to the terrace with its spectacular view of the craggy Pacific coast. He leaned his tall frame against the balustrade to admire a huge gravity-defying metal sculpture that seemingly sprouted from an upper retaining wall, and waited.

"Pleasure Point, by Nancy Rubins," a slightly fatigued voice behind him said. He turned, smiling broadly, "I really enjoyed your lecture," and then placed his long-fingered hand upon his heart. "As an avid collector of antiquities, I am completely ignorant about modern art. I only wish you had the time to tell me more about this wonderful place."

"You are English," she said, as expected, and he introduced himself. "Edward Guernsey-Crock, Antiquities and European Estate Jewelry, at your service."

She thought for a moment, "Any relations to Ray?" Betsy kept herself carefully informed about the upper crust of La Jolla and Rancho Santa Fe, dead or alive.

"Ray?" Edward drew a rare blank.

"Ray Kroc! You know? Founder of McDonald's!"

"Oh, good old Ray!" Hamburgers! That American affliction! Quick to grasp a proffered straw though, he whispered in a conspiratorial tone, "You have heard of Guernsey cows. Where do you think all that ground meat comes from?" His voice trailed off as if embarrassed to flaunt his meaty connection to the beef-patty mogul. He doubted the woman knew where and what Guernsey was. To her credit, she put up a stolid front and dropped further inquisition.

"I am Betsy. Betsy Bunting. Well, actually, Mrs. Joseph Bunting."

After that defining tidbit, he invited her to lunch. With its breathtaking view, George's was an infinitely more elegant restaurant where one overlooked the cliffs of La Jolla Cove from linen-topped window tables. Edward apologized and easily lied that his car—a temperamental Jaguar XJ6, if you please—had just been towed to British Motors downtown and that he had walked down to the museum from the Village. As he had expected, she offered to drive the ten blocks north saving him the parking fee, or possibly a ticket on tightly-packed Prospect Street. The burgundy late-model Lexus convertible fitted her as little as did her exquisite too-tight blush-pink St. Johns knit. Edward could at least be sincere to admire the strand of Golden South Sea pearls buried in her short neck. She beamed. Her hubby, when he was still well enough to travel, bless him, had bought them for her in Tahiti. "Twelve millimeter. Perfectly matched." She sighed. "They cost almost as much as this car."

The ever-astute Edward gathered the Buntings' to be new-garnered wealth.

It turned out that Joe Bunting had put down hard-earned monkey-wrench cash on an all-inclusive tour of Cairo and environments. Pyramids, camel rides, Western-style hotel with bottled water, shopping at the Khan Al-Khalili Bazaar, that sort of thing. Then, Southern California's reigning plumbing contractor had fallen too ill for their planned 'third-world junket.' However, he insisted that his wife go and have a good time.

That week, Edward read several guide books on Egypt and during another sun-drenched lunch with Betsy at an ocean-front in-place called Charley's, he confided how much he envied her. Oh, how he wished to return to Egypt one more time. If only he could join her group. That way he would have her delightful company, and she a solicitous and knowledgeable companion.

"I just love Cairo," he raved implying familiarity with the sprawling metropolis. How disappointing that his remittance from Lloyd's of London was held up due to silly exchange-rate fluctuations.

After sipping a bit more of her heady Napa Chardonnay, the smitten Mrs. Bunting hit upon a brilliant idea. Would he be willing to take her husband's place on the tour—in a strictly platonic sense, of course? It was all paid for, non-refundable. He could repay her after they returned.

That afternoon, the dapper Edward Guernsey-Crock, Esquire, bought himself a pith helmet.

The Marriott Cairo in the Zamalek District was originally a palace built in 1869 by the Khedive Ismail. Its rooms are appropriately luxurious. Still, it wasn't difficult for the ever-solicitous Edward to persuade a travel-weary Mrs. Bunting to upgrade her pre-paid double to a suite in one of the hotel's new twin towers.

While an exhausted and Champagne-drowsy Betsy floated comfortably on her king-size bed eighteen stories above the Nile,

Edward rode the elevator down to the Omar Khayyam Casino, part of the hotel. After checking out several roulette tables, he went to the bar and took a stool next to an olive-skinned man sipping on a beer; obviously not a tourist. You could always find one or two enterprising locals hoping to bump into foreigners. They usually had something to sell or knew someone who did. After Betsy's interminable chatter, Edward yearned for a relaxing smoke. Besides, a local connection could be helpful in the coming days. He struck up a conversation with the taciturn man who, it turned out, was employed by the Cairo Museum. After loosening the man's tongue with several bottles of strong dark Stella Premium during two hours of intense conversation, the British Edward Guernsey-Crock and the Turkish-born Karakurt Tiryaki shook hands. They had a gentleman's agreement.

*

Lulled by the rhythmic purr of the twin Rolls Royce jet-engines, Edward imagined a panic-stricken Betsy Bunting fearing him lost or murdered in some back alley. However, once it dawned on the plump woman that her wad of travelers checks had vanished along with her charming companion, as had her strand of Golden South Sea pearls, she would undoubtedly lose the carefully maintained illusion of good breeding and turn into a vengeful shrew, making Cairo off-limits. Too bad that his passport had remained locked in the hotel safe. Luckily, he had managed to extricate her digital camera as well. It wouldn't do to have pictures of him and the gullible Mrs. B flashed across the Interpol network. On the bright side, he had traveled under American documents with a rather fuzzy photograph of a much younger, hairier Edward. His more current British passport was safely tucked into the false bottom of his carry-on. If he ever got back to California, a visit to Carlos in Tijuana would be in order. The good man could procure anything from genuine python loafers, to US green cards, to slightly used passports. He also sold excellent weed.

Edward opened his left eye just a slit and squinted at Naunet as she leaned over her laptop. *Such a fine neck*. He might have to part with the pearls for a short time. As if she sensed him looking at her, Naunet lifted her head and smiled at him. He was confident that he could beat out the young lout who tried so hard to play protector to his sophisticated older colleague.

Edward nodded across the aisle and stretched his long legs with a contented sigh. Provided he could keep the Turk in line, he had finally hit the big time. Egypt was a veritable goldmine.

The sleek Gulfstream landed at Luxor International with nary a bump. A mustard-colored older-model Mercedes pulled up as soon as the stairs hit the tarmac and the driver welcomed the three scientists into the broiler oven of Upper Egypt.

"I am Ahmed Sharkawy, Director of the Laboratory. I am also the Overseer of the Nekhen site." He shook hands all around and added with great emphasis as if to alley any doubts about his authority, "Dr. El-Masri is my very great friend."

After a brief discussion with the pilots, the rear baggage stairs were lowered and Dr. El-Masri's obliging great friend collected the luggage. A van drove up and screeched to a halt by the rear gangway. Karakurt appeared and motioned the guards to come up. The three scientists wondered with what payload they might have traveled. Two slim boxes were hauled out to be loaded into the van. Even before their own bags were stowed in the trunk of the Mercedes, the pilots secured both gangways, shut the doors and rolled back onto the runway, ready for takeoff.

"You don't mind giving me a ride to my hotel after you drop my friends at theirs."

Edward smiled at Ahmed Sharkawy and pressed something into the stunned man's palm. Without waiting for affirmation, he walked around the hood of the car and slid into the front passenger seat.

The Overseer was confused; he had been told there would be three Americans.

Jonathan, who was the only one who had noticed the surreptitious exchange, admitted to himself, *The guy has balls.* He was glad for their private accommodations. *That should rid us of the pest.*

To his dismay, he heard Naunet ask, "Edward, where are you staying?"

"The Hilton Luxor," Edward replied easily and turned to smile at her.

"Oh, and I'd like to invite you all for drinks. Shall we say, around six tomorrow? I'll be in the lobby."

He was glad that he had researched Luxor hotels in more detail than simply looking up his own, The Boomerang, which served his budget as well as his plans. 'A backpacker's haven' the brochure said.

What amused Edward was that it stated the two owners were Australian and Nubian. That notwithstanding, one of their conditions admonished they would not accept mixed couples without a marriage license. Edward shrugged. What would these race-conscious owners make of Karakurt who was to join him in his room after delivering the two Saqqara tablets to the well-guarded archaeological compound near Luxor.

* * *

Chapter Six

Their accommodations in the walled-in compound were spacious and comfortable in a Spartan sort of way. The air-conditioning worked overtime. Despite its noisy motor, it was a blessing as the outside temperature had climbed to forty-one degrees Celsius. This was the beginning of Upper Egypt's off-season when only a handful of wilting tourists ventured into the arid region enticed by colorful brochures and cheap package deals.

Jonathan decided to check out who else might be prowling around the compound. They knew that there were several active excavations going on in the area, mostly sponsored by European funding. When he stepped outside the freestanding villa, he was stopped by four armed men. It did not take him long to realize that apparently his team was to stay put until someone escorted them to a workshop. Several hours passed with the guards rotating on the hour. So far no one had appeared to show them to a laboratory, or to talk to them, or bring them any kind of food or refreshments.

Naunet decided to explore the kitchen and discovered that the refrigerator was stocked with fruit, several kinds of soft cheeses and flat bread as well as cold meat of an indistinguishable nature. There were also bottles of light and dark Stella. Though not overly fond of beer, Naunet was glad that she would have something to wash down the cheese. She noticed that at least it was not green. She knew that Bill and Jonathan would greatly appreciate and enjoy a couple of bottles each, so she grabbed what she could carry and took five bottles out.

After their improvised lunch, they were even more eager to look at the promised tablets from the Nekhen excavation. Instead, they had to wait another couple of hours for anybody to show up. Meanwhile, they tried to establish an Internet connection on their laptops. However, they could not find any wireless hotspot. Nor was there a telephone in the whole place. Nor did their one cell phone work. It was Cairo all over again. They spent the rest of the day working on their laptops, intermittently trying to establish an Internet connection. Late in the evening, they gave up and went to bed.

Mid-morning on Wednesday the obviously intentional isolation infuriated Bill. He was about to storm outside to find someone to complain to when the front door opened. Hot air rushed in distorting a billowing form that stood out eerily against the rectangle of brilliant light.

"Are you well enough? Then I will take you to the laboratory. It is close-by." Karakurt said, talking straight ahead.

Bill was no longer surprised by the Turk's ghost-like appearances. As he was the only one within earshot, he growled, "We were never unwell. And we have been ready for hours." He called out for Naunet and Jonathan to hurry up, and to grab his briefcase from his room.

The laboratory was housed in a low-slung building. Two guards were stationed at the entrance. With all that supposed gold inside, it was a wonder that the Egyptians had not called up an entire division. Perhaps, because the new dig was not yet common knowledge in the area. With everybody claiming to be everybody else's cousin, word would get around soon enough though, and Jonathan wondered how long they had to work in peace and quiet.

The large room had no windows. Instead the old-fashioned neon-fixtures practically screamed 'there is no place to hide in here.' Tables and porcelain sinks were dust-caked, and laboratory paraphernalia lay strewn about in hapless fashion.

"Oh, boy," Jonathan sighed. "It must be the maid's day off."

Stepping further into the room, they noticed the massive door at the far end.

"Now we wait." Karakurt said which forced them to stand around idly once again. To their relief, it was not long before Ahmed Sharkawy rushed in. He went straight to the back of the lab and studied the massive combination lock with intensity. Then he exercised his fingers as if he were a concert pianist about to perform a difficult sonata. Instinctively, everyone counted the forward clicks and reverse turns until the Overseer threw the door open and proudly pointed to the thick bolts imbedded in two-inch steel.

"The vault," he said, and gingerly pulled on a string that dangled from the ceiling. A bare bulb flickered on.

They saw tablet after tablet, stacked on robust metal shelves that lined the small space on three sides. Blackened and mute, they were intriguing only to a scientist, but very tempting to those in the know about their worth.

"Oh boy!" Jonathan said again, this time with wonder in his voice.

"When you have finished for the day, Karakurt will fetch me and I shall lock up."

They automatically looked back at the Turk. 'Who is this guy?' they wondered. Obviously, he was more than a lowly staff member working in a museum basement. Somebody trusted this man with a heck of a lot of gold. Or perhaps feared him enough.

Naunet recalled insistent rumors about Egypt's ex-first lady wearing priceless late-dynasty necklaces from the Cairo collections, which were apparently not on loan to the State. Opponents of the autocratic Dr. El-Masri had been quick to point a finger at him without being able to substantiate their allegations. Mainly because no one knew the exact contents of the treasure trove packed away in those dusty basement storage rooms. Yet someone always knew something. It would have to be someone who was free to rummage through those cases. Someone able to break old seals on half-forgotten crates. And someone authorized, or ordered, to reapply the resident official's seal which always had the mark of the current museum director. Now, conceivably and by indulgent ministry members, such historic donations could be viewed as promoting their country's heritage through diplomatic channels. These donations undoubtedly cemented beneficial friendships of the highest order. However, it would inevitably open the gift-giver up to certain criticism and possibly some pressure such as blackmail.

Naunet meant to talk to Bill and Jonathan later that evening regarding her rising misgivings about the Turkish 'Black Wolf,' although she did not like the idea that it could throw doubt over Edward because of his acquaintance with Karakurt. Jonathan's dislike of the enigmatic Antiquities dealer had not escaped her. If she was honest with herself, it annoyed her. Or was she angry with herself for beginning to like the tall man who was ever polite, ever solicitous, and a welcome change from the practically hermitic existence she had led over the past few years.

On closer inspection, the lab contained first-rate albeit neglected equipment and instrumentation. Bill asked himself again why the Egyptians had called for their assistance. No doubt, their own people could have hit on an effective solvent given enough time and patience. Egypt certainly had the know-how. Besides, there were several qualified foreign archaeologists in the region who would jump at the chance to cooperate on such an enticing project. With the seemingly abandoned facility, it crossed Bill's mind that someone might have had ulterior motives to involve outsiders. Had Bruno von der Heide's college friendship simply been a smokescreen to keep this extraordinary find from the scientific community—or the world, for that matter? Or was there a problem with the provisional military government presently in power? He had the uncomfortable feeling that the three of them had been dropped into a political powder keg. Bill abandoned his ruminations when he heard a muffled "Wow!" coming from inside the vault. He followed his young colleague back into the strong-room pulling Naunet along with him.

"Twenty-three, twenty-four, twenty-five," Jonathan sang out. "Wait! Those two crates over there. They look like the ones they carried off the plane."

"Could be the Saqqara tablets," Bill guessed. "That means we have twenty-seven to work on." It could take weeks to clean and decipher them all, if they worked non-stop.

"Well, the sooner we start," he said and rolled up his sleeves.

With his entrenched Bostonian mannerisms, Bill had never adopted the short-sleeved fashion of the young, although his concession to casual dress was to do away with a tie whenever he could. And being 'mad scientist Bill,' he almost always could.

On a side-table, they found containers with tightly packed ingredients for Bill's solution, their quantities neatly written out on each label. Large glass bottles had been provided for the solution itself. Once mixed, it was too acid to be stored in anything other than glass or porcelain. Someone obviously was getting messages and instructions through from Cairo without any trouble. Unless these supplies had been transported on the jet from Cairo. Bill shrugged. It was immaterial. They were here for them to use.

Interrupted only by a spare lunch brought in by Karakurt, they mixed and soaked and cut until late evening when, at last, the bottom half of a gleaming tablet emerged. Dr. El-Masri had been correct. It was solid gold, covered with tiny squares. Some of them had horizontally etched lines, and others had vertical ones. It reminded them of a miniature rattan mat, though the pattern seemed random. The reverse side was inscribed with cursive symbols. They were precise, sharp and minute.

In her element now, Naunet bent over the tablet and traced the lines admiringly with her index finger. "Hieratic," she said reverently. "Old form. Definitely pre-dynastic."

They looked at each other, elated. This changed everything. Their projects at the Institute could wait.

Early Thursday morning, unimpeded by their guards, they walked to the lab where Ahmed Sharkawy again worked his artistry with the combination of the vault. They labored all day with a good measure of success. They found that the unguent stayed pliable for quite a while after a tablet had soaked in the solution for several hours. For expediency's sake, Bill decided to work only on the side that contained the Hieratic script, once they determined which that was.

Two tablets, one side cleaned, were now laid bare for Naunet. She deciphered the familiar symbols first and then tried to match similar ones from her extensive computer indexes. Painstakingly, she filled in more and more of the texts which, so far, seemed to be some kind of travelogue across a vast green savannah. Bill continued his precision slicing and gentle prodding and peeling, and Jonathan began to analyze the ancient resin.

"Simply amazing. And so amazingly simple," he mumbled. Still, he had trouble identifying the precise origin of the natural substance and was especially stumped by another elusive ingredient until Naunet mentioned that she remembered large deposits of natural bitumen that had been found in the Dead Sea.

"Bitumen!" Jonathan hit his forehead. He should have guessed.

Their work was interrupted when Ahmed Sharkawy arrived with another man in a dark business suit and tie.

"Mr. Mahmoud Zawwam, Head of Luxor Antiquities. The boss." The important official inquired if they had everything they needed, if they were comfortable in their quarters, and if the food was adequate. They asked about an Internet connection and again encountered the indigenous shoulder-shrug.

"We are working on it." It was as evasive as it was definite. No Internet.

Bill changed the subject and explained their progress.

"Excellent," Mr. Zawwam said. "Cairo will be pleased." Again, they realized that there had to be some connection for him to inform 'Cairo.' It was curious that he had not said 'Dr. El-Masri.' After all, this was supposed to be the Minister's own well-guarded project.

Before the two men left, Ahmed Sharkawy turned back and said, "My chief digger Wamukota will bring more tablets from the site."

"You found more? That's fantastic." Naunet said, at the same time hoping that a so-named *left-handed* digger would not lose his way in the desert, given that he was transporting slabs of gold.

"We found another five," the Overseer confirmed and, as if he had read her thoughts, added, "Wamukota is completely trustworthy."

Sharkawy stepped closer to a table with an exposed tablet. For someone used to handling important finds he was in complete awe, perhaps because of the enormous value of the slate, which easily represented many times his entire life's earnings. It was also obvious to Naunet that the lab director was unable to make any sense of the ancient symbols, although he tried to cover his deficiency admirably.

At last, the two officials left and the three scientists went back to work, again interrupted only by Karakurt who wheeled in a trolley with a more palatable lunch this time, as well as three large cans of the popular Stella brew. Jonathan would have preferred a bottle of ice-cold Meister Max, with its eight percent alcohol content. Although, with more work ahead of them, he knew that the lighter choice was the better one.

Naunet glanced at her watch. It was a quarter to five.

"Oh my goodness. This is Thursday! I completely forgot. Edward invited us for drinks this evening."

"I'll pass," Jonathan said immediately.

Bill declined as well, but then had a thought. The exclusive Hilton Luxor Resort was bound to have Wi-Fi wafting through its halls. If not, there surely would be a live connection in a guest's room.

"Naunet, you go," he said ignoring the glare Jonathan shot at him. "And take your laptop."

They put their heads together and drafted a detailed message to Dr. Bruno at the Institute with a copy to his home, just in case. That way, Naunet could send the e-mails within seconds, preferably unobserved.

"You can send it from the Ladies'." Bill hoped she would not have to use the guest-room option. It could complicate things.

Overseer Sharkawy reappeared for the locking-up ritual and they left the lab with him, nodding to the ever-present guards outside. Parked in front of their quarters was the mustard-yellow Mercedes. Karakurt leaned gingerly against the blistering hood and informed them that he would be pleased to take Naunet to the Luxor Hotel as soon as he got back from dropping the Overseer at his home.

Bill had that spooky powder keg feeling again. He would ask the technologically more adept Jonathan to look for a hidden mike in the lab. In addition to being trusted and extremely well informed, the Turk apparently was also their designated chauffeur-around-town. *Warden is more like it*, Bill thought. The man probably wore a sidearm stuffed in the belt of his khakis. *No wonder he isn't wearing his galabya.* Bill grinned at the image of Karakurt fishing a handgun from under an ankle-length shirt. Although, the result would most likely be less amusing.

Naunet was almost an hour late since she had showered and changed, and then piled her hair into a complicated French twist. Edward was in the hotel lobby, seated comfortably in one of the overstuffed chairs. He sipped something and appeared neither anxious nor impatient.

"You look beautiful," he smiled. "I hope you are hungry. You choose. A bland dining room," at which he wrinkled his nose slightly, "or a delightful patio I just discovered." She chose the patio. It never failed. Women invariably went for 'delightful,' which kept his expenses down.

Immersed mostly in her career over the years, Naunet had almost forgotten how pleasant an evening with a charming man could be. After an aperitif, she finally allowed herself to relax. Edward was a good listener. He was interested in her career, and he was amusing. A couple of hours went by before Naunet remembered to excuse herself, ostensibly to find a ladies room.

It would still be early morning in Boston. She set her laptop on the marble counter and moved it around to find a Wi-Fi hotspot. "Bingo," she said and was about to sign into her e-mail account, when two women burst in. Animated and perspiring in polyester, she couldn't miss—Americans. Too late to hide her laptop, she closed the lid halfway not wanting to break the connection.

"Isn't it terrible," the blonder of the two cried. "We don't know what's going to happen to us now." She pointed at Naunet's laptop. "Oh, you can pull it up."

Was the confounded woman asking her to check on their flight?

"Yahoo News," the second woman directed, adding cryptically, "I hope they haven't started a civil war."

Now alarmed herself, Naunet opened the laptop and quickly changed to the Yahoo homepage. Scrolling down, the headlines screamed 'Soccer coach scandal,' and 'Kardashian sisters launch plus-size denim line.' Finally, she found 'Egypt in turmoil once again.'

"There it is!" The excited blonde poked at the screen.

Naunet was tempted to slap her red-tipped finger. The article filled in and their heads almost touched as they drew together over the laptop.

'Demonstrations in Cairo. Presidential candidates battle for votes. Ministers resign. Among them, previously fired and re-hired Chairman of the Supreme Council. Cairo Museum looted. Curfew reinstated. Military fires into crowd. Casualties in Tahrir Square protests.'

The women nodded a smug 'told you so,' and then remembered why they had come in. As soon as they had installed themselves in their respective cubicles, Naunet brought up her e-mail again, added a few sentences to the drafts, and pushed *Send*. Dr. Bruno and the outside world likely knew a lot more about the situation than she and her isolated colleagues did. Why hadn't Edward said anything? The hotel was full of televisions and international newspapers.

Naunet quickly brought up the English version of the Arabic-language newspaper, *Al Jazeera*, and gave its headlines a cursory glance searching for headlines with politics in it.

Had she been alone, she might not have missed a small article about a former presidential jet missing from Almaza Air Force Base. It had apparently gone down somewhere in the desert during a routine training flight. The G-4 pilots, Col. Rahman and Lt. Col. al-Husri, were missing. After an extensive search had turned up nothing, they were presumed dead.

Naunet slid the laptop back into her bag and left the still conversing duo to their pressing business. She decided not to mention the encounter to her engaging dinner companion. Just how much did Edward and Karakurt know. And what did they not tell? Was Dr. El-Masri's position in jeopardy again? If so, what would become of their project? More importantly, what was to become of them, practically imprisoned in Upper Egypt?

Anxious to get back to the compound, Naunet diplomatically brought the evening to an end, and agreed to another *delightful* evening with Edward. When she suggested that she would simply love for Bill and Jonathan to see this beautiful resort hotel, Edward immediately agreed. He would be most pleased to meet them again. Would Saturday suit them?

For a second, Naunet was taken aback by his enthusiasm. Had she misread his interest in her? Not once during the evening had he come up with an old and overused pretext to get something from his room. Would she care to come along, the view from his balcony was breathtaking. On the one hand, his good manners were refreshing. On the other hand, she was disappointed. At the very least, she would have liked to be able to say 'No thanks.' Or would she have?

* * *

Chapter Seven

On Friday afternoon, they had one complete tablet exposed. Naunet inspected it closely. She noticed the minute outline of an inverted horseshoe-like sign on the lower rim.

"Ten," she cried.

"Dream on," Jonathan mumbled, bent over his vials. "So far, I think we're only about half through with two."

"No. Look! Down here, along the rim. There is an inverted U. That's the number ten. Wait! Here is another. No, there are five. Fifty! Oh, and to the left of them are three pairs of three straight lines. Fifty-Nine!" Naunet fairly trembled with excitement. She straightened up to look for a magnifying glass.

"Good Lord," Bill said and shut off his laser.

"Oh, now I see." Naunet bent lower again with the magnifier pressed against her right eye. "A mouth-sign above the Fifty. Which is 'part of.' Nine of fifty!" Her excitement caught on and both Bill and Jonathan stepped over to take a closer look. "If these tablets are numbered, this could mean there are fifty in all. So, this one would be number nine of fifty."

"Wow," Jonathan breathed. "Fifty slabs of pure gold! That's more than some small country's GDP. Actually, not so small, these days."

"Wow indeed. If they manage to dig them all up, they may keep us here forever." If Bill's reality check veiled his enthusiasm, his mind was already back on the project. This was fantastic. "Why don't we clean off all the lower rims first. That way, Naunet's translation might make more sense. If indeed there is some sort of chronological story here."

Naunet was already back examining the exposed lower rim. "There is another mark. About a centimeter to the right of the number," she cried. "Jon, quick, hand me the magnifier again."

Jonathan loved seeing her all flushed and eager, even if the reason for it was an inanimate—albeit priceless—object. "I don't think it's going anywhere, my dear," he grinned and slowly handed her the magnifying glass. When she reached for it, he pulled it smartly back.

"One day, Jonathan, I am going to punch you," she laughed, her eyes wide, her cheeks the color of his mother's Pink Lady roses, and the bun of her shiny dark hair in danger of coming undone.

"Yes, now I see it," Naunet breathed. "It's a tiny winged scarab."

Jonathan let go of his daydreams and slipped back into his role as scientist. "Say, didn't Dr. El-Masri mention that one of the Saqqara high priests was practically covered with the bug?"

"That's right," Naunet agreed. "Those tablets could have been his. Perhaps that was why he took them to Memphis when it became the new capital, he being the High Priest of Ptah in the pre-dynastic Ineb-hedj."

"That was during the Old Kingdom, wasn't it, Naunet?" Bill looked at her. She simply nodded, searching the tablet's rim for more inscriptions.

"Possibly," Jonathan mused, "they carried some unusual messages or meaning for him."

"Either way, let's uncover the Saqqara rims first," Naunet suggested. "If they are part of the fifty, there had to be a reason why only those two were taken to Memphis and then buried at Saqqara."

"Good point." Bill said. "We'll ask Karakurt to uncrate them. It'll take a crowbar to loosen those nails."

They worked through until Saturday afternoon to around four o'clock when Karakurt arrived without Ahmed Sharkawy. He said that he could close up the lab himself since he did not need the combination to lock the vault. Besides, he added, the Overseer had been called away and would not return until Monday. "You have Sunday off. Like in America," he grinned.

When he saw all the tablets spread out on the tables and noticed that only the rims had been exposed on some, he furiously waived his arms.

"Why you do this? You finish one. Then you work on another."

The scientists ignored his rudeness.

"You tell me why," the taciturn man insisted.

Bill's "No, we'll talk to Mr. Sharkawy, or better yet, to Mr. Mahmoud Zawwam. You ask them to come here," was definite enough for Karakurt to realize he was not going to be told anything more about this change in procedure.

After folding the long white damask table cloth, Karakurt used the same trolley on which he had wheeled in their lunch to haul the tablets they had worked on back into the vault. With undue emphasis, he slammed the heavy steel door shut and turned to leave. Jonathan had stepped up behind him and, reaching past the Turk, twisted the combination several times. The simple gesture earned the Boston metallurgist a murderous look.

To soften the obvious dent to the man's pride, Bill asked Karakurt very nicely if he would drive them to the Luxor Hilton that evening to meet Edward. The simple request improved the man's mood as if it were his pleasure to take them into Luxor.

He must like riding around in a Mercedes, Jonathan thought.

As they were going to the hotel for casual drinks the two men did not want to appear with shoulder bags stuffed with their laptops. Dr. El-Masri had admonished them not to invite anyone's curiosity. In that respect, Jonathan wondered about Edward's connection to Karakurt. Naunet had stashed her laptop in a large tote, again with e-mail drafts to Dr. Bruno ready to be sent. They hoped that his reply would come up in her Yahoo mail which was not exactly a secure way to communicate. At least the browser was universally accessible.

Edward again waited for them in the lobby and steered them to a pleasant swimming-pool bar where overhead fans distributed fine mist over the sparse afternoon crowd. A couple of drinks relaxed everyone.

Even Jonathan had to admit that this was a pleasant interlude to their back-bent toiling in the stuffy lab. He turned around and motioned the waiter for another round and, as if by accident, slightly brushed Naunet's arm. She smiled and excused herself. *Good girl.* He quickly engaged Edward in some meaningless conversation about the market for counterfeits of Egyptian antiquities.

Once in the ladies' restroom, Naunet prayed that she would be alone for some time and opened her laptop which started purring right away. She quickly brought up Google and typed in 'Egypt plus Cairo plus Unrest.'

The latest news was a couple of minutes old. The first headline to scream from the page was, 'To prevent looting, Cairo Museum rehires Dr. Jabari El-Masri.'

Without stopping to read the article, Naunet brought up several other pertinent headlines, U.S. as well as Egyptian, and with a quick copy-function, pasted them into a blank Word-document. They would read the details later. Then she signed into her Yahoo e-mail account. There were several messages from the boss back in Cambridge. She did a cursory reading and realized that she should make some changes to her drafts. Just then, several women came in and she quickly pushed the send button. She would have to find another way to ask Dr. Bruno to send them all the news he could of political developments in the besieged capital. Naunet considered the obvious alternative to getting an Internet connection. She just hoped it wouldn't bring unforeseen complications.

When she got back to the bar, she pushed her drink away and said she was so sorry. The heat had given her such a blasting headache that she wished she could lie down for a bit. She lightly tapped her satchel. Both Bill and Jonathan realized that she needed another hotspot.

Edward jumped up and immediately said that, in this case, they had better return to the compound at once. "We wouldn't want Naunet to suffer needlessly. This heat can fell the best of us. I'll see if I can find Karakurt."

Jonathan could not believe the man would pass up the opportunity to offer his air-conditioned hotel suite for a lie-down, as the British called it. Inwardly, he was relieved that Naunet's ruse to get into the man's room, but hopefully not his pants, was dismissed so cavalierly. The bloody man was either dense or he had something to hide. Hopefully, he was gay. Jonathan wished he had his laptop with him so he could do a quick search on the slippery Brit.

Edward came back to the table and sat down again. "By the way," he said in his languid annoying fashion, and fished an ice cube from his fresh drink. He wrapped it in a napkin which he then pressed against the back of Naunet's neck, "I did not want to alarm you, my dear. The provisional government seems to have shut Cairo down completely. The city is under military rule. It may take some time for them to sort themselves out. Even up here, I have heard rumblings of an insurrection against this state's governor."

"Have you heard anything about the Antiquities Department and our mutual friend, Dr. El-Masri," Naunet asked innocently and, remembering her supposedly splitting headache, thanked him for the ice treatment.

"I understand that everything is at a standstill," Edward replied lightly and bent down until he was cheek-to-cheek with Naunet, "Better?"

"Yes, much. Thank you." She smiled up, her inviting lips only inches from his. Quickly, she added, "It's getting late. I think we better go. Did you find Karakurt?"

On Sunday, Naunet had planned a visit to Luxor's Museum of Ancient Egyptian Art which was as small and pristine as the Cairo Museum was vast and dusty. Karakurt informed her that it was closed. Not because it was Sunday, but because of the political unrest. It had forced the officials to close all the Luxor monuments to the public. Her insistence that she was not 'the public,' and that he should ask Mr. Zawwam for special permission for her, met with shrugs and eye-rolling.

"Not allowed," Karakurt repeated stubbornly.

Again, they sat around without being able to work since the tablets were locked up in the vault. At least, Naunet was able to compare her computer lists against what they had uncovered so far. She wished she had also brought her new lightweight laptop. Its Webcam and Outlook program would at least have given her a chance to get in touch with her father. Not having foreseen their forced isolation, she had only packed her older Mac since it contained all her translation programs.

On Monday, the five tablets from the Nekhen excavation did not arrive as promised by Ahmed Sharkawy. Nor did Mahmoud Zawwam meet with them, as requested. It made them wonder if possibly he had been removed from his position as Head of Luxor's Antiquities.

At least, Ahmed Sharkawy showed up to unlock the vault so that they could continue their work in the lab. With the supposed reinstatement of Dr. El-Masri, albeit only as the Museum director and not as a member of the Supreme Council, they were hopeful for some news regarding their own situation and the future of the project.

That hope was dampened on Tuesday morning when Karakurt came to their quarters announcing that the Nekhen site had collapsed. Thieves had broken through the shuttered entrance during the night. Their unqualified digging through a side chamber had caused the collapse of the main tunnel after the regular crew had begun work, somehow unaware of the previous night's mischief. Wamukota, the chief digger, had been killed. Karakurt did not elaborate.

It was now Wednesday, the twenty-third. They had been in Egypt for two weeks. The outside temperature rose to one-hundred-and-ten degrees Fahrenheit. They continued their work on the tablets exposing one rim after another. Finally, a reluctant Karakurt uncrated the two Saqqara tablets.

Each night when they returned to their quarters, they found the refrigerator restocked with fresh produce and plenty of beer. At least, they had not been forgotten.

On Thursday evening, the Turk handed Naunet a cream-colored envelope from which she pulled a single sheet. It bore the Hilton Luxor Hotel's letterhead, and was signed "Your devoted friend, Edward."

In the note, Edward was sorry for his week-long absence. He had been in Port Safaga and also that, because of his connections, he had learned that things would likely be back to quasi normal after the weekend. He would be back by this Friday. Would she please come to the hotel to have dinner with him that evening at seven?

Karakurt wheeled in an early lunch on Friday, and after they had finished eating, they placed the two Saqqara tablets upright in a porcelain basin to soften the pitch around their rims. It would take until the next morning at least for the pitch to be cut safely with the laser.

Naunet asked to have the Saqqara ones cleaned off completely before tackling any more of the others. She still maintained that they had to be special. Bill insisted that they get all the numbers sorted out first. He was of course right even if she was dying to awaken the ancient secrets from their golden five-thousand year old slumber.

Around four in the afternoon, Ahmed Sharkawy rushed in, visibly agitated. "I am here only for a moment. I must lock up now." He pressed Karakurt to hurry up loading his trolley to wheel the tablets back into the vault. Then he practically herded the three scientists out the door before they could clean up.

Karakurt was the last out the door. He glanced back at the two Saqqara tablets left soaking in their basin on a corner table. He also noticed the laser on the table next to them.

If Edward was annoyed to find the three of them again entering the Hilton lobby, he did not show it. He kissed Naunet on the check and jovially pumped Bill's hand while slapping Jonathan on the shoulder with his left, laughing, "They say, the more the merrier." After his initial disappointment, he was actually relieved. These people had expense accounts, and he was sure he could get the old guy to pick up the tab again.

Before they went on to dinner, Edward asked if he could take some pictures of the three of them to remember his lovely time in Luxor. He took one of Naunet in the middle of the two men, of Naunet with Jonathan, of Naunet with Bill. And, of course, of Naunet with him, arm possessively draped around her shoulder. Then he asked if Naunet would pose for a picture by herself.

"Oh, wait," he said. "I have a favor to ask you. Would you model a necklace for me?" He casually pulled Betsy Bunting's precious pearls from a pocket. Naunet gasped. "Golden South Sea," she breathed and put her hand in front of her lips.

Before she could recover from her awe, Edward had them around her neck, expertly fastening the clasp. "There," he said. "Fit for a queen. Now, why don't you stand against this marble wall right here. I don't want any distracting scenery for this nice close-up." He snapped and sighed, "When I tell them back home that I met Nefertiti in the flesh, they won't believe me without proof."

"You really know how to charm a lady." Naunet looked up at Edward from under half-closed eyes rewarding him with one of her rare coquettish smiles.

"Not just a lady, my dear, but a queen." Edward took her hand, leaned over and brushed a kiss against the back of it. As he held onto her hand, he smiled and looked into her eyes.

"Let's eat," Jonathan growled. "I'm getting sick."

After they were settled in the dining room, Edward mentioned that he had been in Safaga during the past few days, making new contacts. Business was good. He rubbed his hands, apparently pleased with himself. "I must tell you, Safaga is perfect right now. Cool sea breezes, beautiful beaches, and few tourists. It's the greatest spot for diving, if one is so inclined." He leaned back in his chair, satiated with good food and plenty of wine. Ever alert to someone else's mood, he sensed that Bill and Jonathan had glanced at Naunet who kept her eyes fixed on her glass. "Did I say something wrong?"

"No, of course not," Naunet assured him quickly. "It is a great place. I wish I was there rather than here suffering from heatstroke."

"That's just it." Edward pounced at the perfect opening. "I have a friend there who offered me his villa for the weekend. It overlooks the Red Sea. I was hoping to persuade you to accompany me. I have to go back there tomorrow." He spoke directly to Naunet so as not to give the two men any ideas. "Just until Sunday. It would do you good. I suspect you have been working much too hard."

"Oh, heavens, I still have your necklace on." Naunet reached back to undo the clasp. Quick to seize an opportunity to endear himself to a lady, Edward put his hand on hers.

"You keep them until tomorrow. That way, I know you'll come." Turning toward Jonathan, he added quietly, "Too bad, old man. The villa only has two bedrooms. So, be a good chap and find something to dig up in the meantime."

"I might do that." Jonathan poked Edward in the chest. "And perhaps I just might find me some dirt."

After they got back to their quarters, Naunet went straight to her room slamming the door behind her. It left no doubt how furious she was with her younger colleague for his behavior. Bill diplomatically mumbled something about being dead-tired and he, too, retreated to his bedroom hoping the two would mend fences sooner or later. Most likely, he feared, not before Naunet went off on her little junket to Safaga. At the moment, Jonathan did not like himself very much either. He went to the kitchen and took a Stella from the refrigerator unsure if he wanted to go to bed or not. He decided to stay up a while and went back to the living room, finding a few choice descriptions for his opponent, the least offensive of which was 'dandy.'

"I think we need to talk." Naunet had changed into a light-grey tee and the same-colored tricot shorts. She had loosened her hair which fell in dark waves over her shoulders. Jonathan could see the bumps of her nipples and all he wanted to do was to take her into his arms. Actually, it was not all he wanted to do. He quickly slumped down on the well-worn leather couch embarrassed by his rising desire.

"You know how much you mean to me. As a colleague, and a friend."

Jonathan winced.

"I hate to be at odds with you, Jon. Please, do understand. I am driving to Safaga tomorrow with Edward. I am sorry if you are not okay with this. It is my decision. And it is my life." She wished she hadn't added the last words. An overnight trip hardly constituted her life.

"And I hate to see you get all flustery and flirty with a guy like that. I'm telling you, he is no good." Jonathan was getting hotter under his collar.

Naunet felt bad for him. She wanted her old Jonathan back. "Flustery and flirty?" She batted her lashes at him and swiveled her hips. "You mean like this?" Her blue eyes were large and innocent. Then she fanned her face with her hand like an overwhelmed beauty queen.

They broke into gobs of laughter.

"You are too much." Jonathan finally managed to say, but turned serious again. "I am just worried about you with all that's going on. I am sorry if I upset you. I don't trust this guy. If you asked me, which you did not, he has something up his sleeve." Jonathan got angrier by the minute. He breathed deeply to calm himself. "I realize that you also want to visit Safaga because of your mother. I hope this will bring you closure."

The mention of her mother dissipated the last vestiges of

Naunet's anger. She sat down next to Jonathan and he put his arm around her genuinely wanting to comfort her.

Akila Klein had vanished during a cave dive off Safaga. The intricate reefs there were riddled with deep crevasses and the experienced woman simply never surfaced. Somehow she had become separated from her local guide who swore that he never lost sight of her until she rounded a large outcropping. At first, it was feared that she was the victim of a shark attack. The notion was quickly dismissed, however, as no trace of her or her equipment was ever found. At the time of the accident, Naunet was visiting her father's excavation site on Crete and the tragic news did not reach them until a week later. Leopold Klein immediately flew to Hurghada alone not wanting his daughter traumatized any further. He telephoned Bruno von der Heide in Boston and his old friend was only too pleased to be of assistance. To the curator's delight, Naunet was not only a dedicated and capable young woman, she had turned out to be a most pleasant addition to his staff. That she was beautiful to boot did not escape the virile man. He only hoped that this would not prevent some of his male assistants from keeping their fertile minds on their work.

"Mother is the main reason why I want to go there," Naunet said. She got up and went toward the door of her bedroom. Before she stepped inside, she turned and, flashing him one of her brilliant smiles, said, "Thank you, Jonathan. So, you'll see me off tomorrow?"

"You bet," Jonathan grinned back. What was a man to do?

* * *

Part II - The Storm

Chapter Eight

Naunet was waiting outside with her overnight bag when Karakurt arrived promptly at eight to pick her up. After the upsetting confrontation with Jonathan the night before, she was eager to leave and quickly stepped up to the softly humming Mercedes. Because of it being an older-model, the trunk lock popped readily under the pressure of her thumb and she lifted the lid up. Two flat boxes covered the floor of the trunk and for no reason at all, Naunet wondered if Karakurt was taking two pizzas for their lunch. She bent over the large space and tried to put one on top of the other. They would not budge an inch. So she placed her bag on top of the one on the right, just as Karakurt shoved her roughly aside. He slammed the lid down so hastily that he almost closed it on her hand.

"We are on time, aren't we? Edward won't be going anywhere without us," Naunet said. She hoped her driver wasn't in one of his dark moods. Road rage in Egypt more often than not turned deadly. She was glad that it would not be too long before they were to pick up Edward at the Hilton.

She had settled herself in the backseat just as Jonathan came running out of their quarters. Naunet hoped that he was not going to try and stop her from her weekend again. She really looked forward to getting away for a couple of days. *My goodness, I have been slaving from morning 'til night without much of a break, talking to no one except an old man and a boy. Well, that is a bit unfair*, she thought. To her, Jonathan was more often than not too boyish and exuberant to be taken seriously. She had always enjoyed the company of, and occasional involvement with, a more seasoned man. A man who was, for lack of a better word, worldly without being pompous; assertive without being pushy; and one who knew how to treat her like a lady without exposing her to wind and salt spray on a sailboat. There had been times when she had wanted to cry. Out of her liking for the fervent young skipper, she had hidden her true feelings from him. But if the truth was known, she did not particularly like sailing, especially in the rough waters off the New England coast.

Edward was seasoned, good-looking and from all appearances financially well situated. Naunet suddenly wondered where he lived. God, she hoped not on that stormy namesake island of his in the English Channel. I'll find out during the next two days. She smiled and rolled the window down to see what Jonathan wanted. Then she saw that he had her laptop-bag in his hand.

"Hi. I just wanted to make sure you didn't need this."

He appeared to have forgotten all about their disagreement from the night before. As she told him that, no, she would not need her laptop, she knew that he must have been in her room after she left. That was Jonathan. Impetuous; but most of all, caring. She smiled again to make sure he knew that everything would be a-okay, as he used to say, waving unimportant matters aside in his carefree way.

"Don't forget to write," he smirked. "And have a drink for me on the beach." Quite unexpectedly, he reached into the car and stroked her hair. "Off you go now. You got your passport?"

Naunet nodded, relieved they were friends again. With Karakurt impatiently racing the motor in neutral, she rolled the window up and waved.

Jonathan, his hair tousled, wearing his favorite Newport-Bermuda race tee shirt, looked at her through the glass with that lopsided grin of his. Although at that particular moment it appeared sad. As the car pulled away, Naunet saw his lips move.

She thought he mouthed 'I love you.'

Inside the air-conditioned Mercedes, the 125-mile drive through the ancient Wadi Hammamat was comfortable. Karakurt, whose mood had improved considerably after picking up Edward, said that they could expect to arrive in Safaga by late-morning.

"Imagine how long it took the ancients to travel through this Wadi five thousand years ago," Naunet mused. "This was an extremely important trade route connecting the Nile with the Red Sea. Traders came down along the Red Sea, or they sailed across from the Arabian Peninsula, and many traveled through the desert from deep inside this continent. The Egyptians also mined quite a bit of gold in here."

Edward, who had listened with only half an ear, perked up. "Gold? Now that's the best reason I can think of for a dig," he joked. They drove on in companionable silence until he casually asked, "Speaking of gold. How come you people didn't complete a whole tablet before working on the next?"

Naunet bristled slightly. 'You people' did not sit well with her, and she was alarmed by Edward's apparent knowledge of their progress. She fixed her eyes on the back of Karakurt's reddening neck noting that he watched her through the rearview mirror. "There is a reason." Her tone was cool. The silence between them became less comfortable.

After a while, Edward took her hand in his. She loved a man with beautiful hands. His certainly were, with elegant long fingers and well-polished nails. Naunet was suddenly conscious of her own neglected nails. She desperately needed a manicure. Sloshing around in Bill's solutions had not helped one bit. She promised herself to go into one of the resorts and get herself presentable again. Embarrassed, she tried to pull her hand back. But Edward held on tight.

"I have a surprise for you," he said easily and then tapped Karakurt on the shoulder. "We'll stop at the marina first."

Port Safaga had slowly metamorphosed into a low-key holiday resort in contrast to Hurghada which lay some miles to the north with its superior dive sites. Safaga still had a sizable commercial harbor where vessels stopped to provision before transiting the Suez Canal, and mid-sized cruise ships stopped routinely to disgorge their masses for land excursions to Luxor and the Valley of the Kings. Small fishing vessels still made it their homeport. They had built a modern small-boat marina which lay separate from the huge piers. An array of pleasure yachts were for hire, mainly through worldwide franchises, such as the Moorings. Here, sailors also found safe haven from arduous circumnavigations after cheating violent storms and Somali pirates, or both, if they had been lucky.

After they arrived, Karakurt sped off. Edward explained that he had to go on some errands in town. Naunet's eyebrows went up as Edward steered her down a dock rocking slightly with every step. Naunet remembered that she should look at the horizon, not down at her feet.

"Don't tell me you chartered a boat," she said anxiously.

"No, this is better." He grinned back at her in that disarming way of his. He took her by the elbow and then slowed her down in front of a bow that jutted out a couple of feet over the wooden dock.

The wide-bodied sloop sat low in the water. Even though her dark-blue boot stripe and sail covers were somewhat bleached out, she looked seaworthy. Several orange canisters and a small red gas can were strapped to the lifelines. The hump of a dinghy lashed to the foredeck took slightly away from her elegant lines. On the whole, however, the vessel looked well cared for. Blue sailcloth shielded the cockpit from wind and spray and curious eyes present in every marina. Jonathan would have pronounced her shipshape. The man really loved boats.

"Ahoy there! Permission to come aboard?" Edward called out gamely. A couple emerged from below.

Naunet looked up in surprise. *Good heavens, they must be in their seventies.* Oddly, they seemed dressed for land, including street shoes. Naunet always noticed shoes, a habit left over from when her father had told her to take note of a man's shoes. 'You can always tell if someone takes proper care of himself by the heels of his shoes.' Jonathan was almost fanatic about not letting anyone on his boat without soft-soled footwear. Looking again at the nice couple, Naunet wondered if they were to join them at the resort for lunch.

"Edward! Glad you made it," the man's tanned face broke into a relieved grin.

The woman extended a sun-freckled hand to Naunet. "Come on aboard. I hope you'll like our *Tumbleweed.*"

"Naunet," Edward said, "Meet Edith and Harry Jenkins."

After introductions all around, Edward explained, "Harry and Edie are flying to the States and I agreed to take care of their boat until their return. He added, "hopefully soon," and thumped Harry, who was a head shorter than he, on the back.

The two men were soon involved with motors, batteries and shut-off valves.

Edie winked at Naunet, "It's what cruiser-wives call bilge-talk. It happens every time one skipper meets another. They just talk and talk until cocktail time. Then they go on to harrowing tales from their last passage. We all love it. Now, why don't we go below and I'll show you around my little world."

If the hull's paint job looked understandably sea-worn, below-decks was spotless. The many teak cabinets and cubbyholes as well as the double stainless steel sink were polished, and the cabin-sole gleamed with high-gloss varnish. Inviting forest-green velvet covered the horseshoe settee that wrapped around a good-sized table dissected by the sturdy keel-stepped mast. Other than two over-stuffed duffle bags and a backpack on the opposite banquette, everything was neatly stowed.

"It's beautiful," Naunet complimented the obviously proud Edie. "How long have you been sailing?"

"Do you mean us in total? It seems, forever. This was our big adventure. We bought the boat new in Texas and had it trucked to San Diego where Harry spent almost a year getting familiar and outfitting it. It also gave us a chance to visit with our kids who live there and in Arizona."

"I can't imagine living so close with someone for such a long time," Naunet said, never having had to share her own space for more than an occasional visit from an admirer. And no matter how idyllic or exciting the weekend had been, she was always glad when the man finally left.

Edie stepped closer to Naunet and pointed discretely forward. Her husband was kneeling, squeezed into what appeared to be a small closet, with Edward hanging onto its outer doorframe, looking slightly disgusted. They heard Harry explain the flushing mechanism of a marine head.

"It helps if you like your man," Edie chuckled.

"Apparently," Naunet laughed. "I imagine anything less could be a nightmare."

They stood close together in the tiny galley and Edie showed her how to open the cabinets above the double sink by sticking her finger through a hole, releasing the latch inside.

"Your bottles have socks on!"

"Keeps them from rattling. Besides, Harry gave up wearing socks a long time ago. That is, unless he gets cold. Then we have to empty a bottle." She winked.

"It seems so comfortable for such a small space." Naunet liked this woman and wished she could get to know her better. If only she liked boats as well.

Edie sighed, "It's our home. We love it. And we are so lucky to have met Edward last week. It is such a relief to know we can leave our boat in good hands. I know you two will take good care of her. He told us that you have sailed together quite a bit."

Edward stuck his head through the hatch. "I am afraid you'll have to hurry to get to Hurghada in time for your flight. Karakurt is ready to take you now."

"Oh, before I forget," Harry said to Edward. "Could I see your passport? Just a precaution. You understand."

"Of course. Not a problem." Edward rummaged in the pockets of his carelessly tossed jacket and produced a burgundy British passport. Once he realized that Harry was copying his personal data onto a sheet of paper, he seemed disconcerted, Naunet thought, then dismissing it as natural. No one enjoyed this sort of information floating around another person's luggage.

Naunet climbed back out, glad that she was spared to comment on Edie's earlier remark. She and Edward were about to step off the boat when Harry popped his head out from the cabin and asked—almost apologetically—if he could take a look at Naunet's passport as well.

"Oh, I am not staying on the boat. I need to be back in Luxor by tomorrow evening."

Edward patted her hand. "No problem, dear. I'll go back with you." To Harry, who was hoisting two duffle bags into the cockpit, he said, "I can leave the boat for a night or two, can't I, Harry." It was a statement.

Tumbleweed's owner did not reply and only Naunet saw a quick frown cross the man's sunburned face.

Edward gallantly helped Edie, carrying a backpack, off the boat.

"I wish there was more time for you to get to know this delightful lady of mine."

They all smiled at Naunet who was unsure of what was going on. It certainly would not have been any problem to leave Luxor in plenty of time to have visited with this nice couple a bit longer.

Harry lowered their bags onto the dock, and Karakurt stacked the two duffles on the front passenger seat. When he reached for Edie's backpack, she shook her head and hugged it closely to her. Just then, Naunet remembered that her own bag was still in the trunk. No need to worry about it now, she thought. Karakurt would be back to take them to that friend's villa later. Handshakes all around again, and the Turk herded the Jenkins's none too gently into the Mercedes. As they settled in, Naunet heard Edie ask her husband if he had their tickets and passports since his mind was obviously still on his beloved boat.

"Edward, I couldn't get a slip with electricity," Harry called out the open car window. "It wouldn't have done any good anyway. Someone stole our extension cord a ways back. Besides, their voltage is two-twenty here and this boat is wired for one-ten dock power. If you can get a transformer and a new cord, I'll reimburse you when we get back."

Edward started to look bored as Harry went on, "Don't forget to charge the batteries once a day by running the motor. Make sure you open the salt-water intake first, or you'll burn it up. I've left detailed instructions on the nav-table."

Naunet almost expected him to add, 'The numbers for the pediatrician and the grandparents are on top of the list.'

Harry did add, "Our slip is paid up for two months. We'll e-mail Mohammad, the marina manager, as soon as our return is firm. Oh, and Edward, I paid a local diver to scrub her bottom. He works for the marina. The guy is supposed to come early Monday morning. If he doesn't show up, let Mohammad know." As the car pulled away, Harry stuck his head out the open window again and wagged his finger at them. "Just don't sail off with her."

It was the first time that Naunet had heard Edward laugh out loud. The laugh was infectious and made her laugh as well. She wanted to kid Harry if he meant his beloved boat or her. Instead, Karakurt accelerated and roared off. The last glimpse she caught was of Edie placing a hand over her heart and looking back through the rear window like a worried mother leaving her child in a stranger's care.

"So, Edward, are they friends of yours?" Naunet hoped he would explain why he had told them that they had sailed together.

"Not exactly." With his long legs, Edward easily hopped on the boat and reached back to pull her up. Plopping down comfortably on the cockpit's cushioned starboard bench, he rolled up his pant legs to the knee, kicked off his loafers and wiggled his bare feet in the sun. He nodded for Naunet to do the same. "I met them last week when I was here."

"They are leaving their boat with someone they hardly know?"

"Well, they didn't have much choice, did they now? Apparently, he needs some kind of surgery and you can understand that they don't want him under the knife in Egypt. It was either me or leaving it unattended. Not a good idea around here, wouldn't you say."

"What about the marina? I imagine they take care of unattended boats all the time. Wouldn't they have taken care of *Tumbleweed*? Odd name for a boat."

"They are from Nevada. That's why it says 'Reno, Nevada' after the boat's name. Get it?"

Naunet hesitated for a moment at his tone before she figured he might be teasing. "Got it," she smiled back. 'You've got to loosen up,' Jonathan more than once had told her. He liked to tease her too, his voice always gentle and never with a trace of sarcasm.

"I just thought people usually named their boats for something to do with the ocean, or at least their realized dream to be on the water."

Jonathan had named his boat *Solace*. To her, it conjured up comfort and warmth and dockside conviviality. It was a misnomer. The Hinckley was a beautiful wooden classic with an elegant, and now unpopular, overhang. Her cockpit was wide open and the low cabin barely serviceable. A sailor's challenge and pride; a woman's nightmare unless she liked getting her bottom wet from constant spray.

Edward broke through her thoughts, "I guess Harry named his boat to be reminded of dry land. You can get too much ocean after a while, I guess. Don't you worry about all that. I thought we'd have a delightful lunch on board. A little champagne, a nice cheese, fresh dates. And, let's see if Edie kept her promise to bake bread for us before she left."

"For us? How did she know I was coming?"

"Ah, because I am a scheming sort of guy."

Edward's appealing grin made her laugh again. She felt the gentle breeze coming off the water and turned her face up toward the sun with eyes closed. Through her lids she saw a shadow and felt it block the rising warmth. She looked up, right into Edward's eyes hovering close to her face. He bent down and brushed her cheek with his lips. It was a sweet gesture, a pure and simple 'I am glad you are here' kind of gesture. It made her feel safe and content. She was lucky to be with a man like him.

Naunet stopped thinking of the 'why' and the 'how' and all the other questions she had meant to get his answers to earlier. She smiled at him and fingered the pearls around her neck. He was right. It was going to be a delightful day.

* * *

Chapter Nine

It was an odd sound. It gurgled and slapped, and ebbed and flowed. Her head throbbed and her mouth felt like a grotto fouled by bat guano. Nausea rose high in her throat and she had trouble opening her eyes. When she finally could, her pupils did not want to focus but she thought she lay stretched out in a dark tomb. About twenty feet beyond her toes, a rectangular light-tunnel held a promise of brightness. The rushing sound grew louder. The tomb was flooding! Naunet sat up with a jolt but had to lie back again. Or she was going to faint. Or die. Perhaps she was already dead.

"Time to wake up, dear." A cool hand cradled the back of her neck and lifted her head a few inches. The rim of a glass touched her lips. She drank in greedy gulps, the effervescent liquid calming her rebellious stomach enough for her to glance around. This was not a tomb. It was a boat. And it was apparently underway.

"What's going on," she croaked. "Are you taking Harry's boat out?"

"Just charging the batteries. As for you, my dear, I am afraid you had a little too much Champagne. Let's get you out into the fresh air. You'll feel better, you'll see." Edward helped her to her feet.

As the boat lurched off a swell she fell hard against his chest and he put his steadying arms around her. She was grateful for his presence. If only she could stay like this, wrapped in his safe cocoon, at least until she could collect her wits about her.

"You look a real fright." Edward flipped a strand of lank hair from her face.

The tone of his voice was so caring that she was neither offended nor embarrassed about the remark. Instead, a new intimacy toward him surged up inside her. She hoped that she did not look as awful as she felt.

"I am sorry. I didn't think I drank that much. I'll be all right," Naunet assured him. She needed to pull herself together. On the opposite bench, half hidden by the folded-down leaf of the salon table, sat her overnight bag.

"Oh, good," she said, loathe to push herself from the haven of his warm chest. She unzipped the top of the bag to find her cosmetics. The Turk must have brought her carry-on after he returned from taking the Jenkins's to Hurghada airport. Vaguely remembering Edie's comment about good skippers, Naunet did not want to appear completely clueless. She squared her shoulders and asked, "Where's the head?"

"Lucky for you, still firmly attached to your shoulders, my dear," Edward smiled benignly and patted her on top of her head. Good puppy-dog.

Naunet bristled slightly. "I need to freshen up."

"Oh, you want the *Loo*? Up front. On the left. Mind the instructions. What a fuss those people made about their bloody commode. Open this, pump that. Do you know that Harry actually told me that this tub could sink if I didn't shut some valve or other after using the toilet. Can you believe it!"

Naunet was too wobbly on her feet to comment though she appreciated that he tried to humor her in landlubber terms. There had been no reason during their brief acquaintance to tell him that she had picked up a fair amount of sailing jargon from Jonathan. Dear Jonathan. He would have liked this boat. During one of their longer outings along the rocky Maine coast, he had told her that his dream was to sail from Turkey to Crete someday. He had gone on and on about how nice it would be to putter around the Med, stretched out on deck, sipping something cool, chasing the sun into another sequestered anchorage. She knew he was testing the waters with her. Reinforced by their common interest in Turkey and Crete, he thought to sail around the Aegean would be a perfect way to spend a holiday together. 'Of course, we would be working,' he had added. In his enthusiasm, he never noted that she had been less than responsive to the idea. Yes, Jonathan would like this boat, if not its present caretaker. Despite her lingering malaise, she had to grin. That would be something, those two men on the same boat.

When she reemerged into the salon it was empty. The light-tunnel she had squinted at proved to be the main hatch above the few steps leading out into the cockpit. Handling herself along by numerous well-placed teak handholds, she propelled herself through the narrow space, past the galley which was opposite a chart table. The compact navigation station was a bench seat with a built-in chart-table, not unlike a child's school desk. The lip of the slanted table held pencils, a spike-ended pair of compasses, a wooden ruler, and a stack of folded papers. She assumed them to be some sort of charts. A panel with navigation instruments and switches sat above it. Intent on her progress, she barely noticed the built-in short-wave radio with a mike dangling from an overhead clamp.

The gangway steps were hemmed in by a hanging locker—Edie had shown her their foul-weather gear stowed in it—and the exterior wall of the private captain's quarter-berth. They formed a convenient way for her to brace herself without the boat's motion throwing her off-balance as she was still disoriented and none too happy with the condition of her stomach.

Half the cockpit was taken up by the compass pedestal, with the large wheel mounted on it. Edward sat on the high side, cradling a winch for support in his left arm, holding a bottle in his right hand. Karakurt was at the wheel, intently watching the close-hauled jib as they beat into a stiff breeze that blew out of the north.

"What's he doing here," Naunet sputtered.

"Sailing the boat. And quite competently so, I might add." Edward lifted his beer in an appreciative toast to the Turk's seamanship. The dour man stared ahead without acknowledging Naunet. He had on dark slacks with a tight dark-blue sweatshirt. On his head, he sported a jaunty black yachting cap.

Naunet clambered into the cockpit. Despite the blue canvas that skirted the whole stern, the wind took a hold of her hair and whipped it loose. She shivered. This was a far cry from the sunny calm of Port Safaga.

"Where are we?"

"Sailing in the ancient waters you love so much, my dear."

Naunet could not recall if she had told him about her mother drowning off Safaga. If she had, his comment was in bad taste. Even if she had not, the way he said it sounded as if he was mocking her.

"Edward, I don't think Harry would appreciate your taking his boat out."

"Harry's long gone," Edward drawled seemingly having lost most of his clipped British accent.

Naunet looked at her watch. "Please, Edward. Let's get back to the marina. Darkness falls quickly around here. It's four o'clock already."

"Sorry, darling," Edward sniffed and stared at the horizon hoping to keep his beer down. "No can do. By the way, you are obviously not aware—having knocked yourself out on Champagne and all. It is four o'clock all right. But Sunday, May twenty-seventh. You have been out cold for twenty-four hours, dear heart."

There comes that moment in life when an awful truth dawns upon a person. It is the moment when one's insides seem to collapse. Naunet did not scream. She did not cry. Nor did she rage against this ominous turn of events. She simply sat down hard.

Oh my God. Jonathan was right.

Sailing in the Red Sea can be pleasant or terrifying, depending on the capricious northerlies. Naunet had heard the tales of horror from her mother's diving friends. They always said that the wise sailor opted to anchor at night rather than chance running into one of the many uncharted coral reefs. Another worry, especially when slowly beating into the wind, was to be overtaken by a larger ship. There had been accounts of low-riding tankers that arrived at Port Suez in the morning with loose rigging dangling from their bow. Their crew never knew that they had cut a sailboat in half.

With descending darkness, the wind subsided and Karakurt turned the motor on. He told Edward to douse main and jib, and to un-bag and hoist the smaller staysail already hanked-on to the inner forestay between mast and jib stay. It would steady the boat as they cut through the chop. Edward yanked, and hauled, and swore. He slipped several times on the leather soles of his Gucci loafers and once came close to falling overboard. Karakurt shouted warnings and orders from the cockpit. Exasperated with the Brit's fumbling, he told Naunet to take the wheel as he went forward to take over.

Naunet realized that Edward had absolutely no clue about boats, or boat handling for that matter. With both men on the cabin roof struggling to bring the sails under control, she prayed to her namesake goddess for an abrupt change in the wind. All she needed was one violent jibe. A boom scything across from one side to the other could sweep these guys off the cabin roof and toss them into the water. Unfortunately, Karakurt obviously knew his stuff. The boom was sheeted in tightly with a block-and-tackle boom-vang. Besides, she had no idea where they were. Simply to sail west toward the coast, alone at night, could end in disaster. The reefs were numerous and unforgiving. Besides, she asked herself, would she have the stomach to let two men drown?

"Feeling any better?"

She jumped. The two had made their way back into the cockpit while she, heaven forgive her, had been planning their watery demise. Edward patted her on the head again, all solicitous, as if they were on a pleasant Sunday cruise. Well, she thought bitterly, in a way they were. After all, it was Sunday. Her knees would not stop trembling, her hands were ice-cold and she feared that if she said anything, her teeth would chatter. Naunet forced herself to sit quietly and to calm down.

"You are freezing." Edward ducked below and reappeared with a thick cable-knit sweater for her to put on. It smelled slightly musty; the fit was tight. One of Edie's. After that, Edward brought out a plastic tray with cellophane-wrapped pita sandwiches, fruit and three cans of soda. Not having had any food since—ah, yes, since their 'delightful' lunch—she accepted her share. They ate in silence until Karakurt declared that Edward was to stand the first watch until midnight. Then he, Karakurt, would take over until the next morning.

"The autopilot is off so we are not draining the batteries. The alarm on the radar is set for a one mile-radius. You must look behind you at least every ten minutes. Big ships come up fast."

"Hell, I won't see them in the dark," Edward said not too happy in his subservient role.

"We are at the western edge of the shipping channel, going north. If you see a red light coming from behind, they will pass us in the middle of the channel, to starboard. If you see green, you call me at once. Do you hear! At once," Karakurt warned.

"What if I see red and green together?"

"Then we die."

Naunet noticed that Karakurt had lost most of his halting English together with his formerly humble demeanor. There was no doubt who would be boss on this journey. Mostly to calm herself some more, she said, "Karakurt, your sailing vocabulary is very good. And you seem to know your way around a boat."

The man turned toward her with a sneer that apparently was to pass for a grin. "In Turkey, I was a sought-after charter captain. I steered many boats. Big, small, I can handle them all. I learned my sailing vocabulary from those rich clients. The less they knew about sailing, the more they wanted me to use proper boat-talk. It made them feel competent." He sneered again, remembering the overbearing Germans, the snotty French, and the all-too familiar ways of the Americans who always tried to become his buddies.

"You learned very well," Naunet nodded.

Karakurt shrugged and turned back to Edward to explain to him the direction in which the compass needle should be pointing. "Head north-northeast," he said.

Edward repeated it slowly. His knuckles stood out sharply as he wrapped his hands around the wheel, his knees seemed to flex more in tune with the boat's motion. Naunet thought he suddenly held himself taller as he stared ahead in supposed deep concentration. Karakurt was right. Steering a boat did make a man feel more competent; and it was easy—unless of course the wind came up.

Even without the motor running, a sailboat never cuts silently through the water. Yet, apart from the even hum of the Perkins Diesel and the rhythmic squeal of the hydraulic autopilot as it adjusted their course against wind and current, the icy silence in the cockpit was palpable.

Naunet, still shocked to the core, sat rooted on the foam cushion, not knowing what to do or say. The only words racing through her mind were *Why? Why, Edward, why?*

"It's getting chilly." Edward kept his eyes fixed on the fading horizon ahead. "You should go below and get some rest."

She considered spitting him in the face; the wind was right for it.

Her mouth was dry and it would not be worth the effort. She would be better off to curl up in the tight little cabin and think. Think and plan. Perhaps she could use the radio to send out a Mayday. The thought gave her some comfort. 'There is always something you can do in any situation,' Jonathan had said when she had asked him, 'What if...' Her silly questions had included capsizing, being stove in by a whale or boarded by pirates. She even included being dismasted and, as a joke, being chased around the coffee table by an ardent suitor. How they had laughed when Jonathan had pointed out that, alas, the latter event could not happen. His classic sloop was not equipped with that convenient piece of furniture.

Before she went below she forced herself to look at the bastard, as she had begun to call Edward in her mind. "So, where are we headed?"

His answer was as brief as it was telling. "Suez."

Without a glance back, Naunet slipped below and went into the cramped captain's cabin immediately to the left of the steps. In order to close the folding door for privacy, she had to crawl up onto the quarter berth. Edie had made the bed up with fitted dark blue sheets. A large comforter lay folded against the foot of the bunk below a small porthole facing out into the cockpit.

Curling herself into the fetal position, Naunet finally let go. After she had cried the fear from her pounding heart, disgust welled up in her. How could she have been so blind to trust this man? How desperate for love was she? She had not even suspected anything out of the ordinary when they were headed for the marina for lunch instead of the resort. At least, the cockamamie story about taking care of *Tumbleweed* during the Jenkins's absence should have given her a head's up. He stole this boat. He and that creepy Turk. But why? And why take her along? He had never tried to seduce her nor—come to think of it—even touched her for that matter. So, all-consuming love was hardly a motive. She was missing something. The question was, what?

A perfectly laughable thought occurred to her. No! Ridiculous to consider white slave trade. She almost giggled. Those perverts wanted fourteen-year-olds. Her hair was not even blond. Well, that could always be remedied to fool an aging sheik into paying a higher price.

But not for a woman her age.

Naunet promised herself to try and find out more what made those two do what they did. Perhaps if she played along, they would tell her more. Not that the prospect of knowing more made her feel any safer. She needed a ruse, effective but not too obvious. Conmen had a sixth sense when it came to deception.

Still battling residual sluggishness from having been drugged so heavily, she fell into a fitful slumber. When she woke the next morning, her nausea had ceased and her head was clearer of the cobwebs from the day before.

It was at that moment that anger set in. Her own, unexpected hatefulness shook her to the core and she had to sit back on the bed to collect and—more importantly—to calm herself. It would do no good for her to go storming about screaming her head off. Although, she thought with a jolt, that is exactly what she needed to do. The radio! Only three steps away, at the other side of her door.

Once she had teased Jonathan about the oxymoron (she clearly remembered using that word) of state-of-the-art electronics on a classic Hinckley such as his. He had winked good-naturedly, and told her that he might be a fool about his boat. But he was not foolhardy about his life. At once, he had proceeded to show her how to operate the shortwave, flipping this switch and that, punching up noisy channels, and clicking the mike on and off.

'If I fall overboard, always go to sixteen. Everybody listens to it. It's the emergency channel.'

'Mayday, Mayday,' she had cried into the dead mike in a falsetto voice. Glancing mischievously back at Jonathan, he was dead serious.

How she wished now that she had paid more attention then. Very gently, she peeled the door back and, barefoot and still fully clothed from the day before, slid one foot before the other into the narrow hallway leading from the steps to the salon.

* * *

Chapter Ten

I shall kill the swine with my bare hands!"

Even at home, it would not have been a particularly pleasant way to be awakened at four in the morning. Isolated in a walled compound in Upper Egypt, it was downright alarming. They had stayed up late on Sunday night worrying about Naunet and trying to come up with more or less plausible scenarios why she had not returned from Safaga. The eerie howl outside turned decidedly ominous when the entryway to their quarters splintered open. Ahmed Sharkawy rushed in, a rotund dervish tangled up in his oversized nightshirt-like *galabya*. It would have been comical had he not been brandishing a machine gun.

"Ahmed! What's going on?" Bill rushed out of his room fearing the worst. Did Naunet meet with an accident? Had political unrest erupted into bloody revolution? Had last night's consumption of beers placed them into the free-to-kill realm of offending Infidels?

"They are gone!"

"Yes, we know." Bill breathed a sigh of relief. Ahmed simply, albeit a bit too vehemently, seemed to have misinterpreted Naunet's extended absence.

"You know about it? Then I shall have to kill you too," the Overseer wailed distraught.

Bill assumed it was over his failure to guard all of the confined Americans. "Of course, I know about it. Ahmed, listen to me. Karakurt drove Dr. Klein to Safaga for the weekend. We expect them back any time."

Ahmed Sharkawy's moon face turned into a ripe eggplant ready to burst. He threw his arms up and swiveled the gun over his head. "They stole the tablets," he howled.

"What? Who stole the tablets?" Jonathan, roused by the ruckus, had come out of his room clad in dark-blue running-shorts and a white crew-neck tee shirt. Over his left chest, it was embroidered with the official 'Newport-Bermuda-Race 2012' logo; a lighthouse crossed by the US and Bermuda flags. "Did someone break into the vault?" He looked like a sleepy boy with his tousled shock of light-brown hair, yawning and rubbing his eyes.

"I went to count them this morning." Ahmed's distress accelerated. "Two tablets are missing. Gone. How can it be, I asked myself? There was no break-in. The vault was locked. I am the only one with the combination."

Trying to avoid the whirling gun, Jonathan stepped closer to the agitated man. "Ahmed! Stop that! Are you telling us that only two tablets are missing?"

"Only two? Only two?" the Overseer sputtered with indignation. "Yes! Two! That is two too many." He collapsed onto the couch clasping his gun like a crutch.

"Oh God, don't tell me." Bill looked at Jonathan, and both realized it at the same time. If no one had broken into the vault, there were only two tablets that could have been taken.

"Ahmed," Bill said quietly, "do you remember when you rushed us out of the lab late on Friday afternoon? Well," he paused trying to figure out how to put it best to avoid an explosion either from Ahmed or his gun. "Because of that undue haste, two tablets had been left to soak in a tub. Outside the vault. On the table in the far corner." So far, no reaction from Ahmed.

Bill continued cautiously, "Karakurt never wheeled them back into the vault. We were going to work on them Saturday." Bill paused to let Ahmed absorb what he was saying. As a precaution, he placed his hands on the man's shaking shoulders. "But Karakurt and Dr. Klein left for Safaga on Saturday morning. And with you gone as well, we couldn't get back into the lab."

"The swine! He stole them." Ahmed exploded again and Bill stepped back a few paces to escape the man's wrath, or at least the spittle from his lips.

"I will kill them. Him and your woman!"

Bill took another deep breath. "There seems to be an awful lot of killing being planned here, my friend. Let's discuss things a little more calmly. Let's see what we can come up with."

The Overseer shot Bill a withering look. How could the American think of discussing matters more calmly. His head was in a sling. Worse, he was as good as dead.

"First of all," Bill continued, "Dr. Klein is not a thief. She loves Egypt. Did you know that she is half Egyptian herself? Perhaps they came back really late last night and checked into the Luxor."

"Dr. Klein and Karakurt Tiryaki?" Ahmed was so deeply shocked that he momentarily forgot the missing tablets.

"Now there's a happy thought," Jonathan grumbled and went to the kitchen. He came back with three bottles of beer. "Desperate measures, and all that rot," he scoffed and handed out the bottles.

The older man felt sorry for his disconcerted colleague and thanked the younger man for the beer. *What the hell*, he thought. *Who ever said you had to have coffee in the morning.* He watched amused how eagerly the Muslim had reached for the proffered bottle and, with a brief "Allah forgives me," sent most of its contents gurgling down his brown throat.

"No, Ahmed. I meant Dr. Klein and another friend of hers."

Visibly relaxing, Ahmed propped his gun against the arm of the couch and settled back in its faded cushions. He smoothed his *galabya* over his knees and—with a quick gesture that startled the two men— he suddenly stuck his arm under his long garment.

"I call Hilton." Ahmed said and waved a cell phone in front of them with a satisfying burp.

"Ask for Edward Guernsey-Crock." Bill ignored the curiosity in the Egyptian's widening eyes.

The following palaver seemed to last forever, and they barely made out 'Gournsa' and 'Kleen.' At last, Ahmed snapped the phone shut and placed it on the couch next to him.

"Not there."

"They haven't returned?" The pit in Jonathan's stomach took on added weight, and this time it was not caused by jealousy.

"Not there," Ahmed repeated. "Never was."

"What do you mean?" Jonathan lunged for the couch leaning so close over the seated man that Ahmed pressed himself deeper into the cushions as if he expected to be punched.

"Gournsa. He was never a guest, Mr. Jonathan."

Bill felt he needed to break Jonathan's threatening stance which had turned their gun-toting accuser into a rather frightened man. Both personas could be equally unpredictable. The new development was also apt to put a lovelorn Jonathan over the top.

"Tell me. Did Karakurt have a room in the compound?"

"I checked. Nothing in his room. No clothes. Nothing."

"I think it's time we talked to Mr. Zawwam."

The Overseer shook his head. "Mahmoud was arrested on Friday afternoon. That's why I rushed off. You probably have not heard this," he looked around as if he feared a hidden microphone—while Jonathan snorted a cynical "Well, duh"—"that President Mubarak was sentenced over the weekend. Now the candidate for The Muslim Brotherhood and most of the others are marking those of us opposing their bid for the presidency."

"What do you mean by 'marking you'?"

Ahmed looked up in surprise. Were the Americans really this dense? He slid his stiff four fingers across his throat. Then, quite unexpectedly, he sobbed, "If they don't, then for certain Jabari will kill me."

"Ah, yes, Jabari." Bill sighed. In their desperate attempts to find out more about Naunet's disquieting absence they had overlooked that little complication.

"Ahmed, can you get in touch with Jabari El-Masri?"

"Of course." Ahmed brightened and he hastily picked up his cell phone—which he thankfully had left sitting on the couch next to him. Just as quickly though, he laid it down again. "He is in his car right now."

"How do you know that?" Jonathan asked sullenly.

"All night, he must drive. But the jet is not far from here. We meet him there with his tablets. Please, we must hurry. I have loaded the tablets into the truck."

"Are we going anywhere?" Bill asked gently so as not to aggravate Ahmed.

"You loaded all twenty-seven tablets into a truck?" Jonathan bit his tongue. "Sorry, I mean, all twenty-five. That's a hell of a lot of weight for one man to haul around in such short time. You did that by yourself?"

Ahmed shook his head, "Not by myself. Two loyal guards helped. They are going off duty at six. After that, there is no one we can trust. With Mahmoud in jail, a new man will be sent this morning. He will inspect the vault. Most likely, one of the Usurpers." He begged them again to hurry. Then he remembered something and turned to Bill. "Do you have your laser tool? I could not find it in the lab."

"Don't tell me!" The loss of the laser prototype could mean a proverbial nail in William Jefferson Browning's scientific coffin.

"I'm getting a distinct twilight-zone feeling here. How about you, Bill?" Jonathan was not trying to be sarcastic. Actually, he was becoming increasingly suspicious that there was a lot more to Dr. Bruno's little venture than their boss had told them or had himself anticipated.

This early morning of theirs was taking on decidedly ominous proportions. Trucks, guns, driving off with golden tablets weighing a thousand pounds. Oh, and what about the story of yet another jet waiting. It was all too mysterious and none of it made any sense.

"Where is Indiana Jones when you need him?" he mumbled.

"At el-Kharga," Ahmed replied quietly.

"Oh, of course. Why didn't I think of that," Jonathan called back over his shoulder as he walked toward his room.

Then it hit him. Ahmed could simply be telling the truth. During some *National Geographic Special*, a reporter had joked that Jabari El-Masri was Egypt's very own Indiana Jones, not in the least due to the jaunty Fedora the Egyptologist habitually wore when traipsing about his oft-filmed excavation sites. Had the good doctor another private jet stowed away just for eventualities? And if so, was he planning to take the tablets somewhere for safekeeping? Quite likely, Jonathan surmised, Cairo would not be on the flight plan. There was always Oman. Or Kuwait. The Saudis, if well-greased, could be receptive to someone's gilded exile.

That familiar prickly feeling of excitement mixed with intense stress crawled up Jonathan's neck. A sense of danger he loved and loathed just prior to the start of a race when skippers madly tacked back and forth in over-crowded quarters; sails snapping, winch monkeys paddling like mad, tacticians hollering, all intent not to hit any of their likewise frantic competitors or crossing the invisible starting line early.

No! He and Bill were not going to be rushed off to some abandoned airstrip where a little puddle-jumper was revving its engines, ready to haul contraband and them across international borders; even if it were for supposedly patriotic reasons. On the other hand, a few men in the know could live very comfortably on such a hoard. *Forgot about Monaco!* Jonathan jerked his thumb at Bill before he walked into his room.

"I am not going on some hair-brained boondoggle unless we talk to El-Masri first. Or, better yet, to Bruno," he spat as soon as Bill joined him. His broad-legged stance told Bill that this time, Jonathan was dead serious.

"I agree. Now, let's assume for a moment we can't get in touch with either El-Masri or Bruno. Or that Ahmed won't let us. Which amounts to the same thing. What are our options here?"

"I suppose hitting Ahmed over the head and hijacking the truck is out of the question." Jonathan was now certain that Naunet was being detained against her will, likely by someone with two golden tablets strapped under a *galabya*. Ahmed's cell phone retrieval gesture flashed before his eyes and despite their dilemma he grinned briefly. When he saw Bill's raised eyebrows he just waved a quick 'never mind' and went back to assessing their options. Come to think of it, he wondered how the dandy Mr. Pith-Helmet fit into all of this. The snob seemed awfully cozy with a supposed lowly Turk. *And let's not forget the missing laser*, Jonathan thought, and then realized something which gave him hope. That thing could be used as a weapon if it was trained at someone's eyes. *Please, my darling Naunet, for once, don't be your restrained lady-like self. Use it. Gouge the bastards' eyes out if you have to.*

"What about Naunet?" he asked Bill, desperate for an answer he knew he could not get. "We can't just leave her realizing she might be locked up somewhere in Safaga! I tell you, Bill, something is very wrong here. I hope you realize that."

Bill more than understood. By now, he was extremely worried himself. Naunet had an ironclad reputation of always showing up when and where she was supposed to be. Yes, he was plenty worried all right, and just as frustrated as Jonathan by their inability to do something about it just yet. For that reason, he felt that going to meet

Dr. El-Masri might be their best bet if the prominent man was still on their side and was not laying the blame for the missing tablets squarely at their feet. Hopefully, he could get some information from Cairo, or the embassy, or his friends in the military, Interpol, anyone.

"What about her things," Jonathan broke into Bill's thoughts.

"Take her laptop, just in case. Leave her clothes. I'm sure she won't be back." When he saw the rising panic in Jonathan's eyes, he put an arm around the younger man, an uncharacteristic gesture for him. Feeling really bad for his younger colleague, he said, "I meant that I assume she won't be coming back here. That's all."

When the two returned to the living room, Ahmed stood up, stretched leisurely, smiled and cocked the machine gun again, with none of his actions easing the tension. He told them that his efforts to raise anyone with his cell had met with utter failure, not in the least due to a dying battery. Still smiling, he glanced at his watch. "It is almost six. Please, it is time for us to go."

It was difficult for Bill and Jonathan to turn down an invitation delivered by someone with a loaded machine gun. Even if the guy holding it was smiling now.

With a flawless dawn chasing them, they cleared the outskirts of Luxor where the road soon became a one-lane sand-swept path. Ahmed stopped the truck in a turnout and performed some sort of gyrations. Jonathan, who sat practically on the motor hub in the middle of the snub-nosed truck, feared that the man might have a scorpion crawling up his shirt.

Quickly, without any sting-induced fear, Ahmed roll up the hem, then lifted his bottom from the deep indent in the driver's seat, and finally pulled his *galabya* over his head. To the relief of the Americans, he wore lightweight khaki pants and a polo shirt underneath. He flung the discarded garment onto a small bench in the back and then roared off at a speed that sent the truck slithering over the endless sandy stretches of the barely visible road.

After an hour's drive, the ancient truck rumbled to a stop. The landscape looked as if giant prairie dogs had burrowed under it. Bill and Jonathan knew a dig when they saw one. Ahmed jutted his chin at the remnants of some low ramparts.

"Nekhen," he told them.

A man stepped from behind a low wall. He was hunched over the handles of a wheelbarrow, desperately trying to keep it from digging itself deeper into the sand.

Ahmed grabbed his gun from under his seat and jumped out. "Quick. We need your help," he called back over his shoulder.

Bill and Jonathan were glad to leave the stifling cab and sprinted after Ahmed. Sand invaded their footwear as they dashed across some dunes.

Ahmed introduced them to the tall man garbed in the customary coarse worker's *galabya*. "Bill. Jonathan. Wamukota." In the desert formalities tended to be brief. And in their present circumstance, they were understandably even briefer.

"Wamukota?" Jonathan could not help himself. "Of death-by-tunnel-collapse fame, I presume?" This was getting beyond weird. This was getting dangerous. *Hell, it already is dangerous.*

"Looks like this guy is joining us for the drive to el-Kharga," Jonathan half-whispered to Bill.

"Given that he is supposed to be dead, I should think, he'd have to," Bill whispered back.

Jonathan couldn't shake the strange feeling that Wamukota had already been dead for thousands of years. Once he let go of the rough wheelbarrow handlebars, the dark-skinned yet not black man stood tall and erect. His features echoed the full-lipped statuary faces strewn all over Egypt. As the wind wrapped his long shirt around his body, Jonathan could see that he was lean. *Take off his clothes, tie some feathers around his long neck and a penis-tube around his middle, and you have the perfect specimen of an ancient Noba.* Jonathan wished Naunet were with him; she would not only agree, she'd want a DNA sample. *Damn Bruno. Damn Egypt.* They had enough work in Boston to keep them busy for a couple of years. He could just kill somebody. Jonathan shot an absentminded glance at the Overseer's gun.

Ahmed had watched the younger man become visibly agitated. Instinctively, he changed his weapon to the shoulder away from the American.

After the three settled back into the hot cab, sure enough, Wamukota squeezed in on Bill's side and practically sat on the slightly embarrassed scientist's lap. To his credit, the tall digger tried to lean his torso out the open window as far as he could. The aroma in the steaming cab grew riper by the minute, enough to put odor-challenged Americans under. Bill and Jonathan were no exceptions. Mesmerized by the roadway dropping away under the front of the truck, they took shallow breaths, and soon nodded off.

The first thing they saw after regaining groggy consciousness was a brown Fedora bobbing alongside Ahmed's window as he shifted the truck down to a halt.

"Indy to the rescue," Jonathan whispered, rubbing his burning face.

Bill leaned forward to see for himself and stuck his elbow in Jonathan's side. They were squeezed in too tight for a proper jab. Then he turned his head for a sideways glance at Wamukota who was now clad in khakis and polo shirt identical to Ahmed's outfit. How the man had managed to divest himself of his *galabya* in this sardine can while Bill and Jonathan had dozed defied imagination.

Ahmed and the very much alive head digger jumped out of the truck. Their hands performed some complicated Arabic gestures as if greeting their Master and Savior of all Treasures. Dr. El-Masri, who had not bothered to greet them in return, was shooting off questions in his staccato fashion.

Looking abject, Ahmed started to speak slowly. Then, suddenly, he and Wamukota launched into a high-pitched duet.

During the gesticulating palaver, Bill and Jonathan thought they heard 'Gournsa' and 'Kleen.'

There was much arm waving. Then came fist shaking. At last, the word "Karakurt" accompanied by high-velocity spitting left little doubt that the presumed loyal Turk was being dissected in rather uncomplimentary terms.

Then, right after they distinctly heard the word 'Saqqara,' Jabari El-Masri went into a monumental rage. His stocky body firmly planted in the sand, he thrust his head forward. Due to an underbite, his strong jaw jutted out more than usual against this new misfortune heaped upon his head. Like an English bulldog, his trembling body emanated a clear warning: Never—ever—cross me.

Bill and Jonathan decided to stay in the truck a while longer despite the almost unbearable heat.

Luckily, both Egyptians had left their doors ajar so that the hot desert breeze took the worst of the odorous air out into the open where it would cause less olfactory mischief.

* * *

Chapter Eleven

Morning. Sleep well?"

Naunet almost jumped out of her skin. She had been so focused on getting to the radio that the voice floating through the semi-darkness of the salon took her by complete surprise.

Edward was lounging on the settee, knees bent to fit the shorter banquette halfway comfortably. His head was propped against the back of the navigation station, close to where she needed to be. He was all la-di-dah, so quasi civilized! Hot anger welled up in her and for a brief moment she considered picking up the scissors which protruded temptingly from their holder on the chart table.

"I made coffee," he said, "but I am afraid it is a bit salty. They did not tell me how to get fresh water out of that silly pump. That is your department anyway," he continued lightly as if yesterday had never happened. "So, I am going to have a beer instead. How about you? Just hand me one, will you. I hope there are some left in that ice-box."

Naunet was still speechless. She also considered breaking a bottle over his head. Just when she thought she had recovered, Edward added, "Karakurt could use one too. Be a good mate and hand him a beer while you are at it. He's been out there at the wheel forever."

"Sure." It was all she could manage, and even that surprised her. She had no intention of becoming their galley slave. Except that this might give her an opportunity to move around more freely. Anything, that helped her figure out what these guys were up to, and what they planned to do with her. Besides, a full stomach might help improve their manners, if only temporarily, she was certain. It was best never to upset unstable people. And to her, these two scoundrels surely were—well, she thought—not exactly unstable. They were insane, and unpredictable, and therefore very dangerous.

After she supplied them with their beers, she turned a knob on the gas stove and held a match to the burner. Nothing. Having learned from Jonathan how explosive Propane could be if handled carelessly, Harry had most likely shut off a main valve somewhere. She looked around. That's when she saw the small twelve-volt coffee pot, still warm from Edward's sorry attempt, having tossed the half-full can of ground coffee carelessly into one side of the deep double sink. Naunet emptied the dregs from the pot and hoped that she would not plug up any sensitive marine plumbing. When she stubbed her toe on a foot pedal, she figured that it might be for getting water out of the faucet. She pumped tentatively and tasted the water gingerly with her finger. It was salty. Finally, she turned the right knob in the back of the sink. It dispensed freshwater! *Who knew*, she marveled. *Just like home.*

A ship's clock chimed. How many bells? What time? She had no idea and squinted at the clock. Seven in the morning. Monday! They should be missing her by now. Surely Jonathan would not think that she had returned from Safaga and had stayed overnight at the hotel in Luxor with Edward. Oh, God! If he believed that she was with that man, he would be too upset to think of any other reason for her absence. And what about when she did not show up at the lab the following day? Would he think that she had simply left with another man? 'Middle-aged spinster-Egyptologist, overcome by latent romance, runs off with two men.' Not one but two, if indeed Bill and Jonathan connected the Turk to her disappearance as well. What a juicy headline that would be for the tabloids. More importantly, how distressing to those who thought they knew her. With the speed that headlines traveled around the globe these days, there was little hope that her father, or Bruno, would not be informed. Then she remembered that they had practically been cut off from the world. If Luxor was still under that mandatory curfew and the political situation were to worsen, her colleagues might be in trouble themselves. The thought made her heart sink even lower.

The aluminum percolator bubbled and the aroma of freshly

brewed coffee brought her back to her own dire situation. Edward seemed happy enough sucking on his bottle. She could hear Karakurt move about overhead, probably adjusting things to take advantage of the freshening wind. Then, suddenly, silence. Their self-appointed skipper had shut off the motor. Once again, she became aware of the sloshing and slapping against the hull. It was the same sound that had awakened her on that first awful day. When was that? According to her kidnapper it was Sunday. Yesterday! As distasteful as it was to her, she knew she had to do something to lull these guys into complacency. Make them think that she had given up her fight; that she was not going to make any trouble.

Cooking had never been her thing and she was not even sure that she could manage to produce anything edible from Edie's stores. Some women could do magic with practically nothing. That was certainly not her. At home, it was yoghurt for breakfast, a crisp salad for lunch, and something light for dinner, equally vegetarian, like fruit or at most spaghetti with a nice tomato sauce, or store-bought pesto. It was not that she did not eat meat out of conviction. The stuff she produced simply always tasted like shoe-leather. So why bother.

"I found pancake mix and powdered milk. Oh, and here is some egg substitute. If you can figure out how to turn on the Propane, I'll try to make us some breakfast." Her voice was toneless and she was tempted to cross her fingers behind her back as she said it. She also never realized how tough it was to be civil to someone whose head you wanted to rip off; whose black heart you wanted to rip out; and whose despised guts you wanted to see spilled.

"That would be great." Edward, shaking off his beer-induced drowsiness, jumped up. In three steps, he leaned out the top of the main hatch and hollered to Karakurt. "You get us Propane, skipper, and I promise you breakfast."

It was a hazy morning as they slowly made their way north, averaging a good six knots with a south-southeasterly breeze pushing them along. Karakurt felt safe enough to hoist all the sails again. He had decided to sail wing-on-wing, explaining the configuration impatiently to Edward. The two finally had the main hauled way out to port, with the jib billowing out to starboard. The only danger was a sudden wind change causing an uncontrolled jibe. Such an unintended maneuver could actually bring the mast down, not to mention a wildly swinging boom lopping off someone's head. Other than that, it promised to be a perfect day for sailing.

"What are you feeding the crew for lunch?" Edward asked in late morning directing his question decidedly at Naunet. Generally useless in boat matters, he had adopted what he thought of as an old-salt stance. Every time he said something pompous, he glanced at Karakurt as if to elicit the Turk's approval.

"Let me check around below." Naunet was quick to grab the chance to go into the salon alone. "There should be a lot of things," she called back over her shoulder. "I'll take a look in those cubbies. Edie told me that she had an inventory somewhere. Just give me a few minutes." She slid down the stairs and breathed a sigh of relief, hopefully to be free for a time from her detested captors. Then she had an idea to keep them away even longer.

"While you are waiting." She handed the pleasantly surprised men the last of the cold beers to keep them occupied and, more importantly, out of the cabin. The icebox was now out of bottles and she wondered where Harry might have stashed the rest of his supply. For as long as she could keep these guys in their mellower beer-humor, it was better for her. She glanced nervously out the cockpit. From where she stood, five feet below them, all she saw were legs. One brown and sinuous pair securely placed on deck in rubber boots. The other pair was long-shined, wrapped in makeshift espadrilles with the toes hanging over by about two inches. It was obvious that they had belonged to someone with much smaller feet. Edward had found them in Harry's locker after his leather-soled loafers had become waterlogged and too dangerous to wear around the slippery deck. Karakurt had forbidden that they walk around barefoot which could bring its own mishaps of stubbed or even torn-off toes.

Rattling with Edie's pots and pans, Naunet made what she hoped the men would take for proper galley-noises promising food. Her hands shook and were ice cold from nerves. On tiptoes, she sidled over to the navigation station and, leaning over the chart table, stared at the shortwave radio. It looked less complicated than the one Jonathan had on his boat. Still, there were several dials and toggle switches. She bit her tongue and cautiously flipped the first of the switches. Nothing. She tried several others. Still nothing. *Power! There is no power.* She glanced to her right. On a separate board was a whole array of more toggles. Luckily, they were all labeled. Third row down, she saw the word 'radio.'

She flipped the switch. A green bulb on the shortwave blinked to life. She took another deep breath. Reminding herself to make more noise, she turned back to the sink and banged another pot against the shiny aluminum. Then she tried the toggles on the radio again. A faint crackle came to life. Naunet held her breath and hoped that it was the one. In slow motion, she reached for the clamped-on mike overhead and pulled it loose. Just as she had seen Jonathan do it, she held it close to her mouth which was bone dry from frayed nerves. She had to lick her lips several times before she trusted herself that she could actually produce any sound.

"Mayday. Mayday," she whispered into the mike, holding the speaker button down so hard that her thumb cramped up.

"Mayday, Mayday. Can anyone hear me?" She listened desperately for an answer. Sometimes, Jonathan had to repeat his call several times to raise another boat. Of course, it had never been to call for help. Just to inquire about uncharted rocks, or the weather. Often just to hail another beautiful boat on the horizon, or a nearby friend challenging him to a friendly race into the harbor. If he were only here to help her now.

Again she whispered, a little louder, "Mayday, Mayday. Anyone. Come in, please." She repeated the words several more times. The radio remained silent. Finally, she remembered that she had to release the button in order to hear. Cold sweat trickled down her back, and her thumping heart made her so dizzy that she feared she might faint.

"Vessel calling Mayday. Identify."

The voice shrilled through the cabin with such great force that Naunet fell back a step, straight against a warm body.

With the instinct of a wolf scenting a kill, Karakurt had slid down silently and now stood behind her. Furious that he had come too late to prevent her from her treachery, he spun her around by her waist. The quick slap from the back of his hand left a red welt on her cheek. His eyes were wild. His lips were drawn back in a snarl. He grabbed her by her hair with one hand, and ripped the mike clear off with his other. Staring at the radio, he slammed the toggle switch over so violently that it snapped off. His face was a brutal mask. Squeezing his eyes into cold slits, he raised his hand again.

Naunet winced. Was he going to hit her a second time? She did not recognize the words he spat at her in Turkish. All she knew was that she did not need to add them to her vocabulary—if she lived.

"You! Out there! Get down here," the enraged man shouted out to Edward, stationed at the wheel feeling empowered. "Find some tape. Your bitch just broke the radio."

Too late Naunet realized that Karakurt was not planning on using the tape for the mike or the broken switch. Instead, the men taped her hands behind her back and then tossed her onto her berth. Karakurt ripped slats from the varnished cabin sole's bilge access and somehow barricaded the door with them. Furious, she slid off the bed and banged her toes against the louvers, unleashing her hate at the uncaring men on the other side.

After a while, the enclosed space threatened to suffocate her. Without her hands free she could not open the small porthole to let in some fresh air. Defeated, exhausted, and tortured by a sudden thirst that arises from great fear, she was close to panicking.

"Jonathan. Please. Help me."

Edward's voice came through the barricaded door, ripe with mockery, "He can't hear you, dear. I suggest that you be a lot nicer to me from now on."

* * *

Chapter Twelve

The only sign of a fair-sized airplane broiling under the desert sun was a tail sticking up from an enormous sand-colored canvas staked in tent-like fashion that covered the rest of it. Along its side was a dark brown stripe oddly out of place with the rest of the jet's smooth color scheme. Someone had done a rather bad paint job.

With the ingrained habits of a navigator, Jonathan noticed that the plane faced south. There was no sign of an airstrip that he could see.

If it was the same jet that had brought them from Cairo to Luxor, it was almost unrecognizable. The previously luxurious cabin had been cleared of any unnecessary items and the heavy leather seats had been replaced by cheap ones usually found on dilapidated charter planes.

Dr. El-Masri explained, "A question of too much weight in the tail." He then apologized that the air conditioning was turned off. "We cannot run the engines under this tent," he shrugged. After settling his accidental guests around the cabin table which had escaped the purge, he produced semi-cold beers and, having sipped some thick cold coffee himself, made his excuses. "Must oversee the loading of our cargo," he put it. There was no apology for Ahmed practically having kidnapped the two American scientists at gunpoint.

"Gentlemen, welcome aboard again." Col. Abdur Rahman smiled at them. He wore a tight-fitting black turtleneck and the same color slacks. Behind him, through the open cockpit door, Bill and Jonathan saw another familiar figure. Lt. Col. al-Husri was also clad in black down to his shoes.

"Very Ninja," Jonathan said out of the corner of his mouth.

"I have had about enough!" Bill slammed a fist onto the table. He was hot, bothered, and very worried. If the sudden outburst startled the Egyptian pilots, they only shrugged their shoulders and went palms-up. Jonathan was pretty sure that the pilots were pawns in the same game as they were themselves. And he did not have to wonder whose turn it was to declare checkmate should they not cooperate. Still, he couldn't agree more with Bill. It was about time for them to take a stand, at least in theory. In the meantime, perhaps he could try a different tack with these fly-boys, use a more folksy approach—one young guy to another.

"Hi there. So, we meet again." If it was corny, he hoped to appear casual. "Say, how's your radio communication holding up? Battery power still ok? We'd really like to get a message through to our boss in Boston."

"Sorry, Sir. Radio silence. At least, until we are over water," was the not-so-young reply.

"Would that be Red-Sea-over-water?" It couldn't hurt to ask.

"Try Mediterranean-over-water." Dr. El-Masri stood behind them in the open door rubbing his arms. "Finished. We will leave after nightfall."

"Good," Bill nodded, having regained his composure. "Then we'll have some time to talk. Right, Jabari?"

If the accolade-accustomed Egyptian was surprised by the sudden change in the older American's demeanor, he did not let it show. He removed his hat, wiped his thick brows with an already moist kerchief, and sat down heavily. He suddenly looked tired.

"Yes, we better talk," he sighed. "First, we shall eat."

The pilots did not join them, and there was no sign of Ahmed nor of Wamukota. Dinner was a concoction of cold rice, the ever-present sliced cucumbers, goat cheese on unleavened bread, and melon cubes with dates. A fizzy orange soft drink rounded out the meal. Imperceptibly, the temperature had dropped a few degrees, and they heard a kind of scraping and slapping against the plane. The enormous tarp was being taken down.

"Dr. El-Masri," Jonathan said, not feeling entitled to follow Bill's example, "I didn't see a runway."

"Oh, there is an airstrip. The truck will pull us onto it after Wamukota and his friends finish with their sand-sweepers. It's quite good. And luckily long enough for us. Left over from the bloody British, you know."

"How convenient. Yet, you don't seem to like the British very much. Why is that?" Jonathan ventured, though he was not too fond of certain Brits himself just then. Probably for the first time in his life, he cursed his genteel upbringing. Had he grown up in Boston's North End with all those Irish and Italian urchins roaming the alleyways, none of this would have happened. Because then he would have had enough gumption to break the dandy's neck in Cairo, right after he tried hitting on Naunet.

"During the war, the British imprisoned General Aziz El-Masri who was then Commander of the Egyptian Army. If better luck had been on his side, he would have liberated my country from its dictator, the Germans, as well as the British."

"Any relation of yours?"

The answer was a shoulder shrug.

Jonathan pressed on. "Did the general survive the war?"

"Evidently," El-Masri suddenly grinned. "I was born in forty-seven."

Bill cleared his throat. "What are you planning to do, Jabari. You do realize that you have practically kidnapped us, which has the makings of an international incident, I might add. And I assume this plane is still the property of the Egyptian military, or at least of whoever claims to be the leader of your government these days. And once the existence of all these tablets becomes public knowledge, no doubt they will be classified as national treasures. So, it comes to mind—forgive me for pointing this out—that you are about to steal both."

"Steal? Steal!" The Egyptian jumped to his full five-foot seven-inch height. As the Americans were seated, he towered over them, all indignation and spitting rage.

"You dare to call me a thief, when your woman absconded with my Saqqara tablets!"

"My woman did not steal anything," Jonathan exploded trying to jump up as well but failed, being hemmed in by the table and by Bill.

"Let me correct you, my young interferer."

"Now hold on." Bill was turning red himself now.

"No! You hold on. The world has been stealing from Egypt forever. They all came supposedly to explore and study. And then went back home with loot from our ancestors crammed into their lorries. Shiploads of sacred mummies, carted off to Europe for fertilizer. Fertilizer!"

"Mummified cats, I think," Jonathan dared. A jab from Bill, and a scornful look from *The Pharaoh* made him retreat deeper into the hard seat.

"You cannot really believe that the likes of your glorified Carter and Champollion did not take whatever they wanted before leaving us the pittance of their finds. The British, the Germans, the French and, oh, let us not forget the Americans. What they did not damage and destroy, they grabbed with both hands. And now, that I have discovered the most incredible writings since the Rosetta Stone."

Jonathan squirmed. This was not the time to point out Jean François Champollion's ground-breaking contribution to Egyptology.

"But now, my own people aim to steal from me. They have stolen before. Yes, I admit, I was forced to make some deals. Negligible objects, of course. What was I to do? To go against those in power would have been suicidal. The secret buyers came in droves.

"The Japanese in their private jets. The South Americans, mooring their ostentatious yachts off Alexandria. Too much money, and no respect. All they wanted was to squirrel away our antiquities in their private collections.

"And now this! My own people ordering me to melt down these tablets to finance their corrupt campaigns. People who assume that they are the next president.

"Such blasphemy! I cannot let this happen. I must save these treasures for Egypt. They are my heritage. They are," the Egyptologist paused, seemingly exhausted. "They are my nemesis. I will safeguard them to the death."

Stunned silence followed Dr. Jabari El-Masri's impassioned testimony to his almost fanatical belief in his country's glorious heritage. The man before them was neither a thieving scoundrel nor an uncaring zealot. He was through and through Egyptian. He was a world-renowned Egyptologist. And he was willingly endangering his professional credibility. Most likely he had already made personal sacrifices preserving the legacy of this awesome land of his. His whole life, he had painstakingly labored to unravel the enigma of a great bygone civilization, unequalled anywhere. The man standing before them was an Egyptian patriot who, in their eyes, now lived up to his name. It translated into *Brave Egyptian.*

The Gulfstream jerked forward, pulled by the straining World War II truck. The engine thrust increased. The plane shook like an enraged bull ready to burst from its holding pen, hoping to shake the extra weight from its tail. It lumbered along and slowly gained enough speed for the pilot to pull the yoke up. They were airborne, flying south over a shadowy landscape. After a few minutes, the plane banked sharply into a tight U-turn.

Jonathan looked out the window by habit, not expecting to see anything. "There are lights," he said, surprised. "What is that down there?"

"It is el-Kharga. Did you know that over one hundred thousand people live there now? Mostly native Khargans belonging to the Beja ethnic group. They still speak in their own Afro-Asiatic tongue. Of course, Arabic is their official language. It is all modern conveniences now and, unfortunately, there is practically nothing left of the old architecture except the ruins of some forts built by the Romans. The oasis certainly is no longer the romantic crossroad of the caravans you read about in your novels."

"There is an airport. I can see the tower. Wow, we must be really low. That's not the one we took off from is it, Dr. El-Masri?"

"No, Jonathan. That's the one we are trying to avoid." Jabari El-Masri smiled and hoped that his pilots were flying low enough to avoid detection by a sleepy air controller.

"Since we are in this little venture together, Jonathan, isn't it about time you called me by my first name."

"Thank you. I am honored," Jonathan replied. His opinion of the man had increased immeasurably within the last half an hour. He tried it out.

"Was that Ahmed driving the truck away from the jet, Jabari?"

While looking pointedly at Bill, Jabari told Jonathan, "By the way, the 'J' is pronounced as in 'yak.'"

Point taken. Bill grinned. *Though considering that you are essentially carrying contraband, I'm thinking of a mule rather than a yak.*

Having set the Americans straight, Jabari smiled. The lad was all right.

"No, Jonathan," he said. "Ahmed is in the back. We need all the strong arms we can muster."

Jonathan could visualize the portly Overseer huffing and puffing, as he unloaded the tablets. He remembered the sinewy digger.

"What about Wamukota? He is supposed to be dead."

"He is from el-Kharga. His people will take care of him."

Jabari El-Masri reached into a corner cabinet and produced three crystal tumblers with a half bottle of Remy Martin VSOP.

"Leftovers," he sighed. After he poured two fingers' height into each of the exquisite glasses and settled himself back into his chair, he took a deep breath. "Suppose I start at the beginning."

"I was overseer of the Giza plateau when we opened the mastabas of three early-dynasty priests. I did not think they were related, though I still believe that they were close to each other. Perhaps the oldest, Badar, had groomed the most splendidly wrapped high priest, Ramose, who was quite old when he died. It appears that he survived the third, Tasar, who died fairly young. Oddly, he had the most astounding golden mask wrapped up on his chest." Jabari paused and looked at Jonathan. "The death mask of the Princess Nefret, daughter of King Aha. Perhaps you noticed it? You had to pass right by it on your way to the lab in Cairo." He wanted to add something but then thought better of it.

"Anyway, there were so many tombs, so much to catalog and display. So, we put the two blackened tablets into storage. Only after the recent find in Nekhen did I realize that there might be a connection. And I was right."

"How did you realize, apart that they were pure gold underneath, that there was also writing?"

"Well," a vein on Jabari's forehead welled up slightly, "because of the broken corner piece. A sliver of the pitch splintered off when it fell onto the stone floor."

"Do you still have that corner?" Bill asked innocently.

"No!"

"Do you think Karakurt might have it?"

The vein stood out angry now. "That pig of a Turk!"

Bill, afraid of a repeat explosion, quickly changed the subject. "Can we assume that the newest Nekhen tablets are onboard?"

"Ah, Wamukota. A good man. Yes, he saved the latest five for us to work on."

"There is just one slight problem," Bill said as calmly as he could. "We now have thirty tablets. But no solution. Oh, and no laser."

It was not the threatening vein exploding. It was Dr. El-Masri himself. He jumped out of his seat, stomping two paces back and forth. In the small cabin it practically meant that he pirouetted about like an angry dervish. "You forgot your laser!"

"No, I didn't forget. Whoever stole the tablets, stole the laser as well."

"Then you must order another one at once."

"Jabari. That laser was a prototype on loan from an English instrumentation lab. Besides, we are not exactly around the corner from Silicon Valley where you can snap your finger and someone builds you something." Bill was getting angrier by the minute and about to jump up himself. With his six-foot three frame he might literally have hit the ceiling. This time, it was Jonathan's hand that restrained his colleague.

"Dr. El-Masri, why exactly did you come to us? I mean, we are glad to help. Surely you have excellent researchers and scientists available in Egypt."

"Have you not heard a word I said," the agitated man leaned practically over Bill and stared at Jonathan. "We have a revolution going on. There was no one I could trust. Of course, coming to you was a grave mistake, it turns out."

If Jonathan had not been sitting in the chair by the window, hemmed in by the table and Bill, then surely he would have jumped up as well.

"This is getting us nowhere," Bill said. "Please, Jabari, sit down. First, we need to call Bruno. And we need to find out about Dr. Klein. I have a bad feeling that this Edward Guernsey-Crock was in cahoots with your storeroom keeper. Karakurt drove the two to Safaga for the weekend."

"Who is this Edward—Crook—did you say?"

Good man. Jonathan wanted to high-five the Egyptian. Instead he said, "We were given to understand by Edward, 'the Crook,'"

Jonathan scowled, "that he was a friend of yours. He appeared so completely at ease on our flight from Cairo to Luxor, that there was no reason for us to doubt it." He added, "Ask the pilots."

"I have never heard of the man." Jabari El-Masri jumped up again and stuck his head into the cockpit, apparently to confer with the pilots.

A minute later, Col. Rahman joined them. He said something in Arabic and then switched to English, explaining that they were to take on extra fuel in about half an hour on an old airbase near Cairo.

Bill shook his head and wondered aloud if that was not a bit risky, given the proximity of Cairo International and Almaza Air Force Base. He was assured that they would fly below the radar. Besides, that particular airbase was abandoned after the war. *Most likely built by the British*, Bill thought.

To bridge the ensuing silence, Bill pointed to Jonathan's tee-shirt and asked if he was planning to crew for the Newport to Bermuda Race again this year.

"I was. On a great Swan-Sixty-Five," Jonathan grimaced. "It doesn't look like I'll make it though. The crew list had to be in by now. The race starts on June fifteenth."

Knowing of Jonathan's passion for anything connected with boats and sailing, Bill looked at the younger man with true pity. The famous Newport to Bermuda race was one of the highlights in Jonathan's year. So far, he had always been a member of the crew on a winning boat, and for two weeks thereafter, the lab was treated to blow-by-blow stories, whether they were interested or not.

"I was in Newport for the America's Cup once," Bill remembered.

"The finals? That was in the seventies, Bill."

"Yes, well. Still, it was quite exciting, I thought."

"They are having the first of the World Series there again this year, starting on June twenty-six. Perhaps I can make that one on a friend's spectator boat. And have a hot toddy while I watch some of the races. Rhode Island on the water can be cold even this time of year. The final America's Cup will be held in San Francisco in September next year. Now, that's one race that will be really exciting. That Bay has some of the roughest waters in the world." Jonathan's face was all lit up. "I sure hope that Russell Coutts makes the cut this year with his Oracle Team USA. He's the best we have." Jonathan's mind was thousands of miles removed from the desert sands of Egypt.

"You are a sailor?" Col. Rahman said and suddenly added, "That reminds me. We heard something about a missing American boat on the radio while we were waiting."

"I thought, I had ordered radio silence," Jabari El-Masri reprimanded the tall colonel.

"We were just listening, Jabari. We weren't transmitting. Anyway, there was a lot of chatter about this sailboat having gone missing out of a pleasure-yacht marina in Safaga. A worker had been hired to clean the boat this morning and when he couldn't find it, he reported it to the marina manager. I heard that the manager told police he had seen a man and a woman that Saturday having lunch on the missing boat which he described as a very seaworthy vessel. He called it a...ah...a Veriant?"

"Valiant. Bob Perry design. Great cruising boat. Had a serious blister problem some years ago," Jonathan rattled off automatically.

"Jon!"

When children hear their full first name called out, they usually know that they are in trouble. With Jonathan, it was the opposite, and a stern 'Jon' from his parents always put him on guard. But when Naunet called him Jon, it felt like a caress to him. However, Bill's reminder now for him not to digress was far from that.

"What? Oh, sorry. Bad habit," Jonathan apologized.

"That was it, a Valiant." Rahman nodded appreciatively to the young sailor. "The owners apparently had paid two months ahead for the slip as they were flying back to the States. The lunching couple definitely was not them, the manager swore to the police. Of course, he felt responsible and is now worried he will lose his job."

Jabari turned to Jonathan having established himself as the apparent sailing expert. "What do you think, Jonathan? Could your friends have taken the boat out? To where? And if they stole the Saqqara tablets, would they sail down the coast of Africa, say to Cape Town?"

Jonathan shook his head, somewhat annoyed with Jabari implying again that Naunet was part of the theft.

"Much too risky. Hypothetically, if it were me, I'd motor up the

Read Sea and hope to transit the Canal into the Med. After that? Your guess is as good as mine. I doubt that the crook knows how to sail. I have a strong feeling that your Karakurt would be the skipper on that particular cruise."

"Speaking of whom, Jabari," Bill broke in and scratched his chin. He hadn't shaved that morning and felt grubby. "How come you trusted Karakurt? What was he to you, precisely?"

"Well," the Egyptian hesitated, "it is a long story. Let me just say, he was useful to us. When we were in trouble, financially speaking, he got me in touch with some South American billionaire who then bought several things from us. Worthless trinkets, by any standards, you understand. Nothing important. It simply helped us out at the time."

"Now I ask myself, how would a guy like that be friends with a billionaire?"

"Oh, I doubt that they are friends. I remember Karakurt letting it slip that he crewed on the guy's yacht lying off Cyprus some years ago."

Jabari suddenly slammed his right fist into his left palm. "That is it!"

"The billionaire?"

"No! Cyprus!"

"Why?"

"The northern part of that island is controlled by the Turks. I bet that pig has relatives there."

"Then let's fly there to find out!" Jonathan was all afire, ready to launch an air raid if he had to. Then he paused. "It'll take a sailboat at least a week to get there from Safaga, provided they have a stiff breeze coming from the right direction. We need to alert the authorities in Safaga, Port Suez, and Port Said, and, of course, the U.S. Embassy in Cairo. Maybe Interpol."

The Colonel looked at El-Masri. Both shook their heads and Jabari told them that, sadly, kidnappings had increased markedly since his country had been left leaderless.

They noted that he did not call it 'Mubarak's ouster,' as almost every news service all over the world had termed it over the last year.

"Every agency, including your embassy, is being overwhelmed by this new crime spree. It is a sad time for my country."

"You better tell us where you are going with all this, Jabari. And then, where we can expect to be let off." Bill said with a finality that was not to be denied.

The Egyptian looked again at his pilot. They nodded to each other. Rahman stood up and headed back to the cockpit to relieve his co-pilot.

"Crete," Jabari said. "I have friends on that island."

"Hot damn," Jonathan cried and slapped Bill on the thigh. "So do we. We have a friend on Crete. Bill, remember, Dr. Klein, Naunet's father, is supposed to be there right now!"

"Not *Herr Doktor Leopold* Klein?" Jabari was astounded that he had not made the connection earlier.

"The very same. I remember she wanted to stop off after Cairo to see him. He is on a dig with a couple he knows there. Mac..., Mac..., McPeal! That's it!"

"I don't believe it! Josef and Mary McPeal are the very people I want to see. This is quite extraordinary." Jabari El-Masri was highly agitated again.

This time, Bill and Jonathan did not have to fear that such excitement might culminate in another explosion.

"I just talked to them a couple of days ago. I met both Bruno and Josef McPeal at the same time, at the University of Pennsylvania, you know. Unfortunately, I never did meet Leopold. Well, now this can be remedied. He is very well respected in his field."

"Jabari, what are the McPeals exactly doing on Crete?"

"They are both renowned archeologists. Been there for years. Some months ago, they were digging for Minoan artifacts at Kommos, on the southern coast, you know, when they stumbled on several flat stones with curious patterns all over them. Small etched squares, dating back to 6500 BC, Josef believes. Definitely not Minoan. Likely from an unknown civilization that existed long before the Minoans.

"Josef e-mailed me photographs. Comparing them to the exposed sliver on the broken piece from the first slate, I found that they looked just like those squares." The Egyptian hardly took a breath. His words gained momentum.

Uh oh, he's gathering steam, just like a Rossini overture. But Jonathan was soon caught up again in the Egyptian's rapid-fire account of the mysterious squares.

"Of course, I immediately e-mailed Josef a picture of the broken-off corner." Jabari El-Masri's mouth turned down as if he had tasted something bitter. "That was when I still had it. And Josef agreed with me. They are the same. Here is what I concluded." His eyes shone and little beads of sweat appeared on his forehead despite the cold air that blew on them from the overhead nozzles.

"I think that what I have is a First Dynasty translation from that lost civilization!" Jabari leaned back, exhausted yet exhilarated. In a perfect world, there would have been applause.

Instead, Jonathan yawned. "Oh, yeah? I bet it's the proverbial old curses that the world will soon end." The moment he said it he knew that he had deflated and angered the eminent archaeologist.

Sure enough, Jabari's eyes sparked. "I do not believe in the proverbial curses of the mummy. It is pure rubbish. And I have never appreciated silly jokes and interminable questions. But I expect those from camera-toting tourists. From you, Jonathan, I expected better. The world still holds many mysteries. And man had better take heed and learn from history."

Jonathan clammed up. Bill tried to hide a grin. He vigorously rubbed his chin pretending that his beard stubble itched.

Luckily, they were about to land for their clandestine refueling stop. The proud Dr. El-Masri held his legendary temper in check. There would be plenty of time to reign in this young wise-something. What was that American expression? *Wise-ass.* That was it. He would be sure to use it on the know-it-all whippersnapper at an appropriate time. He liked Jonathan, though. The lad was good-looking and open, if perhaps a bit too quick with his opinion. *Well, he is still young.* Jabari El-Masri fleetingly wondered if the tall scientist was in love with the Klein-woman and then decided that it was in the young man's favor that Bruno had sent him to Egypt. That certainly would not have been the case if he were not any good at his job.

Bill, on the other hand, was somebody not to be trifled with. If he, Jabari, was successful in pulling this whole madness off, he realized that he needed to do some damage control with the Americans and make them see the conundrum he had created for himself. So far, they had taken the extraordinary turns of their visit pretty well, considering. He just hoped that they cooperated a while longer, even if it turned out that the woman had gone bad. One never knew with middle-aged females. They were so easily duped and swept off their feet by sweet-talking conmen. How that Edward-person had managed to get on the jet in the first place was astounding. It had to have been through Karakurt. Most likely, the Turk had smuggled him aboard through the loading ramp. Rahman had said that the first time he saw the man was in the cabin.

Their refueling stop had to have been the fastest on record. It seemed they were back in the air within minutes. After gaining altitude, Rahman left Lt. Col. al-Husri at the controls and stuck his head into the cabin.

"We land at Nikos Kazantzakis Airport in seventy minutes. Please, set your watches an hour ahead. It is now five-thirty-two a.m., Crete time."

"We are flying into Heraklion?" Jonathan was amazed. "Is that wise, landing at Crete's major airport?"

"Ah, my young friend," Jabari smiled—and Jonathan hoped he was forgiven—"The wise know it is best to hide in plain sight. Besides, Rahman has the necessary clearances, and there is a private hangar reserved in the cargo area where nobody will come snooping." More quietly, he added with a sigh, "I hope. Besides, it is easier to rent a car there. We have to drive down to Kommos."

* * *

Chapter Thirteen

Upon arrival at Heraklion International Airport, their clearance went smoothly just as Col. Rahman had arranged, using contacts his passengers did not ask him about. For them, it was enough that they had landed. The pilots taxied to the assigned cargo hangar where they shut down the G-4. A small truck pulled them all the way in and everyone breathed a sigh of relief when huge steel doors rolled down behind them. According to Dr. El-Masri, the pilots as well as Ahmed Sharkawy, would stay with the jet until further notice—a wise move considering that they lugged about a thousand pounds of gold around in their tail section. The other three hailed a stray cab to take them from the isolated cargo area to the main terminal.

Despite the early hour, Jabari called down to Kommos on his cell. Someone there told him that the McPeals together with Leopold Klein were already out on the dig. He, whoever it was that Jabari spoke with, would make certain that the archaeologists were informed to expect their visitors in a couple of hours.

Since the Egyptian had not exactly been forthcoming to lend his cell phone to 'his visitors,' never letting it out of his sight, Bill went to find a bank of public telephones; a rarity these days almost anywhere in the world. He slid the Institute's high-limit credit card through its slot and placed a call to the States. His call caught Bruno von der Heide—it was still Monday evening in Boston—at his Marlborough Street home where he hosted a small dinner party. From their conversation Bill learned that the guests were Bingham Adams, Hayden Smart and, to Bill's surprise, trustee board president George

Searing, all of Museum of Fine Arts persuasion.

For the following twenty minutes, Bill's increasingly animated reaction to his long-distance boss included more than a couple of juicy curses and several most unlike-William-Jefferson-Browning swear words, his voice spilling out forcefully over the semi-private booth partition. At last, he sputtered that, if the Boston art community was only worried about their Egyptian exhibit instead of his and Jonathan's kidnapping and their missing colleague, they could all go to hell. He mashed the receiver so violently back onto its cradle that the grimy instrument jumped right off again and was left there dangling, an innocent witness to a greatly frustrated man.

Jonathan had pulled up outside the terminal in an Opel Astra hatchback. The three drove back to the cargo area for some coffee and fruit, served by Ahmed from the jet's plentiful larder. Jabari also had Ahmed stow the fully exposed tablet number Nine carefully into the rental car, and personally checked that the hatchback was locked. He was anxious to compare it to the carved stones Josef McPeal had told him about. After they discussed various scenarios for the next few days with the pilots, they grabbed their overnight bags and drove off to search for the road to Matala. Jonathan had been given a tourist map by the rental-car company even though the car was equipped with GPS. Considering the unknown road conditions, they thought it should take just under two hours to drive the seventy kilometers to the protected archaeological site, which was closed to the public.

Jonathan drove, not in the least due to the car's manual transmission. Bill had not driven for ages since a car in public-transportation-rich Boston was a nuisance that came with great expense. And Jabari was used to being chauffeured around. The GPS was out of order but thanks to the map, they found the road and soon saw the sign for Kommos.

Nearing the beach of the McPeals' archaeological site where they and Leopold Klein were excavating Minoan artifacts, they rounded the last sand dune and were confronted by a formidable view of Mesara Bay.

Had they not been so preoccupied with pressing matters to talk to the archaeologists, they would have enjoyed its natural beauty. In addition, there was the feared moment when they would have to confront Leopold Klein and tell him of his daughter's recent disappearance and let him know that some doubt had been cast over her character.

"Jabari! What an honor!" Josef McPeal fit the part of the lanky, sandy-haired, khaki-shorts-clad explorer of the nineteenth century to a tee, down to his knobby knees. *All that's missing is a pith-helmet.* Jonathan immediately damned himself for conjuring up the unpleasant association with the Dandy. His nimble mind would not let go of it until he explored the more satisfying scenario of cramming the bloody thing down a certain bloody Brit's bloody throat. Better yet, he vowed to shove it up the bloody man's something else—if he ever got the chance. Jonathan completely missed out on the introductions until Bill boxed him on the arm and introduced him as 'our dreaming materials scientist.'

A tall, striking woman with red curls heaped high on her head, and the greenest eyes, joined their group. She pulled off and carelessly dropped her handyman's yellow leather gloves and smiled broadly at them, extending both her hands in a warm welcome.

"There you are, at last. I'm so glad to see you again, Jabari. And, of course, we welcome your friends. Do come inside. I hardly slept last night knowing that we would see your tablet for ourselves. Didn't I, Josef."

The look that passed between the couple who, Jonathan guessed, had to be in their late fifties, spoke of immeasurable closeness. There was nothing physical about it, not even sensual, and definitely nothing overtly sexual. He simply sensed a deep unbreakable bond tying them together.

Perhaps it was exhaustion, or the heat, or the pain of missing her. Jonathan was close to breaking down; to cry inconsolably. At the same time, he wanted to fling curses at the ancient monster god who allowed his heart to be ripped to shreds like a storm-tortured sail. His boat was sinking; there were no life preservers; and all on board were lost. He felt numb, and dead-tired, and utterly without hope.

"Jonathan, are you all right?" Bill had watched the increasing pallor flooding the young scientist's face. They had been up all night and he knew that Naunet's disappearance had to weigh heavily on the young man's mind. Out of the corner of his eye, he saw a tall man advancing quickly toward them. Bill judged him to be close to his own age, with hair as full and as white as his own, except that it was exquisitely cut in contrast to the unruly shock he himself sported. Considering the remote location, the man was also impeccably dressed. Bill knew that the older archaeologist had to be the main reason for his young colleague's mounting anguish. *It has to be done, lad.* To pave the way, he stepped forward and greeted Leopold Klein, Naunet's father.

Jonathan mustered his courage. "You probably don't remember me, Dr. Klein." He extended his hand to the man he had met years ago, on this very island.

"Let me see. So many eager young faces. Ah, Wilkins, wasn't it? At the Zominthos site. I remember now. More of an avid sailor than an archaeological student, as I recall."

The villa Josef and Mary McPeal had made their home for many years was modest compared to those of the southern beachfront communities of Matala and Kalamaki, newly popularized resorts with organized beach conveniences and even lifeguards. Nestled among huge sand dunes, the whitewashed house with its soothing blue tile-work suited them. Besides, it was conveniently located in the no-access zone of their large excavation site offering peace and quiet at night.

After they all had been introduced and thanked each other for mutual inquiries about all-around health, they still maintained an outwardly jovial manner and carefully kept to social generalities. To ease the palpable tension, Mary pointed to a hulking mound in the bay and told them that the locals called it Volakas and that it played an important part in Greek mythology. The legends insisted, she explained, that this stone was the top of a mountain supposedly thrown by the blinded Cyclops Polyphemus at Odysseus' ship to prevent the intrepid traveler from escaping.

Jonathan frowned slightly, and Jabari just could not help himself. "That's Ulysses to you. Sorry, Mary. Please continue."

In an effort to keep the lighter mood going, Mary McPeal explained that Kommos was established at about two hundred BC as a port called Phaestus. Several centuries after that, it was destroyed by a horrific earthquake, and later rebuilt by the Minoans.

They listened politely bursting to come to the crux of their visit. At last, Josef jumped up, left the room and came back carrying a tray with four green bottles and a tall glass.

"I don't believe it is too early for a beer. Try this. Greek *Mythos*. It's excellent," he said and, handing his wife the frosty glass filled with a greenish liquid, he added with a wink, "Special occasion, my dear."

She took the glass from him, touching his fingers as she did so, and smiled up at her husband. "Green tea," she explained to the others. "I drink it by the gallon. Well, cheers, gentlemen."

The way she lifted her glass had gusto. She managed to be gracious at the same time. Her four guests bowed to her, taking thirsty gulps from their bottles.

To Leopold Klein's fleeting dismay, it had not occurred to Josef that someone else might have preferred to drink from a glass. "Dr. El-Masri," he said quietly. "I regret that we never crossed paths at U-Penn."

Everyone was acutely aware that the time had come. There seemed to be collective deep breathing and sighs all around, after which they finally talked and listened, explained and suggested, and planned whom they should contact to find out about Naunet's whereabouts. They believed that they needed to be proactive themselves as well. They hung their hopes on the fact that someone apparently had abducted her in connection with the Saqqara tablets. They would need Naunet's expertise. Her chances of being kept alive improved greatly as long as she could delay her task.

Jabari did not think for one moment that the thieves—whoever they were, he said and briefly managed to cast a renewed shadow over Naunet's integrity—might simply melt the priceless tablets down to nuggets. ·

Jonathan was about to protest as far as Naunet's character was concerned when, not too delicately, Jabari reminded them of his mission. He emphasized that he could not risk involving his own government—such as it was at this time. It became apparent that the good Dr. El-Masri had burned his bridges with his country's provisional power-mongers.

Mary gently reminded the men about lunch and led the way to her cheery dining room where her cook, who also took care of the workers and students at the dig, had laid out an array of fresh fruits and vegetables, as well as cold chicken.

It was not all gloom and doom during the simple meal. Everyone listened gratefully to Josef explain that, so far, the excavations had traced the outlines of a harbor complete with shipyards as well as the foundations of several public buildings, oil presses and a courtyard. The conversation became more scientific when Josef excitedly added that they were presently digging for the remains of a primitive temple which had been built on top of the ruins of an older, presumably Neolithic one.

Jabari finally interrupted with a brusque announcement that he had brought one of his own tablets to compare its pattern to those found on the Kommos stones.

"The tablet is apparently number nine of fifty. The only one so far we completely cleaned. I have it in the back of the car," he said. Not a venerable resting place for the precious object, I admit."

"Never mind how you got it here." Josef jumped up. "Let's have at look at it." He dashed out to the car shimmering in the midday heat like a mirage.

"Josef, wait! The thing weighs a ton," Jabari called after him. Too late.

Josef had already popped the Opel Astra's hatch, and was pulling at the tablet. Surprised by its great weight, he lowered it onto the gravel where it lay, golden rays shooting into the high-noon sky. Five pairs of anxious hands reached for it at the same time.

"*Ps'ari!* Eels! Live octopus!" The singsong startled the five men into rigidity. In unison, they straightened up and turned to form a human shield around the gleaming slate.

A leathery grin greeted them. It came from an old man wizened by the wind and the sea. He cackled and pointed to an odorous cart. With the cunning of a simple soul, he wagged his finger and said, "I see plenty. You buy my fish, I see nothing."

"Allah, Ptah and Christ combined! Who was that?" Jabari was shocked to the core. He and Josef had rushed the tablet inside, while Mary shelled out a high percentage of her household money to buy the entire stinking cart of ocean offal from the old man.

"Don't worry about him," she said hoping she was right. "That was Odysseus. He brings his catch over from Loutro." She nodded to her husband. "Josef, do tell them about Loutro."

"It's a small fishing village about seventy miles west of here. It must take the poor man all night to motor his catch over from there. Of course, he could be coming by ferry. It runs almost every day. His village is picturesque and completely isolated, accessible only by water."

Josef was in his element. After archaeology, geology and history were his other passion. But his calling was teaching. After he and his wife were finished with Crete, they planned to publish their findings, perhaps obtain tenure at a west-coast university, preferably Berkeley. He looked over at Mary and, noticed only by her, he pursed and smacked his lips lightly in her direction. She smiled back, content and secure in the 'turkey-wrap of their love,' as Josef had coined their intimate moments.

They talked and compared notes, and fretted about Naunet until late that night, until Mary suggested that everyone call it a day. Josef showed them to a side building with bunk beds and a single shower. As all of them had been on primitive digs at one time or another, they hardly blinked an eye or voiced so much as a single complaint about the Spartan accommodations. Sleep was fitful, and their dreams included mountains of gold.

The next morning, Jonathan had to rid himself of the cobwebs of his nightmares and lessen the yearning in his heart. He needed a clear head if he was to be of any help in finding out about Naunet's whereabouts. When he saw how deeply the three older men were still asleep, he quietly slipped out. A short stroll over huge sand dunes and through a stand of tamarisk trees brought him to a nearby village. Lying on the shores of the Libyan Sea, the beaches of Kalamaki were beautiful and at that early hour thankfully devoid of tourists. He sat down on a sun-bleached chaise-lounge overlooked by local beach boys the evening before. Jonathan stared pensively at the Idaian Mountains that loomed to his northwest. It seemed that he had been away from home for an eternity. Counting the days on his fingers he was stunned. If this was Wednesday, the thirtieth of May, they had been gone for almost a month. He kicked the sand and stomped resolutely back to the Kommos compound.

By the time he got there, the camp was humming with local workers arriving for the day's dig. Vans rattled up to deliver food and other supplies. Josef showed him to a large terrace where Mary had laid out breads, jams and hard-boiled eggs. As soon as he had joined the others, she carried in a steaming fragrant pot. This morning, it was back to coffee for everyone. They set to work photographing and copying the squares from Josef's find.

"Naunet will have some comparison when she gets back," Jonathan said and the other men agreed, and kept their private fears in check.

The work distracted them from more morose thoughts although Jonathan was antsy and wished they would go back to Heraklion and take the G-4 to do a grid-search over the Mediterranean. It was wishful thinking, of course, and he tried to settle down.

Around noon, just when they were about to eat a cold lunch, the old man lurched up the few steps to the terrace.

Josef jumped up to cut the unbidden guest off at the last step. "Odysseus," he said and put a restraining hand on the man's shoulder. "We don't need anything from you today."

The man cocked his head. A sly grin stretched his cracked lips. "But I think you do," he said and looked past Josef to where the others sat motionless. "You need my stillness." It was clear. The man expected for them to buy his silence.

Josef motioned to Jabari to follow him and led him and the smelly fisherman into a small room. Judging from the masses of books and papers, as well as a photocopier and laptop, it was his office. He closed the door behind them. There was only one chair behind a wooden desk, so they all remained standing.

"Odysseus," Josef said quietly, almost gently as if speaking to a child. "You know that we sometimes dig up valuable things around here. After we do, we examine them. And then, they go to a museum in Heraklion. Why? Because they belong to Crete." He stopped for a moment to let the old man digest his English words. "What you saw was also a precious object from the past. But it does not belong to Crete. This gentleman brought it with him to show me. It belongs to..." Before he could say another word, Jabari quickly stepped between them.

The Egyptian trained his dark eyes on the old man and told him, "The whole world will know that you were the first to see it here in Crete. To make sure I have it correct, write your name down for me." When the old man hesitated, Jabari easily lied, "You will be famous. But for now, no one must know about this. You understand?" Jabari waited for the nod and added, "If you keep quiet, I will reward you plenty." That promise, the old man understood perfectly.

They spent another uneasy night at Kommos. Each hoped that the old man would keep the reward in mind, and therefore his mouth shut.

* * *

Chapter Fourteen

The winds were obliging during their two-hundred-mile passage up the Red Sea. They could sail most of the way, saving on diesel. Karakurt had topped off the in-board tanks before they had left Safaga and replenished the spare twenty-gallon canisters strapped to the deck, including the small red five-gallon gas can for the dinghy's outboard that was bolted onto a stanchion-plate at the stern.

Before leaving his boat, Harry Jenkins had pickled the small watermaker to preserve its delicate membranes during his absence. Therefore, all the fresh water on board was in the eighty-gallon tank located under the cabin settee, and Karakurt cautioned that they use it sparingly. Cyprus was over four hundred miles to the northeast of Port Suez and in good weather, averaging an optimistic eight knots, they should have no problem arriving with diesel and water to spare. Still, it was best to stay prepared. The winds of the Mediterranean could be capricious.

More than anything, Karakurt wanted to avoid stopping in Port Suez. In every small-boat marina around the world, cruisers maintained their own radio net. If word had spread as far as the Canal Zone about two corpses having been discovered on the road to Hurghada, there could be inquiries, especially if the marina manager in Safaga had reported a sailboat having left without checking out. These irksome busybody cruiser guys all knew each other. They readily spread news and weather over their ham and shortwave radios and were all too eager to juice up the monotone of their down-days at anchor. Too bad there hadn't been time to paint the sides over. On a Valiant, a double-ender with a rounded stern, the boat's name and home-port are painted along both sides, the lettering nice and big, and easily readable from a distance, especially through quality marine binoculars.

The *Tumbleweed* entered the Canal Zone early Tuesday morning, guided by flaming oil derricks and the procession of boats ahead. Karakurt had taken down all sails and was motoring at reduced speed. As soon as they arrived, they were beleaguered by self-appointed agents and pilots bumping their dilapidated dinghies against the hull, demanding payment for services not yet rendered. Karakurt, only too familiar with baksheesh, threw prepared packets of cigarettes and small bills onto their scruffy decks, and then shouted that they do something to themselves and their mothers. If they had not been hailed by a fast approaching launch, there could have been an unpleasant scuffle. Karakurt idled the Perkins and hove to.

Edward went below. He undid the slats barricading Naunet and ordered her to come on deck. His warning glance spoke volumes. She huddled against the cabin bulkhead to be out of the wind and stared at the horizon. The restless night in the closed-in captain's berth had taken its toll on her stomach again, and the fresh air felt good.

"Harbormaster. Passports and papers." Karakurt nodded toward the fast approaching launch.

Naunet jumped up from her seat. "I'll get mine." A word or two of distress scribbled onto an empty page in Arabic should alert the official to her plight. Maybe she could step close to the lifelines, stub her foot on the toe-rail and, pretending to lose her balance, fall overboard.

With a double-ended cruising boat like the *Tumbleweed*, it was impossible to get back on board without a ladder. The launch, on the other hand, had a low swim-platform off its stern. No doubt, they would fish her out. During the few seconds it took for these possibilities to race through her mind, Edward had ducked down the hatch and came back waving a plastic envelope. She guessed that he most likely rifled through her bag while she had slept. She no longer had an excuse to go below.

The launch had its fenders out and the driver pulled up alongside with a gentle bump. Leaving his powerful engine idling, he hung onto one of *Tumbleweed's* stanchions while the harbormaster asked permission to come aboard. As if they could deny him, Karakurt thought. The portly man gauged the swell and executed a well-practiced jump from one boat to the other. What surprised Karakurt was that he did not press them for the customary gifts. He was professional and courteous. Karakurt pointed to Edward and said in Arabic, "Owner."

Edward handed over the boat's registration papers and crew list, and the harbormaster asked in good English if the boat had a propeller, if they had fire extinguishers, and if the motor worked. Getting an affirmative answer each time, he told them that they passed inspection. Then, as the official leafed through the ship's log, he suddenly drummed a finger at the crew list. "He is not on here." He raised his chin at Karakurt.

"Local pilot," Karakurt replied quickly.

The harbormaster raised his eyebrows, "I have not seen you before. Where did you get on?"

"About half a mile down. I work for the Prince."

"Oh, that scoundrel." The harbormaster shrugged and wondered how much these people had paid the thieving agent who was known to order his pilots to run boats up on the rocks if his outrageous fee was not met; always, of course, at the beginning of the transit.

The 'Prince of the Red Sea,' a well-known scourge among cruising folk, was not a 'to-be-paid-after-services-rendered' kind of fool. Too many things could go wrong in his line of extortion. These unofficial agents and their mostly useless pilots were an age-old custom and though the harbormaster didn't like them one bit, he was not one to quarrel with these bandits. The idea of being discovered floating belly up under an oil derrick was more than enough for him to look the other way. As did his colleagues.

The harbormaster then looked at the two passports Edward had handed him. He squinted at the pictures and smiled at Naunet. "Very pretty, Madame." Then, aware of his importance, he pulled up straight and proclaimed in his official voice, "You are cleared." Turning to Karakurt, he added, "You must go on quickly. A large convoy is coming up behind you. If you do not get out of the way now, you will have to anchor somewhere out of the channel for the next twenty-four hours."

To Naunet's dismay, the portly man handed the boat papers and the two blue passports back to Edward who stuffed them hastily into the waterproof envelope and tossed it carelessly below.

It was her last chance to alert the port official to her plight. Should she jump now? She was on the port side of the cockpit and the harbormaster was already clambering back onto his launch on the opposite side. Besides, she would have to squeeze past the wheel where Karakurt stood broad-legged and alert. She took a deep breath.

Any intent to jump or scream evaporated when something hard pressed against her lower back. It might just be the handle of a screwdriver, or a flashlight. Quite inappropriate for the occasion, an old tasteless joke flashed through her mind. No, she thought, most likely, Edward was not 'glad to see her.'

Yet he slung an arm across her shoulders and called a jovial, "We do thank you, sir," over to the Egyptian who turned back and smartly saluted Edward. The port official then bowed to Naunet and, with his hand cupped around his lips, called back to her, "Bon Voyage, Madame Jenkins." His driver gunned the motor and the launch roared off, fenders skipping.

"One day, he'll lose those," Karakurt sneered and put the engine in gear to motor back out into the shipping channel.

It hit her right between the eyes. *Blue!* The two passports Edward had given to the harbormaster were blue! Her Austrian passport had a burgundy cover, like all within the European Union. And the one Edward had given Harry to copy had also been burgundy.

She stared open-mouthed at the insolent cad, balancing himself broad-legged in the cockpit to match the swell that rocked the slow-moving vessel from side to side. A prickly feeling went from her spine to her hairline. For a second, she thought she might faint. American passports were blue. And the harbormaster had just called her 'Madame Jenkins.'

"You bastard!" Naunet flew at him with clenched fists.

Edward easily caught her slender wrists in mid-air. He twisted her arms behind her and pulled her so close to him that she felt the heat of his body. His breath was moist against her ear.

"We don't want any unpleasantness, do we now. So be a good girl. Do what I say, and you won't wind up like the Americans." He rested his chin on top of her head and rocked her gently until he felt her go limp against his chest. He might be a cad and a thief. And—if one had to be pedantic about it—an accomplice to murder. But no one could accuse Edward Guernsey-Crock of being unnecessarily rough with a woman.

On the other side of the Canal, they picked their way through a large anchorage of merchant ships, wide-swinging buoys and the rusting hulks of half-submerged bulk-carriers. At last, the narrow channel, lined by flame- and smoke-belching oilrigs, spewed them out into the Mediterranean.

"Cyprus, here we come," Karakurt grinned.

Divided into Greek and Turkish territories, the island was a haven for the shady exchange of even shadier goods. In a secluded anchorage near his brother's village in the north, the Turk expected to meet up with his customer, a rich nut on his mega-yacht, the *Bucanero*, out of Punta del Este, Uruguay. The man was driven to chasing down ancient oracles. Whether he believed in them or was hoping to debunk them was of no concern to Karakurt as long as the purse strings of the South American remained loose. After Karakurt had relayed his newest discovery via the Iridium satellite phone supplied by the secretive collector, the billionaire had told him that he would buy as many of the tablets as Karakurt could lay his hands on. On one condition: that the tablets be deciphered and certified by an accredited archeologist.

What a waste of perfectly fine gold! Karakurt adjusted his stance to the swell of the sea. He rubbed a rough palm over the stubble of his chin and breathed a sigh of relief. Thanks to the convoy, their clearance had been a lot faster than he could have hoped for. He had smuggled things out of Egypt this way once before. Transiting the Canal then had been a nightmare of too much baksheesh and contrary winds. If El-Masri had checked the many half-forgotten crates way in the back of the storage rooms himself instead of asking a Turkish immigrant to inventory them, Karakurt might be rotting in some stinking Egyptian jail by now. The man could be positively vicious when it came to his precious hoard of ancient discoveries.

Karakurt grinned. Considering that this was his plan-B, it was his best haul yet. *That goat turd Wamukota! Serves him right to have the tunnel collapse around him. For sure, he tried to steal the tablets.* But Allah was great. He had placed the Brit and the gullible Americans right into his path with a second chance to supply his client. He was not called 'Black Wolf' Teriyaki for nothing. His last name meant 'addict.' True, he was addicted: to becoming rich.

Then he would buy a beautiful boat, and no longer have to cater to the whims of those detestable Germans and the pasty-white Brits. He could sail off in style. Maybe buy a little island. Karakurt glanced at Naunet. If the woman did not cooperate or was not able to complete the cleaning and translating of his payload hidden in the bow, there was always his brother's kiln. He looked at Edward. The arrogant cad had come in handy in getting the woman and the boat. But he would no longer be of use on Cyprus.

Karakurt told Edward that it was time to hoist the sails. He ordered Naunet below to feed the stored jib back out onto the deck through the forward hatch.

The forepeak was not a nice place to be for a queasy stomach, and more than once, Naunet was slammed against the bulkhead as the boat rolled and sea-sawed. She grabbed a cushion from the V-berth to prop against the paneling. Laid bare was a flat object wrapped in white damask. It looked just like the tablecloth in the trunk of the Mercedes. She lifted the second cushion. There was another packet. Naunet glanced behind her. Nobody was in sight. Out the main hatch, she could see Karakurt's stringy legs as he braced himself against the wheel. Outside above her, Edward struggled to raise the mainsail and she heard him curse. Something about stupid people, and why they couldn't have automated roller reefing. Naunet pulled the cloth of one package back. The tablet had a corner missing.

"Now you know." Lying spread-eagle on the deck above, Karakurt glared at her through the forward hatch, his reddening face inches above hers as her head jerked up.

"I'm ready," Edward called and Karakurt got up. He told her to start feeding the sail out, tack first. *Lord, which corner is the tack?* Jonathan had made everything look so easy when he hoisted the sails all by himself while she was at the wheel nervously following his instructions. She heard Karakurt stomp about and then his brown hands reached down, "This," he grabbed onto a point and yanked half the jib on deck.

Edward grunted and struggled to hank the salt-stiffened cloth onto the forestay. More than once he swore as he wrestled with the sail. If Karakurt hadn't caught the whipping jib halyard Edward might have been garroted.

"Hand me the clew," Karakurt called down to Naunet and she pushed the last corner out. Kneeling on the V-berth, she stuck her head out the hatch.

Edward had lurched back to the wheel and was ordered to 'hold her into the wind,' as Karakurt quickly knotted the jib sheets through the metal eye with perfect bowlines.

"That's the clew," he told Naunet. "So you'll know next time."

After feeding the lines through the blocks and around the winches, Karakurt was back in the cockpit. He took the wheel from Edward and turned it until the sails filled. Then he cut the engine and set a northeasterly course. "Stay on this heading," he told Edward. "With the wind out of the west, we should make good time. I am going below to sleep."

If the Red Sea had been unusually benign, the Mediterranean now proved querulous. Mid-afternoon, the wind changed to a strong easterly breeze. As the wind backed the sails, Edward remembered that they should tack. He asked Naunet to loosen the starboard lines and pull in the port sheets. "Well done," he praised her. His arms soon ached from forcing the wheel to keep the compass needle in its northeasterly direction without stalling the boat.

Naunet stayed in the cockpit and stared out to sea while her captor managed to hold the compass on course. Unfortunately, he had no idea about the effect of slippage, the imperceptible sideways crabbing of a vessel due to wind and current while the needle still indicated a correct course.

"So, Edward," Naunet forced herself to appear calm. "What happens now?"

"Naunet, my dear, I am so sorry. I am as much a victim as you are. I swear I had no idea what Karakurt was up to. All I wanted was for you and me to have a nice weekend."

"So you stole a boat."

"No, no. Karakurt suggested we go for a sail. I thought it would be fun."

"You drugged me! And what about Harry and Edith?"

"Ah, them. An unfortunate accident, I assure you."

"You call that an accident? He killed them!" She breathed deeply to stay calm. "You knew it, didn't you!"

"Work with me here," Edward said lightly. "If we play along and keep our heads then—well, we will keep our heads. Just as certain English queens should have remembered when they would not play along with their ruler."

The joke was as old as it was tasteless. However, it made Naunet think about her chances for survival. And her only chance indeed was to keep her head. For sure, Bill and Jonathan were by now upending heaven and earth to find out what had happened to her. *Oh God, I hope they don't think I ran off with this guy. Or worse, it suddenly occurred to her, accuse me of stealing the tablets.* Yes, she would at least try to play along with the taciturn Karakurt and the ever so charming Edward, as revolting as the idea was.

When night fell, Karakurt came on deck, refreshed and happy with Edward's proud declaration that the compass needle had never veered much off-course. They ate whatever they could find in the icebox: cheese, hard salami, soggy crackers. There was plenty of beer they had found stored in a dry bilge compartment.

Karakurt took over the night watch.

Naunet was forced back into the small cabin. After a while, her confines became so claustrophobic that she thought she would lose her mind. Locked up for the next two days, she waited, plotted, and finally did some long-forgotten praying.

To calm herself to sleep, she imagined the mountains of her youth. There had been no ocean for her until her mother was sure that her daughter had learned to swim properly. At the age of six, Akila took her to Egypt for the first time. The little girl, bundled up in a stiff life-vest, became a darling member of the dive boat crew, and Akila called her 'my little baby-shark.' To be honest, Naunet thought drowsily, I liked the mountains better. During summer vacations, her father would take her on weeklong hikes, often just the two of them, singing along on a high crest, or cautiously traversing an eternal snowfield. She smiled at last, remembering the green mountain meadows dipped in blue gentian and pink laurel. 'God's own tapestry,' her father called it. Still, he would always return to the dusty plains of yet another excavation. Those were the worlds she grew up in. How had she ended up this way? Partly, she admitted to herself, because she had been a gullible spinster, too eager to believe the sweet talk of a confidence trickster. It was difficult for her to believe she could have been so stupid to fall for a conman.

Sleep came only reluctantly. When it did, it was fitful with nightmarish dreams.

* * *

Chapter Fifteen

It was Edward who suggested untying Naunet to have her work on one of the tablets while they sailed along in surprisingly calm waters. To save time and keep her occupied, he told Karakurt. Actually, her tiresome riling against her confinement and the frequent requests to have to use the head—or else—were getting on his nerves.

"I suppose she won't run off with our gold," Karakurt sneered.

They untied her and then pummeled her up into the forepeak. The relatively fresher air there was deceptive. Doing things such as reading or knitting or—a highly unusual scenario on a sailboat—squinting at hieratic Egyptian writing, could be thought of as a soothing diversion for a troubled mind. Until one became aware of the bow's pronounced sea-sawing. Up and down. Up and down. Then it was quickly apparent that the forward cabin should be the last place anyone would wish to be when underway and even the most intrepid sailor would prefer to doze off in the cockpit.

Naunet was no exception. After enduring the bow's exaggerated motion for fifteen minutes, she stumbled back out to the open cockpit.

"I can't do this down there. You've got to let me work some other place."

They ordered her back into the salon where she slid behind the U-shaped table. Karakurt issued a stern warning for her not to touch the electronics again. Or anything else, for that matter, or he would throw her overboard. When she defied him with a sardonic, "Oh really, and who'll work on those tablets then," he changed his threat to cutting off her hair. It was an odd thing to say and Naunet wondered if, perhaps in Turkey, this was a shameful thing to do to defiant women, although she had never heard of it. Considering other odd and demeaning customs most Muslim countries thought of as normal when it came to the treatment of their womenfolk, she was not surprised. At any rate, life with short hair would be better than drowning—she hoped.

Karakurt hauled one of the tablets from the bow and cushioned it with a towel so it would not slide off the table with the next swell. It was the tablet with the missing telltale corner. Number One, Naunet noted.

The Turk went to his satchel and rummaged through it for something as he cast pieces of clothing aside. To get to the bottom he stuck his arms up to his elbows into the mottled canvass. It looked like an old fashioned World War II barracks bag. At first glance, the object he hauled out resembled a small handgun. Her eyes widened in alarm. Instead, what he laid in front of her was Bill's handheld laser.

"You think I am stupid, I know. But not enough to forget this," he sneered.

She remembered noticing his interest in everything they did at the Luxor lab. How he watched intently until his curiosity became too distracting to them and one or the other of her two colleagues shooed him off. He would leave reluctantly, scowling and muttering, as he pushed the empty lunch trolley out the door. At the time, she wrote it off as being keen to learn from them. After all, he would presumably be working with all sorts of scientists in the Cairo lab again. If he wanted to advance at all, he naturally would be interested and want to observe any new methods.

Karakurt jutted his chin at the tablet. "Start work!"

She had no choice but to get to work. That previous Friday afternoon, when they were asked to stop their work at once and leave the lab, the two Saqqara tablets had soaked in the solution for the pitch to become pliable enough for them to continue the following Saturday. Of course, that had been before they went to dinner at the Luxor Hilton, and before Edward came up with his Safaga invitation. She briefly recalled how charming he was, and how eager to take all those photos; especially her close-ups. Now, she was certain that one of her pictures made it into Edith's passport. Karakurt had probably gone into one of Safaga's hotel kiosks where tourists could have their digital photos printed. Except that most people did not ask to have this done after murdering two innocent people!

Her hackles rose again. To clear her inner eye of the grisly image, Naunet bent closer over the tablet and discovered that the unguent was still fairly pliable. The solution must have a longer lasting effect than they had previously assumed. She switched the battery-powered laser on and hoped for the best. Never actually having done any cutting herself, she was nervous about making a mistake. She always tried to excel in everything she did. This time, however, she wished Bill would be looking over her shoulder, guiding her, chiding her, and finally patting her on the shoulder with his appreciated *well done*. Her first cut went shallow. Better than to cut into the unguent too deeply and damage chunks of the writing. Bill would have raised his eyebrows, always the first indication to an assistant or intern that matters had not gone as expected.

Take a deep breath. Adjust the measurement. Go carefully over the line again. With the constant motion of the boat, it was near to impossible to cut in a straight line.

"I can't do this with you breathing down my neck." She looked up at Karakurt who held on to the table's edge, glaring down at her. "I need a ruler, and something pointed to peel the pitch back."

She looked around. "Over there. The scissors or better yet, the points of the compass might work."

He followed her eyes to the chart table and swore at her not to try anything funny and reluctantly handed her the needle-sharp instrument with a wooden ruler. Naunet ignored him for several more minutes and concentrated on the delicate task. She heard him huff before he turned abruptly and hawked. Loathing welled through her whole body. If he spat his phlegm onto the cabin sole, she swore she was going to do something irrational. Unrestrained spitting by crass people was one of the things she could not endure without grimacing or exclaiming disgust. Despite having had to endure the filthy habit on dusty excavation sites it remained one of her pet peeves.

Karakurt climbed back out into the cockpit where he spat again.

Pig. Naunet shuddered.

After a couple of hours her stomach threatened to give up

whatever little food she had been lucky enough to keep down. The laser stopped working. Reluctantly, Naunet stuck her head out the main hatch. The fresh air was heaven and she breathed deeply, and stared out over the stern to keep the horizon in her sight hoping to calm her queasy stomach.

"What?" Karakurt's sneer startled her.

"The laser quit."

"You broke it!" He let go of the wheel, leaned down toward her, caught her by her wrists, and twisted them until she cried out in pain.

"No! Stop! The battery went dead. Did you bring the charger?" she whimpered.

For a moment, the Turk's look went blank. He let go of her, staring. "What charger? There was no charger with it."

"Not in the lab." Naunet was glad that she could point at his stupidity. Perhaps this would dampen his new insufferable attitude of trying to appear superior all the time. "Bill kept it in his room. He always charged the laser overnight."

"Then you will finish without it." His black eyes had narrowed into malevolent slits and turned even colder than his voice.

Naunet looked up at Edward who had quickly positioned himself behind the wheel and now stared intently at the fluttering telltales sewn high up near the luff of the sails. Self-absorbed and pretentious, he busied himself and adjusted their heading to keep the colorful yarn streaming back in a fairly straight line. He had found something to be proud of. He steered the boat, and was learning fast. He wanted no part in her quarrel with the upset Turk.

"Why don't I start translating some of it," she said. "I have enough writing exposed to make a good start. Then, after we get to Cyprus, perhaps you can get a new charger."

She tried to keep her voice even to sound detached and professional; anything to soothe the angry man's quick temper. She would not cherish a welt on her other cheek. Nor most likely tolerate his raising a hand at her again. Involuntarily, she brought her palm up to her right cheek. The swelling was still there. And so was the hurt.

Karakurt pointed for her to get back down below.

Reluctantly she slid down backwards into the salon and wedged herself against the banquette's cushioned back once more. While she worked out the most familiar sequences and styles of the cursive symbols from memory, she wished she had her laptop with her. How much good it would have done her. On a good day, the old battery lasted for two to three hours before she had to recharge it. And just as with the laser's transformer—if they had it—her own transformer would not have done her any good either.

Most of Europe, as well as Egypt, ran on a two-twenty to two-forty volt current. They had brought specific travel transformers for their laptops and the laser with them. However, a boat's house battery ran on twelve volts only unless plugged into shore power. So, even if she had a transformer to the called-for electrical house power, somehow she suspected that she would be blowing some fuse or other on a boat, or even ruin the laser. Did she really care about this now? If she was honest, she had to admit that she had no illusions about the outcome of this particular venture. She knew she was in mortal danger and, likely, that it was just a matter of time. The time they needed for her to clean and translate the two tablets. *With what? And how? And after that?* A heavy sigh escaped from deep within her soul.

Bent over the first tablet, Naunet started to decipher the last few inches of the hieratic text she had exposed: *And now, you know from where we hailed so long ago.*

"No, I don't," she cried, exasperated. Where the supposed name of their homeland should have been, that corner had been broken off. And since she had not been able to remove all of the pitch above it, there was only the last half of an apparently extraordinary story. She had to write down what she read so far. Naunet slid out from behind the table and grabbed a book off a shelf above the chart table. The inscription on the cover read in gold lettering. 'Logbook of the Valiant-40, *Tumbleweed,* 2006-to—.' Hesitating for a moment, she breathed a quiet "sorry" and then turned it upside down. She flipped to the last page making it now her first, which she titled *Saqqara Tablet Number One. Hieratic Inscription, 3080 BC. Translated by Dr. Naunet Klein, June 2012.* Then, reading the words to herself Naunet, once again the consummate Egyptologist, slowly wrote down what she thought would best depict the meaning of the ancient writing:

I am the oldest surviving the fires from the mountains. The roiling waters ripped us from our island and sucked us out to sea. For many days, we clung to the floating forest which the angry gods had ripped from our hills and spewed into the Great Green. We wept and called out to our island, but it was no longer there. Burning ash rained from the sky. We drifted for many days and nights until those who lived came to a new empty land.

It was a green savannah with a great river. We named it Sahari. For years, we lived well and prospered. Many children later, our people turned bad with avarice and strife. Then a great wind turned the grasses into sand. With it came the locusts. They devoured the last of our fields. We traveled many risings of the sun until we met another great river. These mats tell our story. But those who come after us must take great heed.

It took all of Naunet's willpower not to run up to the forepeak to get the fiftieth tablet and practically force it to give up its secrets, pitch-covered or not. The old one had talked of mats. Not tablets. Not stones, nor slates. But mats. She turned the heavy piece over and studied the minute squares again. It suddenly occurred to her that what she had deciphered could already be a translation, most likely by that high priest, Ramose. That would explain why his seal was stamped on the rims following the numbering of the tablets.

This could mean that the original story was thousands of years older than the tablets were. The squares could have been copied onto the gold from those mats the old one spoke of, with the high priest's translation on the reverse. *My God*, Naunet marveled and squinted at the tiny squares again. It would have taken years to do just one slate, if the inscriber's eyes had not given out before finishing.

She was dying to tell Jonathan. And Bill, of course. The more she thought about it, the more certain she was that the irregular groupings of the squares were some sort of code, each representing a sound or a word perhaps. Much like a Morse code. If she would be able to decipher that code—following the high priest's ancient translation—these tablets very well could become her very own 'Rosetta Stone.' She would be feted as a modern-day Champollion, with another important milestone in Egyptian archaeology. If—and this was a very big if—she survived her ordeal.

As a scientist, Naunet had always scoffed at the stories that were circulated about a sunken Atlantis and its outer-space inhabitants. However, the Mediterranean was known to have endured many volcanic eruptions, with numerous islands that imploded and sank into the sea. Quite likely, something like that had occurred on this unknown island and its ancient people. It could not have been Crete, nor Cyprus, she thought, since they still existed.

Again, she wished she could share her thoughts and assumptions. Dr. Jabari El-Masri's dark eyes flashed before her. Oh, how she would love to have a debate with him and prove to him that she was to be taken seriously.

"How about dinner? We're getting hungry out here."

Naunet's head jerked up. She had been so wrapped up in her findings that she completely forgot where she was. Now, staring her in the face again, was that big *If*.

* * *

Chapter Sixteen

Ideas and plans were formulated and tossed aside like pointless chapters of a manuscript. Josef provided his Iridium satellite phone and there were many calls to and from the Institute's director. Bruno von der Heide apologized to Bill for their recent somewhat heated conversation. It had not been like either of them to use such language and be curt with each other. However, Bruno explained, there had been too many ears that had pricked up at his dinner table. His research director, naturally, was likewise sorry for losing his temper and the use of colorful vocabulary. Bill was glad when Bruno assured him that he was in touch with the U.S. Embassy in Cairo, divulging as much or as little as he could at this time, considering Jabari's caper, as he called it, was still in progress.

Incidentally, Bruno told Bill, the First Secretary at the embassy had admitted to him that the name Guernsey-Crock cropped up in one of their complaints received by an American tourist. Luckily, the frantic woman had provided an American passport supposedly belonging to the man. They still had not determined if it was a falsified document or not. At any rate, an alert had been issued through Interpol. If Dr. Naunet Klein was traveling with this man, there was a good chance that they would find her as well. Bruno added as delicately as he could, it sounded to him as if the embassy people believed she was traveling with the Brit of her own free will. The embassy official had stressed that they ran into this situation often enough, especially with middle-aged women. 'Middle-aged! Our Naunet? The nerve,' Bruno had huffed and then continued that those people had given him to understand that the embassy was coping with other, more important concerns at the moment. With a new regime about to take power in Cairo, new alliances had to be forged. Then, as an aside, the trite man mentioned that two Americans had been found. Well—he added as if it were an afterthought—they had actually been murdered. Found on the road, between Safaga and Hurghada.

Interesting thing though, no passports or wallets were on them, but the man still wore a money belt. It contained a piece of paper with that Crock-person's passport data. Except that this particular information stemmed from a British document. An emergency contact list contained in that belt identified the couple as Harold and Edith Jenkins, traveling on their sailing yacht which—the obviously overworked man added in a bored tone—had been reported stolen. The proper authorities in Safaga were handling that case. The embassy did get in touch with the Jenkins's relatives in the States. Really sad. Finally, the man had shown a spark of sympathy, Bruno said. But that was about all he could tell Bill.

It was a lot more than they knew before. After Bill relayed his telephone conversation with Bruno to the others, a feeling of helplessness crept over them. Still, they had to do something.

Armed with new information and renewed hope, it was decided that Jabari and Leopold would take the Gulfstream to Cyprus to see if they could find some trace of Karakurt Tiryaki, his Turkish relatives, or the stolen boat. As it would make sense to land on the Turkish side, Jabari hoped that Rahman could obtain a landing permit there. In order to conserve fuel, it was also imperative to lighten the Gulfstream's load. Josef suggested that they get one of the airport's sealed baggage containers and lock up the tablets in the hangar, together with Ahmed and his gun.

When they thought that they had a reasonably viable plan, Jonathan pleaded that he should fly to Cyprus with them. When he had been there twelve years ago, the dig had been on the Greek side, of course. Still, if—and it was still a very big if—Karakurt and the Brit had stolen that missing Valiant out of Safaga and were headed for the Turkish part of the island he, Jonathan, could snoop around the marinas, and befriend some of the cruisers there. It was amazing, he emphasized to them, how much information ham-radio operators could come up with, especially when asked for help by another sailor who spoke their lingo. He could pretend that the stolen boat was his. He knew enough about a Valiant to make it stick. He should ask Col. Rahman to place a call to the Safaga marina and see if he could get the name of the boat. It was the first thing an owner would mention when searching for his missing vessel. Not unaware of the young man's anguish, Jabari relented. He placed a call to the pilots and told them that they were driving back to Heraklion late afternoon.

"You better hurry. We need to fly this evening," Rahman told him. "The forecast for the Med tomorrow is not good at all."

Jabari told his pilot that they would be there by five. Just in case Rahman needed to call him back, he gave him Josef's number since he could not get a decent reception on his cell.

They were about to leave the Kommos compound when Josef came sprinting down the gravel drive. He waved his arms frantically, calling to them as he ran.

"Jonathan! Stop! I have a call for Jabari." He skittered to a halt and handed Jabari his satellite phone through the window. "It's from a Colonel Abdur Rahman."

"Why aren't you calling me on my cell?" Jabari bellowed into the phone in Arabic, and then, somewhat milder added, "Oh, I forgot."

After mostly listening and saying little, he hung up and stepped out of the car. "We need to talk. Josef, can we use your phone again? Bill needs to call Bruno in Boston."

To most outsiders, the twin cities of Boston and Cambridge were one and the same; and most people from there rarely corrected them—except when it was a matter of civic pride. It more often than not was, especially when it concerned Cambridge's Harvard University or the Massachusetts Institute of Technology.

They went back into the villa and after Jabari found an electrical outlet to recharge his cell phone, he explained the Colonel's urgent call.

"With Greece in the European Union—at least as of this moment—I forgot that the 'Turkish Republic of Northern Cyprus' requires all aircraft to touch down on mainland Turkey first before being cleared into that part of the island. Oh, by the way, Abdur told me that on May twenty-third, the Turkish Cabinet renamed it the

'Turkish Republic of Cyprus.' I guess they no longer liked the 'northern' part. Anyway, Abdur had an idea how we could circumvent the rigmarole of landing the Gulfstream in the North. It would also make the unloading of the tablets unnecessary."

"Do tell," Leopold said, praying this would not delay the search for his daughter on Cyprus.

To his relief, Jabari went on to say that Ercan Airport in the north was close to a town called Kyrenia which had the only good-sized marina on that part of the coast. Jabari hesitated before going on. He would have to choose his next words carefully, in a way that would make Bill realize it was the best and perhaps only way for them to get to Cyprus without having to waste precious time with governmental red tape.

"Abdur got in touch with a private charter-company that flies out of Ercan, Stratos Jets, I believe he said. They fly over to Heraklion by late this afternoon, pick us up and fly us straight into Ercan. It's their home base, and they apparently have good relations with the tower and immigration. If you know what I mean."

Jabari sighed heavily and then spoke directly to Bill. "I would spare no expense out of my own pocket to help you find Naunet Klein, if only I could manage it. Given the present situation with the Euro, the Dollar is back in style."

Bill got the hint. For someone with a thousand pounds of gold practically in his back pocket, Jabari sure knew how to play his hand. And he had conveniently omitted to mention the two missing tablets which he, no doubt, wanted to recover. Bill placed a call to Bruno, who in turn placed a call to Richard *Hobo* Percy in California. Within the hour, there were no more problems, at least not financially.

Jabari El-Masri heaped silent blessings on all American billionaires eager to buy themselves a little culture. The grateful man also blessed the upstart country for not knowing how to separate a busy day from a restful night. Due to their unending working hours, he now possessed the number and security code of a limitless credit card, issued to the Institute with Jabari and Bill as its authorized users.

He would have to talk to Bruno about this Richard Percy. If things went altogether sour with a possibly negative outcome for his own country's presidential elections—which for him meant victory by the candidate of The Islamic Brotherhood—a connection to a generous billionaire in America would be very helpful. He only hoped that it would not cost him one of his golden tablets. This, in turn, reminded him to check that his tablet was in the car. He would feel troubled knowing it left behind in Kommos while they went to Cyprus. His jet was surely a much safer place. That they were leaving Bill behind did not trouble him at all.

While they waited for the chartered jet to land, Jonathan took advantage of the Wi-Fi hotspots floating around Heraklion airport. He searched for information about Turkish Cyprus and was amazed to learn of the political complexity for such a small island. Twelve years ago, busy with his continuing studies, he had paid little attention to the geo-political make-up of the island. For instance, he was surprised to read that the city of Nicosia was termed the last divided capital of the world. Like most, he had assumed that designation had gone out with the fall of the Berlin Wall. An infamous, so-called Green Line, slashed right through the heart of Nicosia with each faction, Greek and Turkish, having built their modern halves on either side.

He was even more shocked when he read about the coastal city of Famagusta and its forbidden suburb of Varosha, a ghost town surrounded by barbed wire. It had been uninhabited ever since the 1974 coup. High-rise apartment buildings stood overlooking the beautiful Mediterranean. Empty and forlorn in the wasteland, it was yet another human folly.

Jonathan shook his head and then searched for information about currents, seafloor conditions and water depth. Anything an approaching vessel would need to know. A long narrow peninsula stretched way out to the east. Given the prevailing easterlies, a boat coming in from the south would have to beat out a long ways and then tack back around to reach Kyrenia.

If Karakurt and the Brit were indeed headed there—which was only an assumption on his part—they would have a difficult time of it, even in favorable winds. At this point though, Jonathan thought, they could not be anywhere near Cyprus yet. It lay a good three hundred nautical miles northeast of Port Said. And that was to Larnaca on the southern coast. He calculated that it would take them at least another day, if not more, to sail all the way around that coast to Kyrenia.

The Stratos jet landed at its home base without having to submit to customs or any other formalities. The Turkish pilots had even arranged for a guide. He waited at the private gate for non-commercial aircraft. An attached small lounge was surprisingly well appointed with leather seats. Despite the late hour, a smiling young girl offered refreshments. Apparently, the super-rich had discovered another low-priced paradise to invade and spoil.

"Welcome to Ercan Airport." The young man shook everyone's hand. He was good-looking in an indigenous sort of way and his English was excellent. "I am Veli Demir, your guide." He suggested The Ship Inn, which he said was not too far from the airport, and close to the center of Kyrenia. He took them to his car which, in contrast to the charter jet and its airport lounge, was neither well appointed nor did it have functioning air conditioning. Though with their late arrival, the evening had cooled down. Remembering their trip from Luxor to el-Karga, it could even be termed comfortable.

With the impatience of the young, Jonathan was hard pressed not to ask if the young man perhaps might be a cousin of Karakurt Tiryaki or at least knew of him. One could never tell. Wisely, he decided to wait for a better time and not to take the driver away from negotiating the potholes on the dark road.

The Ship Inn was a much larger complex than they had expected, or hoped for. Neither of the three was keen on running into curious European or American tourists, always eager to trade travel experiences and talk about the awful local food stuff; for most of them it was de rigueur to complain how nothing was prepared like they were used to at home.

The three men were glad to be shown to a separate three-bedroom villa. After an early dinner, they said good night and hoped to get some rest before their planned busy next day. They would each take on a separate location. Jabari was to make inquiries in town, Leopold intended to wander around the shipyards, and Jonathan of course would go down to the marina docks and talk to some of the cruisers he was sure to find.

Try as he might, Jonathan could not go to sleep. At around nine, he knew it was hopeless and got up. Slipping on his running shorts and favorite tee shirt, he padded out to the lovely terrace overlooking the pool. Only when his eyes had become accustomed to the bluish light that reflected off the chlorined water did he notice the figure sitting by the small rattan table. There was a glass in his hand and now Jonathan could hear the faint clinking of ice cubes.

"Dr. Klein?"

"Hello, Jonathan. Come and join me. Cognac? Compliments of the mini-bar. Quite good, actually."

"Thanks, I will. Let me get a glass from my room." Jonathan quickly came back with a glass and an additional couple of the small bottles in his hand. "No sense just raiding one mini-bar," he grinned and pulled up a creaky rattan chair.

"Santé, my boy." Naunet's father raised his glass and by the soft light of the terrace, Jonathan could see a resemblance. "By the way," the older man smiled. "I feel somewhat left out in our little group."

By the crinkle around the blue eyes, Jonathan knew he was expected to ask, "And why is that, Dr. Klein?"

"You call Jabari by his first name. So why not me? He and I are the same age."

"Oh, well, Dr. El-Masri offered." Jonathan hadn't meant for it to come out like a challenge. Somehow it had, and he hoped the elegant Viennese was not offended.

"He did? Well, *Leopold* it is then. Let us drink to it. By the way, there is that thing we old-fashioned Austrians do when we start to call each other by our first names. Most of the time, we do it with great relish, especially if the other person is of the opposite sex. Always, of course, one has a glass of something alcoholic in ones hand. Even then, it is usually only done after having had a few." He paused and looked at Jonathan. "But I don't suggest we do that."

"I would hope not," Jonathan said rather too hastily before he realized that Leopold was teasing him. He knew all about that little custom. Naunet had explained it to him. Afterwards, she had given him a delightful demonstration. It was the first and, to his great regret, the last time she had kissed him. With that brilliant smile of hers, she had wagged her finger. 'I only showed you because that is what we do at home.' He knew she had been teasing. But to him, that kiss had meant a lot, though he never let her know how much.

"I love her, you know," he said suddenly without preamble or hesitation.

"Yes, I thought so." Leopold had that wan smile of his on his lips; half bemused, half sorrowful. After a few moments, he added, "I am glad. She needs to be loved. Don't let her prickly independence fool you. She truly wants to be loved." *And have lots of babies and ride my horse around my estate*, Leopold remembered her saying so earnestly as a six-year old. Now his little girl was all grown up; there were no babies, and there was no estate. And still, there was no husband. Leopold sighed. He took a long look at Jonathan, and had another sip of his Cognac. For a while, they drank in silence, each immersed in his thoughts; and in his fears.

The breeze was more insistent now and the smell of the sea had become slightly pungent. There was no moon. Jonathan, in his thin tee shirt, could feel that the temperature was dropping fast. He gathered up the empty little bottles and said that they should try to get some rest.

Leopold pulled himself up. "Good night, my boy," he said with that gracious nod of the head older Viennese seemed to do from habit.

"Good night, sir," Jonathan replied. Then he remembered and, with a slight bow of his own, said, "Good night, Leopold. I know there will be news tomorrow."

"I hope you are right," Naunet's father answered quietly. As he walked toward his room Jonathan noticed how his shoulders slumped low and that he walked almost painfully slow as if carrying a great weight. The younger man almost went after him to put an arm around him, to comfort him. He feared that his easy American manner might embarrass the elegant European. With his own heart heavy, Jonathan stepped into his room and threw himself onto the bed. He stared at the ceiling for a long time before he finally switched off the light.

* * *

Chapter Seventeen

As midnight changed the end of May to the beginning of June, the whisper of a breeze crept out of the east. Without much warning, it strengthened into a banshee-like howl that shook *Tumbleweed's* sturdy rigging and tore at the sails. The seas foamed up around the hull, and fierce squalls rolled out of the dark, unseen. Suddenly, heavy rain pelted the deck with ominous drumbeats announcing the full-blown storm.

Karakurt had found a set of yellow oilskins in the wet-locker. Then a pair of rubber boots that fit him reasonably well, as long as he kept his toes slightly cramped under. He stood watch again, and was comfortable and dry until the weather changed so abruptly. This late in the season, there was no reason for him to expect the dreaded southern *Sirocco*. He scented the air like a wolf following its quarry. This storm, howling out of the east, was different. Instinctively, he knew they could expect the worst.

Even experienced forecasters did not widely accept that the Mediterranean Sea occasionally spawned a hurricane. When such phenomena occurred, they simply reported it as 'a tempest in a tea cup.' Of course, whoever was the proverbial flotsam in that cup could not dismiss it as lightly. A sailor knew that it was to be respected and feared, and survived, if at all possible.

At precisely ten minutes into that first day of June the storm intensified. It flogged both fully hoisted sails with malice. Within a short time, the mainsail was screamed into shreds that bandaged the mast. Karakurt cursed himself for running with too much sail up at night. No sailor should ever do that; no matter how light the winds. Well, he thought grimly, at least he no longer had to worry about the mainsail. He turned the motor on to compensate for the loss of stability. Thankfully, it sprang to life, and he felt better. The jib had to come down though, and it would be none too soon.

Below-decks, once again locked in the private quarter-berth after her failed attempt with the radio, Naunet was half-asleep when the sudden turmoil slammed her against the port bulkhead. Confused and frightened, she sat up and promptly hit her head against the padded headliner. The hard bump stunned her for a moment.

"Edward! Karakurt? Let me out of here!"

Only faintly, she heard a straining voice from the cockpit.

"Get your shoes on." Then, louder, the voice hollered, "You, Brit! Get up here! Now!"

When there was no answer from the cabin, Naunet heard a string of curses, mainly in Turkish.

Then, Karakurt hollered again, "You! Brit! Get your English arse up here."

Afraid that the boat was about to capsize, Naunet threw herself against the barricaded door. The flimsy louvers splintered outward and she could reach around to unlock the panels. The salon was semi-dark and she felt her way ahead as best as she could. In the shadowy glow of the red nightlight, she clung to whatever overhead handholds she could grab. Things started to fly off the shelves, and she was unable to duck out of the way of several objects hurtling at her.

Edward lay on the settee curled up like a child, his knees sticking out. Naunet was not sure if he was asleep, had been knocked unconscious, or was simply too terrified to move. When the next swell dumped him onto the cabin sole, she knew it was the latter. She saw him crawl on all fours toward her and hold up a hand for her to help him to his feet. There would be no comfort from that one. The man was a coward.

Despite the secured latches, cabinets started to pop open. Condiment and liquor bottles shattered into dangerous shards on the cabin sole. The two-pronged compass slid off the chart table, missed them, and impaled itself on the floorboards by its sharp points. Books stashed on a shelf behind a horizontal safety bar sailed through the air, hitting the two as they tried to make their way toward the main hatch. The worst was the noise outside. Not knowing what slashed and pounded the deck above them, their fear reached its height. Then the dim cabin light blinked off.

The two clawed their way closer to the hatch where Edward pushed her aside and, halfway up, poked his head out cautiously. Naunet had to give the man a good shove for he did not seem to relish going out into the cockpit. Neither did she, but she did. Naunet sensed rather than saw Karakurt at the wheel. *He still has things under control.* For once, she was glad for his skill.

Salt spray stung her eyes and the fierce wind took her breath away. A cold wave half swamped the cockpit and soaked her through and through. Not dressed in heavy-weather gear like Karakurt, she shivered so violently that she could hardly hold on to the boom straining against the lines tethering it in.

"What's happening?" It came out in half syllables because her teeth chattered uncontrollably.

"Let go of the boom!" Karakurt screamed.

She slid down and hung onto the lowest spoke of the large wheel, impeding Karakurt's effort to keep the boat pointed into the crashing waves.

"Don't do that!" He screamed at her again.

Then he ordered her to go back below and when she crawled toward the hatch, he shouted after her to slide the wide boards into their grooves to close the dangerously large opening from the inside. One more wave like the last one and the boat could take on enough water to render it unresponsive. Maybe even sink it.

Edward had his arms wrapped around a winch that dipped perilously far into the sea. Holding on for dear life and, with the wind raking him from behind, he was violently sick. Karakurt glanced at the crouched figure and hoped that the squirrely gusts would not change direction just then, even though the Brit's vomit would be the least of his problems.

"Get up," Karakurt howled with the wind and kicked Edward in the ribs with his boot. "You have to haul the jib in. Or the whole damn rigging comes down."

No sooner had he jabbed the hapless man again than there was a sharp noise, much like the crack of a whip. The jib halyard holding up that sail had ripped loose from the head eye. Freed from its restraining wire, the hanked-on sail slid down the outer forestay. The wind caught in its folds and billowed it way out over the bow. The pull exerted onto the sail ripped its sheet through the cleat in the cockpit. With lightening speed, the line unwound itself, ripping forward, its bitter end barely missing Edward's face. Had that end been knotted into a figure eight, as most sailors secure all sheets, it would have jammed into the cleat and they could have winched the sheet back in and at least brought the jib under control. As it was, the free-flapping sail sank lower until it dipped into the sea. Not only did this pouch fill with water, acting like a sea anchor, but the other danger was that it could get hung up on the keel or, worse, the jib sheet, now trailing in the water, might foul the propeller. In addition, the loose halyard whipping out of control above the foredeck could easily maim a man.

Acutely aware of these possible calamities, Karakurt screwed his eyes up at the one-inch stainless steel shrouds on either side of the mast which held the massive spar up—so far. If one of the thick wires parted, or if the chainplates securing them to the hull ripped out, he might as well kiss his dream goodbye. Possibly his life.

He clamped his fists tighter around the wheel and prayed to Allah that the rudder pins would not sheer off from the enormous pressure he and the contrary waves exerted against them. At least, the upturned dinghy seemed to hold fast in its cradle. However, with the lifeboat canister stored underneath the strapped down rubber boat, there was no way that the self-inflating lifeboat would pop free as it was designed to do, should this blasted tub sink.

Why had he ever let the fast-talking Brit con him into such a stupid venture? He should have sided with El-Masri and his weird plan. Karakurt had been told that the ambitious Egyptian was planning to transport all the tablets in a jet to somewhere in the desert. His contact did not know where. In any case, their escape would have been a lot faster and a lot safer; alas, not as profitable, at least not for himself. Karakurt clenched his teeth. *Two for me, twenty-five for Jabari. And, quite possibly, five for the digger.* Karakurt had never been convinced that the story about the head digger dying in a tunnel collapse was true. He thought of el-Kharga. Now there was a good hiding place. He should have stayed in Luxor. He was sure that the sly Wamukota was hiding out there, among his strange people, living off the five tablets like some Turkish pasha. It just wasn't fair.

Despite the strain to keep the bucking vessel from turning broadside to the mounting swells, Karakurt leaned forward and again prodded the stricken man hanging through the lower lifelines like a sack of wheat.

"Get up. Go up there. Haul in the jib." No response. Karakurt leaned closer and screamed into the prone man's ear, "Now! Go! Or we'll all die."

Whimpering to himself like a little boy expecting a beating, Edward crawled along the narrow starboard strip of slippery deck. Even though he slithered low along the raised cabin, the wind still caught him. Every time the boat heeled over, he was slammed hard against the inch-high toe rail. What kept him from falling overboard were the stanchions he hit along the way, slamming mercilessly into them with his mid-section. If he was lucky he could grab hold of the lower lifeline and hang on like someone caught in a flash flood. When the boat heeled the other way his whole body was smacked into the rock-hard siding of the cabin with a rib-cracking thud. He thought he would never make it to the bow. Somehow, though, he did.

To haul a waterlogged sail back onboard is almost impossible, even in the best of circumstances. He clawed at the rough cloth, pulling it in inch by inch, trying to spill seawater back where it belonged. It was the toughest thing Edward had ever done. The second hardest was to keep the sail bunched up on deck so that the wind would not rip it out of his stiff hands again. Desperate to tame the large jib, he crawled on top of the sodden mass and stretched out over it, belly-down.

By the way the bow righted itself, Karakurt felt rather than saw that the sail had been hauled back in. If he survived this mad journey, he swore again that he would be better off without the useless dandy barfing his heart out every time the sea got a mite rough. He stretched up from his hunched-over steering position and scanned the invisible sky for any sign of light. Then he promised Allah that, if he survived this journey, he might let the woman live.

Besides, he needed her to clean and decipher the tablets for his South American contact, if he ever made their rendezvous on

Cyprus's north coast. As far as he was concerned, she might as well make up some inane text to save time. Lorenzo Dominguez, as rich as he was, wouldn't know the difference between an Egyptian curse, a dire prediction or a bedtime story.

After she had certified her translation, Karakurt could find some lonely goat farmer up in the hills grateful for a change of pace. In exchange, his cousin living on the coast could expect a lifetime supply of soft white goat cheese; a pleasant arrangement all around. Well, maybe not for the woman. But you never knew with spinsters. She might begin to like it; or at least get used to it.

The vile man grinned contemptibly and, during a careless moment, took his hand off the wheel to wipe the spray from his eyes and the spittle from the corners of his salivating mouth. Damn the woman. He took his other hand off the wheel to scratch at his crotch.

Just then, the wind veered and a violent gust slammed into the boat from astern. The vang's pulley assembly ripped loose from under the boom. Freed, the massive spar scythed across the cockpit. The glancing blow from its sharp end did not kill Karakurt, though it raked a deep gash across his forehead. His eyes filled with blood. His knees gave out. Losing consciousness, he slid into the water sloshing around in the cockpit.

The force of the wildly swinging boom exerted tremendous pressure on the shrouds. With the mast's perilous backward rake, the thick wires were stretched to the limit. Despite the tension, the wind vibrated them into a high eerie pitch. They held.

It was the chainplates that ripped out of the fiberglass hull. At the same time, both forestays tore from their toe brackets. The mast whipped backward. It snapped ten feet above the deck. Forty feet of the fifty-foot spar came crashing down over the cabin deck, taking the boom with it. With a shattering thud, the fused aluminum tubes crushed the wheel, then the stern railing. They wiped out the wind vane, but missed the dinghy's small outboard. The mast spreaders snapped off just where Karakurt had stood. He would have been crushed to death for certain had he not been lying in the bottom of the cockpit.

Miraculously, the compass pedestal held, though its instrument dome splintered into a million pieces of glass. It was that solid base that saved the Turkish wolf's life.

The only thing that died that night was *Tumbleweed's* diesel engine.

They endured for hours, each unable to help the other. To the east, at last, a morose sliver of gray promised that daylight was not too far off.

Edward dared not move an inch. He lay burrowed deep into the folds of the jib, his hands pressed over his ears. He alternately howled with the wind and then riled against it. His legs had cramped up. He was sick again, partly from the boat's violent motion, partly from having his nose pressed into the salt-caked sailcloth.

The quake that the toppling mast sent through the boat almost threw Naunet from her bunk where she had lain curled up like a hibernating hedgehog. Immobilized by her own terror, she waited for the peace of death. Apparently, this death was going to be a noisy one. There was constant loud scraping along the hull, and relentless banging on the cabin roof. She lifted her head and, still not dead, placed her feet cautiously back on the cabin sole. Again, she had to negotiate her way through the splintered door.

"*Verdammte Scheisse!*" She surprised herself by the long-forgotten, never-used obscenity. She had mashed her knee into a wooden edge, and it did hurt. Feeling around, it turned out to be the small door to the wet-locker which had been thrown open. She fingered the sleek foul-weather gear. It had to be Edie's. She pulled the tight jacket over her head but gave up on the pants. Groping for more, she caught hold of a rubber boot. "Forget it," she whispered. It would be way too small. Besides, she could not feel the other one anywhere. Luckily, she had packed her tennis shoes and had changed into them earlier.

After the failed harbor master incident, she had made a mental note of the huge flashlight clamped under the next to last step. She remembered thinking that it was big enough to hit a man over the head. She groped for it now and switched it on just long enough to find her way back out the hatch.

With great caution, hoping no rogue wave was about to overtake the wallowing boat, she slid the two upper slats out of their groove. The glow from the compass mounted atop the pedestal was gone. There was no white stern light. Naunet craned her neck and looked up. The masthead was dark as well.

That's when she heard the moan. "Karakurt?"

More moaning. Then, a weak curse followed by slight movement. Naunet could barely make out the dark mass on the cockpit sole on the other side of the wheel which seemed to be lower now and had an oddly oval shape.

"Karakurt!" She crawled out and promptly smashed into something big and round and very much in the way. To her shock, she found it was the mast.

"Flashlight, stupid," she chastised herself and found it rolling along on the seat next to the hatch opening. The water in the cockpit looked curiously dark. She trained the light beam onto the yellow clump. The prone bundle lifted itself up a few inches.

Naunet had looked into the smashed-in black faces of countless mummies without flinching. Now, she almost screamed. What the ghostly beam of the flashlight revealed was almost too much for her frayed nerves. If she had died, she certainly had not gone to heaven. The grotesque thing before her had to be something from hell.

"Naunet. Help me up."

It was only a whisper. But it was human. Hearing her name broke the terror. She ducked under and knelt beside the man. The water was colored by his blood. There was a nasty gash on his forehead.

"Can you manage to get yourself inside?" With not much help from the injured man, she pulled and pushed, and guided him toward the hatch where she quickly removed the rest of the slats and Karakurt more or less tumbled down the four steps.

Below, Naunet helped Karakurt onto the settee. Then she made her way forward to the head through broken glass and scattered items. She found a first-aid kit and while she had never taken a first-aid course, at least she could slap some gauze pads onto his wound and bind him up to stem the flow of blood. If he needed stitches, he was out of luck.

"Where is he?" Karakurt croaked. Naunet had wrapped his head up and he looked like a turbaned Turkish pasha, except that blood again oozed its way through the bandages. He raised his head from the cushion she had slid under him. His voice was weak and he had to lie back down again.

They both noticed it at the same time. The enervating slamming of loose shackles had stopped. The wind outside seemed to have lessened and even the sea had calmed down. Something scurried along the deck. A few minutes later, Edward slid down the steps. He was shaken to the core and as he reached Naunet's splintered cabin door, he went right through and collapsed on her bunk.

For three days, Naunet rummaged among the shambles left from the various cupboards for anything that they could eat out of the can. She mixed peas with a little mayonnaise, served tuna on soggy crackers, and watered down syrup from canned peaches and pears. She even mixed raw oatmeal with powdered milk and water. Still, they became weaker and more dehydrated, mostly from being seasick.

Their bruises turned into ugly swellings and Edward sported two astounding black eyes, reminding Naunet of a Madagascar lemur; except that she liked those critters.

Dismasted and adrift, the *Tumbleweed* was now at the mercy of the wind and the current.

* * *

Chapter Eighteen

A disabled vessel being towed into port after a storm is a heart-wrenching sight, especially to those who make their living from the sea.

Most of the villagers were gathered on the crumbling seawall that lined the small harbor. They waited silently as one of their larger fishing boats towed a battered sloop to a large inside buoy. It must have been a proud boat once. The hull appeared still sound, with its wide dark-blue boot-stripe hovering just above the waterline. But with most of the rigging downed it reminded them of a seagull with broken wings.

There was money to be made from salvage though. They waited patiently for any sign of survivors of the cruel storm that had battered their coast for the last two days. True mariners, the village people prayed for the wellbeing of those who had sailed on her because no islander ever placed the value of salvage before that of a sailor's life. Except, perhaps, during the southerly *Sirocco*, when minds became muddled and greed sometimes drowned out charity. This storm had been different; this monster had come roaring out of the east. It had just been as fierce as a *Sirocco*, except that it had not been laden with African desert sand, nor had it carried swarms of the dreaded locusts in its gusts. For that they were grateful.

The curious got their answer when a head slowly emerged from the main hatch. "A woman," they murmured when they saw her long hair streaming behind her in the wind. Little boats paddled out to assist the fishermen who had rescued the stricken vessel. Within thirty minutes, she was secured to the large buoy normally reserved for the ferry from Sfakion. It had left that day and would not return until the next.

Two men lying in the swamped cockpit finally managed to rouse themselves from their stupor brought on by exhaustion, seasickness and dehydration. The villagers ferried the three disoriented people ashore and administered a few swallows of fresh water to each. After giving them another few sips, someone prodded them to toss down a thimbleful of something so shockingly vile that it restored them simply by burning its way straight into their empty stomachs.

Karakurt was the first to recover. "Where on *Kibns* are we," he managed to whisper in Turkish, the burning liquid having done more harm than good to his parched throat. His question was met with uncomprehending stares. He tried Greek. *"Kypros?"*

An old man with a deeply lined face stepped forward and shook his head. He opened his arms wide in the direction of the village, "Loutro."

"Loutro?" Karakurt had never heard of a village by that name, at least not on the Turkish side of Cyprus.

"We must have landed on the Greek side," he croaked, still hoarse from the fiery concoction these backwater people had made him swallow.

The man's leathery face slipped into a toothless grin. He pointed to the ground and toward the crowded row of houses along a narrow quay, "Loutro. *Kriti. Kriti.*"

"Shit!" Karakurt spat at Naunet as if it was her fault that they had been blown off-course by hundreds of miles.

"These imbeciles towed us into Crete."

The small village of Loutro lay pressed into the end of rugged southwestern Crete. An eighteen-hundred-foot cliff rose into the sky behind the whitewashed houses. Without a coastal road, it was accessible by water only, unless one were inclined to hike out on foot, over the Idaian Mountains down into the Mesara, Crete's largest coastal plain riddled with recent excavations of ancient sites.

For supplies and news, the villagers depended on their ferry, and on their fishermen husbands and betrothed for their main staple of fish and crustaceans, some of which were reserved for barter with 'the other side.' That this beneficial ferry also took away most of their young meant that the average age of Loutro's population grew older with each passing year.

Naunet could hardly keep her emotions in check. They were on Crete! *Papa*, her heart cried out. He was at Kommos. It was the glimmer of hope she needed. She would survive this ordeal. And she would save both tablets from these grave robbers. Calm! She had to stay calm. She had to find a way to get in touch with her father. What if he had flown to Egypt after hearing that she was missing? The McPeals should still be here. They would help her. She would find a villager to take a message to them. Naunet trembled at the thought of a rescue close at hand.

A ripe, handsome woman with swaying hips and a glistening dark braid halfway down her back detached herself from the knot of curious.

"I am Cassandra," she said to Naunet in accented English. "I have a little villa. You stay there. It has view of water. Cheap."

Despite its isolation, Loutro was not the backwater Karakurt had cursed it to be. What corner of the world was, these days, with fanny-pack girded tourists swarming all over the globe like locusts, defying distance and difficulty, as long as their destination was proclaimed to be exotic, sunny, and on sale.

Edward had at last shuddered himself free from the fog in his head brought on by the local firewater. He stepped between Naunet and the woman. It would not hurt to have a bit of local crumpet on his side for the next few days. So what if she was plump. That had never stopped him before to sow his charismatic pearls before the proverbial...*well, maybe not quite that*, although there was the matter of a black gap in her front teeth. He looked around for tell-tales of a possessive husband. So far, none of the gawking men seemed to lay claim to her.

Karakurt, somewhat recovered from his apoplectic seizure of being on the wrong island, joined their small group.

Cassandra repeated that she had rooms for rent on the very outskirts of the village—a little villa, she called it. Over the years, she had learned that the description warranted a higher rental price. An artist from the mainland had recently died there, she explained. But not to worry, she assured them, it was quite livable again. The smell had gone by now. "We found her after a couple of weeks," she smiled.

'The villa' was actually the upstairs apartment of her home that was at the end unit of boxy white row-houses with blue windows. It was small and enchanting, despite the recent death. Double-winged doors opened out to a terrace in blue and white tiles, surrounded by a waist-high whitewashed masonry wall. The southern exposure with its gleaming horizon of the sea was indeed glossy-brochure worthy. Under normal circumstances—such as a vacation—Naunet could have fallen in love with it.

As it was, however, Naunet found serious drawbacks with the idyllic setting. To begin with, she had no cell phone and no Wi-Fi to send e-mails. For that matter, she had no computer. Besides, there still were those two unscrupulous men, each rotten to the core in his own way, each with his own agenda. How long would it take for them to find her no longer useful? That she was not desirable to either one had been clear from the start. The answer, she knew, lay in the cleaning and her translation of the two tablets. After that? She shuddered.

Naunet was assigned a sunny bedroom, and as she watched Cassandra put fresh linens on the bed and straighten curtains and wipe flecks of dust, she felt the woman lingered for another reason. Curiosity. Naunet smiled. "This is really nice," she said, and meant it.

Cassandra smiled back tentatively and stepped closer. She was about to say something when Edward ambled in. He plopped down on a yellowed rattan chaise-lounge, its long pillow sending up a light plume of dust.

"This is great, Cassandra. Thanks. We'll need a little rest after our terrible ordeal. You understand, ordeal? Terrible journey." He pulled his face into a frightened grimace.

The intuitive woman understood. The handsome man wished to be alone with the tall woman. She nodded and left, smiling, glad to be renting the apartment during the slow season.

Karakurt decided that he had better stay on the *Tumbleweed* to prevent salvage claims and—Allah forbid—the theft of his two slates. The villagers might be keen to strip the boat's valuable hardware during the dark of night; he would use it for barter with these people. He had wrestled the dinghy off the cluttered deck and bolted the small gasoline motor to its stern. Absentmindedly, he noted the name *Thistle* painted on the varnished backboard. Then he pulled the starter on the dinghy motor with no results. Again. And again. He pulled the chord about ten times. The motor would not start. Perhaps it was out of gas. He searched for the small red gasoline can. It was gone— likely ripped off together with the spare Diesel canisters that had vanished as well. Luckily, he found two oars strapped to the dinghy's floorboards.

Held fast to the Valiant by its thin painter the small boat bobbed around, bumping into the stern, then pulling up against the bow. Glad to have independent transportation to and from the boat, he was aware that it would take a lot of muscle without a motor. He hoped no one would row out silently while he slept, cut the line, and steal the dinghy itself. He would keep the oars on *Tumbleweed*. Despite his concern, he decided to catch a few hours of sleep. Bone-tired and still weak, he stretched out in the cockpit. The storm had passed, and even though the night was crisp, the dark firmament was a sight to behold. Star-studded and immense, it stretched above him. Karakurt opened his arms and embraced his new world. And the riches that awaited him.

"Allah be praised."

He was getting chilled and so he got up again and went into the dank cabin to fish around for warmer clothes. He needed to get in touch with the *Bucanero* too. Lying off the northeastern coast of Cyprus, its owner was undoubtedly anxious as to the whereabouts of the enticing Old Kingdom tablets. Karakurt dug the Iridium phone out of his sodden bag.

"Damn." The battery was dead.

Mounted in the cockpit, Karakurt had noticed a covered 12-Volt house battery outlet. Not caring if he drained the darn thing to the point of no return, he plugged his charger into it. One way or another, he was going to get off this tub and reap the reward for all his troubles.

During an impatient hour waiting for the phone to charge, he decided to carry one of the tablets into the dinghy. The Klein woman needed to start cutting off the tar, or whatever the black mess was gumming up the tablets. It would avoid transfer of his precious loot during daylight hours. He knew islands. They had many eyes. And ears. As well as thieves.

He smelled it as soon as he dove down into the chaos that had been the salon. Gasoline! No doubt about it. He sloshed his way through the sodden mess into the forepeak and noticed that the smell of gasoline grew stronger with each step.

"What the hell?" He reached up to open the hatch. It had held up pretty well, considering. Still, something leaked down from above and onto the tablet that was nestled deep into the wedged-in cushion, its weight prevented it from having been tossed off. The other one with the missing corner, though, had tumbled onto the cabin sole. Karakurt grabbed the intact tablet and turned it over. It was slippery and when he drew his hands away, they were covered with slimy black unguent. Swearing to himself some more, he tried again and after some effort flipped the tablet over.

"By Allah," he breathed and drew back as if he had disturbed a cobra hiding underneath. The side that had lain cradled on the soaked cushion shone as bright as the sun. Nay, as gold!

The gasoline! He almost stuck his finger into the smelly mixture to give himself a taste of his fortune. It anointed his soul. It also turned the boat into a potential bomb.

Under falling darkness, he lugged the tablet out into the cockpit. The trick now was to transfer it from the boat to the bobbing dinghy. He wisely refrained from simply dropping it over the side. So he clambered down into the dinghy and tried to pull it down. The problem, of course, was that the little run-about wanted to swing away from the boat. At some point, he almost fell into the water, caught with his feet in the dinghy and his hands holding onto forty pounds of uncooperative gold. It finally occurred to him to look for a swim ladder. He found it in a cockpit locker. After making sure that the dinghy was secured, he hauled himself back onto the *Tumbleweed*.

The phone finally showed some bars. He pressed a pre-set number.

"Lorenzo? Karakurt."

After listening to a rude expletive from the South American, Karakurt asked, "Are you near Cyprus?" More rude language from the other end.

"You have to come to Crete—to Loutro."

"Loutro!" *By Allah, how can a rich guy be this deaf.*

"Lima, Oscar, Uniform, Tango, Romeo, Oscar—Yes. Loutro on Crete.

"Well, look it up." *Damn fool!* With all the electronics that guy had on his monster boat, he should be able to pinpoint this hole of a village in seconds.

Karakurt was proud of himself having learned to spell words out, the seaman's way. Who was it that gave him that huge book to read? Oh yes, he remembered, it was an American who had bought a sixty-five foot boat off some unlucky gambler in Monaco. Then the fool had sailed her to Turkey by the seat of his pants. There, he had hired Karakurt to captain her while he began to study 'the bible of sailing.' Chapman's something or other. Indeed, there were a lot of idiots floating around on the water. In the innermost corner of his freshly anointed soul, Karakurt wondered if he wasn't one of them right now.

"To hell with sleep," he muttered. "I better stay awake to shoot anyone who comes within twenty feet of this wreck."

When the insistent knocking on the hull became loud enough to wake him, Karakurt had a hard time remembering where he was. He blinked his eyes open and realized that daylight must have come hours ago.

"You go now," the same old wizard from the day before called up to him. He stood in a small wooden boat, his brown hands clasping a stanchion. "Ferry comes."

Karakurt understood that he was swinging on the ferry's large mooring, and that the bloody thing was likely expected that day.

"*Tumbleweed*, where?" was all Karakurt could think of to say for the moment.

The ensuing pantomime seemed to indicate that there were no other buoys in Loutro. The local fishing vessels crowded the pier with not a space between them. He had to anchor further out. Apparently, the old gnome was willing to guide him to a new spot. He glanced around. The dinghy was still there. And, thankfully, so was the flat lump lying snug against the floorboards, half-hidden under the straddling seat, covered by random pieces of foul weather gear. Karakurt nodded and pulled himself forward on the loosely dangling shrouds. He knelt on the blunt bowsprit and started to pull on the already slimed-over bowline tied to the ponderous ferry mooring. It was tough going. At last, he caught hold of the mooring's thick wire-loop and worked to undo the unwieldy knots the villagers had tied the day before. The boat immediately swung into the wind, almost fouling the dinghy painter. If the old man and his responsive little craft had not been there quickly to snag the painter and hold it out of the water, for sure it would have wrapped itself around the prop. Karakurt cursed himself for doing things backward, and dashed aft to the cockpit. He pressed the starter button. To his surprise and delight, the motor sprang to life again.

Damn good engine, he rejoiced silently.

The old man led him out a quarter of a mile, where he motioned for Karakurt to drop the anchor in the lee of a small island that sat in the middle of the bay. It seemed a good enough spot, although it was further away from the village than he would have liked. It would be tough going to row the snub-nosed dinghy back and forth.

After Karakurt had reset his anchor, the old man called, "Your chain. Let it out more. But not too much. There is a bad undertow all around." His arms swept wide across the island.

Karakurt gathered that a strong current must swirl against three sides of the island. Once caught in it, a boat could drag anchor and be swept out into the open water. It was the last thing Karakurt wanted to happen. But for right now, the anchor seemed to be holding well.

"Thanks," he called down to the fisherman.

What a pain. He would have to let the chain out by hand since the electric windlass no longer worked. Meantime, he hoped that the anchor was not snagged on the rocks below, or that the flukes would not break loose. Besides, it should not be too long before Lorenzo arrived. Then he could scuttle this thing, or leave it to the village scavengers. *Oh hell, I'll do it later.*

He went below and returned with the last two lukewarm beers from the defunct icebox where they had been saved from breakage.

"Cheers," he said and handed one down to his self-appointed guide.

"Odysseus." The old man grinned and stubbed himself in the

chest with a gnarled finger.

I'll be damned, Karakurt thought in Turkish. *You never know who you run into on a Greek island.*

Even lukewarm, the beers tasted good to the two men, after which Odysseus pulled the starter cord of his noisy two-stroke motor and happily veered off toward the village. Karakurt got busy sorting through the shambles to look for something better to wrap the tablet in. The idea of having to row all the way to deliver the slate to the Klein-woman was not very appealing, but asking the old man for a tow had been too risky at this point.

Karakurt wished the Englishman was still on the boat. He could have used a strong oarsman. At least he hoped that the useless man would have the sense to be close at hand when he rowed up to the quay.

Worrying about the tablets, he forgot about letting out more chain.

* * *

Part III - The Prediction

Chapter Nineteen

Insistent howling and rattling outside his room woke Jonathan shortly after midnight. There was no need to switch the light on. He recognized those sounds. Instantly alert, he got up and padded out to his terrace where he was immediately soaked as he strained against the wind that tried to push him back in. With his sailor's sixth sense, he felt the drop in barometric pressure and smelled the increase of salt-content in the air. Silent lightening flashed far out over the eastern horizon. The island was in the throws of a serious storm.

With rising concern, Jonathan wondered about the stolen Valiant. Whether or not Naunet was on the boat, it had to be sailing straight into this foul weather. Remembering that she did not have the best of sea legs, he surely hoped that she was not. But then, he also hoped that she was. It meant that she was still alive. The scientist in Jonathan had never prayed to any god. Now, if he ever needed to, was the moment for this naked man to turn to a higher force.

Without looking at his watch's glowing dial he would not have known that dawn had come. There was no electricity. And, apparently, the hotel management had shut off the water as well—unless the coughing faucets were a sign of some more serious destruction to the town's frail infrastructure.

Even before Jonathan lifted the receiver of the house telephone, he knew it would be dead. He did it anyway. "Dead."

His murmur was swallowed up by the furious wind rattling

against the double veranda doors. Just to make sure, Jonathan checked that he left the latches hinged securely after he had come back in, sodden and shivering.

Getting dressed without lights was no problem for a sailor. He had done it often enough on a dark wildly bucking racing boat getting ready to stand a cold watch in the dark along a foaming coast pitted with treacherous rocks. Then he went to wake Leopold and Jabari, assuming both were still in their rooms. He was wrong. Wearing a paisley silken bathrobe over black pajamas, Jabari was in an animated but somewhat one-sided conversation with a Pakistani desk clerk. Leopold, fully clothed, stood by patiently. Jonathan noticed his foot. The quick tapping against the high desk's baseboard told otherwise.

"What do you mean curfew? Until when?" Jabari waved his arms at the stoic clerk. Not only were they stuck on the less than friendly side of Cyprus, the powers that be had confined everyone to the hotel for the next two days. Without phone service and electricity. At least, they were promised simple meals with sweet sodas, but no water. The desalination plant had been shut down.

Naunet's father took it like a gentleman, though Jonathan could see that the swollen veins on his neck pulsed in double-time. Jabari, well, amiable Jabari had turned back into Dr. Jabari El-Masri, no longer the reigning, but a still raging *Pharaoh of all of Egypt's Antiquities.*

Jonathan's own mood swung like a pendulum from morose to impatient to desperate, and back to being his youthful, hopeful self again, which ultimately saved a lot of wear and tear on everyone's already frayed nerves.

The worst of the storm only brushed eastern Cyprus as its main fury blew itself out further to the west. On the third day of their unforeseen confinement, Jonathan had enough of their interminable and impotent fretting about Naunet's fate. He could stand the gnawing pain in his heart no longer and decided to brave the last of the squalls. He would walk down to the small pleasure-boat marina. If he could not find anything out about a Valiant cruising around the Med, at least he might be able to help some people to retie their boats or render some other assistance. Sailors are like that; always ready to help one another without much bidding, especially after a storm.

At first sight, Kyrenia's small marina looked a lot more battered than it really was. The whole place actually resembled a giant floating flea-market, with clothes and bedding hung across every boom, strung out over lifelines with old-fashioned clothespins, and in one case the wash had been hauled up to dry high above the crowd.

Jonathan grinned at the yellow long-johns fluttering from a starboard spreader. Just above it, slightly frayed, snapped a triangular club pennant. "Wow," Jonathan said. He had raced under this burgee often enough.

Founded in the late eighteen hundreds, The Boston Yacht Club initially had several sites where it operated its fleet. Now, however, the club had one single station with over five hundred members. And more than four hundred yachts flew the BYC burgee. That station? His own crowded Marblehead Harbor, Massachusetts.

"That's my man," Jonathan sang out loud and stepped close to the boat. "Anyone need help down there?"

It took a while for a black-smeared face to emerge from the cabin. The oily man was holding his even blacker hands stiffly away from anything in danger of being defiled. For his tee shirt and sweat pants, the precaution had come too late.

"Yeah, you want to change the oil for me?"

Changing oil and filters, in the cramped engine room of a sailboat, was more often than not accompanied by lusty curses and frantic demands for old rags and more paper towels. In sad cases, it had spelled the end of marriages.

"Hi! I just thought you could use some help after this storm. Nice boat."

To get on the good side of any skipper the first rule of engagement was to compliment him on his vessel. From then on, no one ever met a stranger. If one could figure out the make and length of his boat to boot, a friend was made forever. However, if in doubt, it was best to err on the larger size.

"Tayana-Forty?"

"Thirty-Seven," the man replied, and nodded approvingly. He cleaned himself up somewhat with some rags and liquid from a can. Not much cleaner, now the smell of turpentine wafted about his wiry body.

Jonathan introduced himself and jokingly pointed to the yellow pair of legs whipping in the wind above them, "I trust that's not a quarantine flag you're flying."

With a chortled, "At your own risk," Jonathan was invited aboard the *Intrepid*. Chuck Reynolds, it turned out, was the current moderator for the cruising net around Kyrenia. He knew just about every skipper in the marina, at least by radio call-sign and boat name. For a confirmed solo-sailor he seemed to have a great capacity for human face-to-face interaction. Over a couple of beers, the two men swapped sailing stories and discussed boat peculiarities. They briefly touched on the always disappointing do-you-know-so-and-so, until Jonathan thought it was time to explain his own boat-less visit to Cyprus.

Chuck listened intently and shook his head several times. To his credit, he did not interrupt Jonathan's selective account of events until his guest was finished with his second beer and with his story.

On a hunch, remembering Jabari's comment about Karakurt getting him in touch with a South American customer, Jonathan asked, "Have you seen or heard of a motor yacht out of South America around these parts?"

"Have I?" Chuck jumped up. "Have I? There's one called the *Bucanero*. Home port Punta del Este, Uruguay. That monster is anchored a ways out from here. Too big for the marina. Listen to this." He bent closer to Jonathan and then sat down again. "A couple of days ago, this guy gets on the radio and asks if anyone here had a spare high-pressure hose. He's on channel sixteen, mind you, and won't get off. Yeah, real classy. Now, I ask you: Do you see any boat around that would have a high-pressure hose lying around for that guy?"

Jonathan smiled and shook his head. "So, he's stuck here?"

"Nah, rich guys like that never are. He had one of his crew fly over to Turkey to buy him one. That's something, isn't it! But wait. There's more. His man comes back, but nobody on that fancy mega-monster knows how to install it. Right away, he's back on channel sixteen, screaming for help. So me and my buddy from *Endless* row out there and splice it in for him. The guy didn't even offer us a beer. Nor his half-naked girls lying around on deck." Chuck grinned broadly and winked. "As I said, real classy."

Chuck looked sharply at Jonathan, "Any particular reason you are interested in this guy? Come to think of it, he did ask about a sailboat called the *Tumbleweed*. Is that the Valiant you are looking for?"

Jonathan could hardly believe his ears.

"You were on his yacht?" "Any chance you could wrangle another visit, say, to make sure the splice is holding?"

Chuck turned cautious. "Maybe," he said and crossed his arms in front of him. "But I think you better tell me first what the real story is here. Because if you think the girl you're looking for is on there, think again. Those three honeys I saw were perfectly content sipping their champagne."

It was difficult for Jonathan to concentrate on the idle prattle. Still, when Chuck had stopped fantasizing over the South American's girl-fortune, he listened up again.

"And if by chance you are planning to beat the guy up or something, I am telling you right now, forget it. He has goons on that boat that would love to finish both of us off in a heartbeat. They looked bored out of their minds. Didn't even look at the girls as they bounced around in their nothing-bikinis. I should think anyone as much as crossing their boss-man the wrong way would make a welcome change in their routine."

Jonathan felt instinctively that he could trust Chuck. It would be all right to tell him everything. Well, as much as he should, under the circumstances. Nevertheless, it was a gamble. But so far, this was his only lead. He had to know if there was a chance that Karakurt planned to meet his buyer here. What an ideal place for shady deals. Jonathan looked at the clearing sky where the last dark clouds scudded off to the west. *Oh Lord. Please, let her be all right.*

Chuck went below and got on the cruiser-dedicated channel eight to call his buddy. The *Endless* was on the end-tie of the same dock from where the whole outer anchorage was visible. Jonathan's heart sank as he heard the reply to Chuck's inquiry squawking back over the mike. "Pulled up anchor. Yep. This morning."

Not one to give up easily, he asked Chuck if they could walk out to the *Endless* to have a talk with her skipper, Nat Szabo. It turned out that the South American had motored his launch over to the *Endless* disgustingly early, as Nat put it, to ask him about Crete. Nat's cruising stop on that island had come up during their hose-installation on the *Bucanero*. It had just been idle boating talk and nobody seemed too interested at the time. Now, all of a sudden, Nat said, this guy wanted to know all about Crete's coastline, Loutro, in particular. Did it have good holding for his anchors, what was the village like. "Strange, for a big yachtie like that wanting to put in at such an isolated village."

Jonathan declined a third beer and spent a few more minutes with the two sailors who soon began to talk about other things, mostly related to the storm and its impact on their local sailing community. Just as he started to say his good-byes, Nat took a hold of his arm.

"Say, when I couldn't get back to sleep this morning, I fiddled with my shortwave. There was some chatter about a sailboat being towed into Loutro. The skipper of an outgoing ferry reported it. Pretty banged up by his account. He also said that, as far as he could tell, there was no one on board."

Jonathan felt he was running a Boston Marathon even though it seemed like hours before he got back to The Ship Inn.

Jabari and Leopold were standing in the lobby, apparently hoping for the utilities to be turned back on.

"Why didn't you tell us!" Jonathan's finger stabbed Jabari in the chest.

Alarmed at the young man's agitation, Leopold put his hand on Jonathan's shoulder. "What did you find out?" he asked quietly.

"The *Bucanero*. Out of Uruguay! She was here! Right here! Looking for the *Tumbleweed*. And you," again, Jonathan stabbed Jabari's chest, "you didn't even care to mention that yacht."

"Jonathan, my boy. Whatever are you talking about?"

To Jonathan, Jabari sounded cautious rather than surprised.

"The South American yacht! The buyer! I'm sure Karakurt was hoping to meet up with him here. For some reason, she left for Loutro. We have to get back to Crete. Now!" Jonathan thought he would suffocate. He had been so close. Shrugging Leopold's hand off his shoulder, he stepped even closer to the Egyptian. "What's his name? Tell me his name!"

"If what you surmise is true, Jonathan, of course, we will try to fly back as soon as possible. But I assure you, I never knew the names of Karakurt's contacts."

"Bastard!"

Stomping off, Jonathan left the two older men to wonder who it was he had bestowed with that moniker.

As soon as the electricity came on again, Jabari got a hold of Sparta Charters, and arranged for one of their jets to fly the three of them back to Heraklion.

Just after take-off, one of the pilots came back into their cabin. He was not the same captain who had flown them over from Crete. Older, with a slight limp, he bent closer to Jabari. "Dr. El-Masri," he said. "Since you were practically marooned for several days, I thought you might not know the latest news from your country. On Sunday, your President Mubarak was sentenced to life in prison."

Jabari El-Masri could not hide the fact that he was deeply shocked. Now, his only hope for support in saving his country's national treasures was the victory of one of the two secular front-runners.

Ex-prime minister and a former air force commander, Ahmed Shafiq, or the former foreign minister, Amr Moussa. Both were good friends of his. Or at least had been up to now. They had always been supportive of his particular kind of patriotism even if it sometimes seemed to touch slightly on fanaticism.

However, if an Islamist candidate won the elections by the end of the month, in particular the candidate of The Muslim Brotherhood, Mohammed Morsi, then he, Jabari, was surely finished. The two had known each other for many years. And for just as many years, they had hated each other's guts. *Yes, then I am surely finished*, Jabari thought.

Jabari, Leopold and Jonathan talked little during the trip. Each retreated to his own thoughts and fears.

They stared out the small windows, perhaps hoping to catch a glimpse of an ostentatious yacht headed for Loutro which, incidentally, would have been way off their flight plan. In their present frame of mind, it was just as well. Because if by chance they had seen the *Bucanero* below the plane, with thoughts of revenge running this high, at least one of them would most likely have forced the charter jet to make a dive for the mega-yacht.

* * *

Chapter Twenty

Naunet discovered the small space off her bathroom by chance. When she opened the narrow door she stepped inside a sunny glassed-in ten-by-ten workshop. It made her feel as if she intruded onto the dead artist's silent world. Brushes, paint palettes, and half-filled canvases lay strewn about. The lingering smell of turpentine assaulted her nostrils.

It would be an ideal space for her to work on the tablets, if and when her captors took them off the boat. She certainly was not going to be working in that sodden environment. Well, at least if she could help it. When Naunet could not figure out a way to open any of the glass-walls, she went back into her bedroom, leaving the connecting doors open. Perhaps that would air the place out somewhat.

As she flung the double doors to the terrace wide, she saw Karakurt and Edward trudge up the quay. At any other time, they would have made her laugh. What a bedraggled pair they made. There was not much left of the self-assured, arrogant dandy who had temporarily swept her off her stupid feet, his lank hair plastered down most unbecomingly. And the Turk was a crumpled mess, especially with the bloodied bandages still wound around his head. Both sported a week's worth of stubble. They looked like two down-and-out men who lived on the street.

Edward was bent over pushing an apparently heavy old wheelbarrow while Karakurt kept shushing curious street urchins away. Every few steps, he urged the Brit on as he might a draft-horse. *All he needs is a whip.* She imagined how an artist would have loved to paint the grim pair: 'Master and slave hauling gold.'

Naunet could hear them trudging heavily up the stairs, one step at a time until an impatient foot shoved her door open.

Karakurt looked around and indicated with a flick of his head to place their burden on her bed. With a flourish that reminded her of the first time they all had met him at the Cairo lab, he pulled the oily rags away. Sure enough, he said it again now. "*Voilá.*"

Naunet gasped at the golden surface. "How did you do that?" she cried and rushed over to the tablet to see if its hieratic script was still intact.

"Easy!" The Turk sneered. "And none of your experts thought of that simple solution."

"How did you do it?" she asked again.

"Gasoline. Actually, a mixture of gasoline and oil dripping on it from the small red canister wedged above it by the storm." He grinned, which did little to improve his mien. "Luckily, it exposed the side you have to translate first. You can work on cleaning up the other side later. I am expecting someone soon to take a look at it." He stepped closer to her and once again pulled her by her hair so that she had to look him right in the face. "And don't even think of making something up."

Edward stood by, shuffling his feet this way and that. "What do you want me to do, Karakurt?"

"You watch her. I am rowing back out to the boat. Somebody needs to guard the other slate." He was going to add that he had hidden it in the chain locker, but thought better of it and instead said, "Meanwhile, try and buy some gasoline and motor oil."

"Ah," Edward hesitated. "There's a bit of a problem. I don't have any money on me."

Karakurt pulled out a black leather wallet and handed Edward a few sodden dollars. "That should do it. I am sure these people take tourist dollars all the time."

Neither man noticed the small card floating to the floor. Naunet took a quick step forward and placed her foot on it. After the two had left, she picked it up.

'*Tumbleweed*, Reno, Nevada. Valiant-Forty. Harry and Edie Jenkins. Call-sign: K17T...' A dark blotch obscured the last letter. Naunet shuddered.

For a long time, she remained as still as if she had been turned into a salt pillar. Then came the shakes. This time they were bad. Worse than the time she had realized the truth behind the blue passports. She barely made it to the bed where she put her hands in front of her face and wept. All the fear, and the hate, and the hope came flooding out of her like a great salty river.

"Madame."

The voice became more urgent. "Madame!"

Through her tears swam two figures standing by the open door. A quick wipe of her face with the back of her hand let her see more clearly. She took a deep breath and tried a wan smile. One was Cassandra, the landlady. The other she did not know. Wait. She remembered him now. It was the old man from the quay whose answer to a simple question had so infuriated Karakurt. Craning his scrawny neck, he intently looked past her.

"This is my old uncle, Odysseus, Madame."

For an old man, the uncle proved as nimble as a weasel. With a few shuffled strides he came to stand beside Naunet and stretched his gnarled hand toward the gleaming tablet.

"No-no-no." Naunet almost flung herself across it. Then she quickly flipped the bedcover over it. She looked at Cassandra. "Please, tell him it is... it is glass. Painted glass. I am an artist too. That is why I like your apart... ah, villa, so much." She had to get the woman on her side.

Next to her, Odysseus rattled off a litany of toothless sounds. Cassandra kept nodding, making clicking noises with her tongue. At last, she looked fully at Naunet. "My uncle says he saw the same, ah, glass, as you call it." A sly wink to Odysseus, then, "The same glass-thing. Over at Mr. Josef and Mrs. Mary. He takes his catch to them every week. The men who drove down from Heraklion had one in their car just like it, he swears."

Naunet slid back down onto the bed. Her heart raced, her hands trembled, and her knees turned to jelly. They had to be the McPeals. And her father! How was it possible for them to have a tablet? Jonathan and Bill? Jabari? Forcing herself to sort through her jumbled thoughts, she reached for Cassandra and patted the bed next to her.

With a woman's intuition for heartbreak—why else would those tears have been shed—the handsome villager swayed over to her new tenant. She sat down and put a maternal arm around Naunet's shoulder. With her other hand, she shooed Odysseus away and waited until he had closed the door behind him.

"He will be handsome again. No? Once we clean him up." Cassandra smiled and thought of the tall stranger. Even in his bedraggled state, there was something about the man that made her tingle. She noticed the way he had looked at her that first time on the quay. *I can forget about the sour one.* She squeezed Naunet's shoulder again.

"Cassandra, I need your help." It had come out too sudden, too fast. *You fool,* Naunet chided herself. "Well, what I mean, how far is this other place where your uncle saw the painted glass? Is it called Kommos? I have not seen any cars around here. How does he get there?"

"Yes, Kommos. No cars. No road. You come to Loutro by boat. Or by ferry, of course."

"Ferry? There is a ferry?" Naunet knew that she was getting too agitated again. She forced herself to slow down. *I have to choose my words more carefully.*

"Cassandra, do you understand everything I say?"

Another nod. Naunet could only hope.

"Good. I would like to see that other piece. To meet the artist if he is there." She leaned closer. "My boyfriend...." it almost made her gag to have to say that, "my boyfriend—ah—he is very, very jealous. You understand?" A nod from Cassandra had her hopes soar. She was on the right track. "Can your uncle take a note to the other side when he goes there next? And tell them about me?" She said her full name slowly several times, thankful that it was relatively simple and not something unpronounceable for most foreigners. Then she had the woman repeat it back.

"If he does that, they will all come here and bring you lots of business." She hoped her last remark would make the woman eager to comply. The prospect of additional business usually prompted universal willingness to do something for it.

The door suddenly flew open, pushed hard by someone's foot.

"There you have it. Two liters of gasoline, and half a liter of motor oil. Man, that stuff is expensive around here." Edward stopped short when he saw Cassandra sitting next to Naunet.

"I beg your pardon." The deep bow, Naunet realized, was of course a thinly veiled mockery. However, it delighted the woman and she could feel Cassandra straightening up: Bosom out, stomach in, albeit not with the same measure of success.

"I must look a fright," Edward said and rubbed his chin. He expected it to be the perfect opening for any reasonable woman to spring into action. As usual, he was not disappointed.

"You can use some of my husband's things," Cassandra said. Seeing his eyebrows go up, she quickly added, "He has been dead for years. I also have a nice room for you downstairs." She stood up, smoothed down her skirt and, taking Edward by the elbow, resolutely marched him out of the room. Armed with useful information regarding a dead spouse, Edward went more than willingly.

Naunet was unsure what she should do next. "What is that smell?" she mumbled. Edward had simply dropped his dirty canisters assuming she would drag them into the workshop. "Typical," she sighed. Now the place would smell twice as bad. She had forgotten to ask Cassandra about opening the glass panes.

Having cleared a wobbly card table of artistic paraphernalia, she went back to the bed to get the slate. Naunet had never handled a tablet by herself and now realized that forty pounds of awkward slab were not that easy to carry around. She finally pulled the cover with the tablet off the bed and hauled it into the workshop. The image of a dead body being dragged off crossed her thoughts and she had to talk to herself to keep her mind on her intended task.

There were plenty of old rags lying forgotten in corners or hanging over the pegs of an easel. She looked around and found an empty glass mixing jar. "That'll do," she said and started pouring gasoline, careful not to spill any. "And a little motor oil." She had no idea what ratio of gas to oil a dinghy motor took. Measuring the shimmering concoction, she felt like Julia Child might have, when she was still alive, preparing her *Coq au Vin*. *Well, not quite*, Naunet shrugged, remembering her own simple meals.

She heaved the tablet onto the table, exposed side down, and started working on the unguent that still covered the mysterious squares.

With an old rag, she soaked and waited. Nothing. She wiped.

Nothing. She scratched. Still nothing. Had the Turk done something to it that he was not telling? From his perspective, it would make sense.

"There is an ingredient missing here. Let me see. What had the Ancients at their disposal to etch or to dissolve?" She licked the corners of her mouth which were still salty from her tears. The palm of her hand flew to her temple. "They had natron. Saltwater! There had been saltwater dripping on it together with the gasoline-oil mixture! I need salt!"

Under normal circumstances, she would have called an assistant, shouted out the door for help, run over to Bill's office to tell him. The circumstances on this island, in this isolated village, were anything but normal. So was the fact that she was being held captive by two unscrupulous thieves. Not to forget murderers. So what was she doing still trying to unravel the mystery of the tablets? She had to be mad.

Yes, it was driving her mad. She had to know what lay hidden under that pitch. Who had designed the original squares, and what was the translation from the ancient high priest? Her madness was caused by the unquenched thirst of the Egyptologist in her.

Against all reason and possibility, Naunet vowed that she would save the tablets. If only Karakurt would bring the damaged one to her. Why was he keeping it on that sorry hulk? She thought about the ferry Cassandra had mentioned. There had to be a way!

The fumes were getting to her. It was neither the fumes nor her nerves, she knew. It was her innate immersion in a forgotten culture.

Naunet left the small room and walked out to the terrace, two floors above the quay. Cassandra had been right. The view was breathtaking. Small fishing boats were tied up along the jetty, except for a large empty space, probably reserved for the ferry. When that ferry came, it would be near enough to run to it, or at least scream for help to its captain.

She had to give Karakurt something—like a small carrot—to keep him out of her hair. Literally. Better leave the reverse side alone for now. She pulled the logbook of the *Tumbleweed* from her overnight bag and went back into the smelly room. Before she opened the log, she gently ran her hand over its title. "I am so sorry," she whispered. In order not to cry again, she bent over the tablet and began to piece words and phrases together. It was very slow going. Soon, though, the scientist in her became so involved with the fascinating script that she completely forgot about her own plight.

Children laughed below her terrace. A little boy cried over something. The hollow clatter on uneven cobbles brought her back. The fumes from the rags were stronger. Perhaps the artist had killed herself accidentally with these noxious fumes. She had better be careful not to do the same herself. No, she decided, she would not give those bastards the satisfaction. Naunet put her pencil down and, crossing quickly through the bedroom, stepped onto the veranda again. A salt-laden mist had rolled in quietly, steadily, and inexorably, until it welled up against the high cliffs that hemmed the little village in. There was no escaping it. Just like fate, Naunet thought.

Along the steep cliffs, dusk infringed upon the waning sun and Naunet realized that she had not eaten all day. Further down from where the children ran in circles, she noticed a sign. *Taverna Kri-Kri*. It was worth a try. She went back in, picked up her scarf and tentatively tried the door. It opened and Naunet tiptoed out. No one barred her way as she went down the stairs, and out into the street. The children looked at her open-mouthed but when their mothers called them for dinner from blue-shuttered windows, they scattered like frightened lambs. Left on the street, forgotten by a child, stood a little wagon. Not one of the shiny red ones with big quiet rubber wheels. This one must have had an earlier life, perhaps as the planks on a wooden fishing boat, or a leftover rafter from a building site. Even the wheels were solid wood. Naunet realized now that it must have been the clattering sound she had heard.

A solid whitewashed half-wall surrounded the *Taverna's* outdoor seating area with its tilted colorful umbrellas shading small round tables from the sun and, less successfully so, the curious strolling by. A man and a woman were seated at a table in the back. He had his back to the street and the woman had eyes only for him. They had their heads together, flirting, laughing, touching each other's hands. Only when the woman looked up, startled, did Naunet realize that it was Cassandra. She fluttered her hand to her neck. The gesture drew Naunet's attention and she saw that the plump woman wore a strand of Golden South Sea pearls. The man with her, dressed in a white short-sleeved shirt and black trousers, slowly turned around. Naunet sucked her breath in.

"Look who's here." Edward stood up and cordially stretched his hand out to her. "Come and taste a bit of local specialty."

"Seems you already have," Naunet answered icily.

* * *

Chapter Twenty-One

The news of Hosni Mubarak's sentencing and the widely assumed election of Mohammed Morsi as Egypt's next president severely affected Jabari El-Masri's mood. He knew that it would change his future, probably his fate, and none too positively. Soon, if he was not already, he would be a man with a price on his head.

Leopold and Jonathan listened intently to his plight. They agreed that he had no other choice than to be concerned with the safekeeping of the golden tablets, unless history was to label him a thief. That was something the proud Egyptian simply could not bear. He would rather die.

The chartered jet landed back in Heraklion during the late morning. Again, they took a cab to the cargo area where the hangar was all closed up. From all outward appearances it looked abandoned. It was of course a relief not to see dozens of police cars and possibly Interpol surrounding the building. Still, they approached it with trepidation. Jabari cautiously tried the small side door that led into the hangar. "Locked," he said needlessly. The same horrified thought raced through their minds.

Jonathan, no longer caring what and who awaited him inside, impulsively pounded his fists on the hot metal. To their surprise, the door was cautiously cracked open. A beaked nose appeared through the three-inch gap together with the nozzle of a gun.

"Ahmed Sharkawy! For heaven's sake!" Jabari exploded, exhaling the fear and his fury from his lungs. He kicked the door wide open and then impulsively embraced his Luxor friend. "Are Rahman and

Husri still here?"

"Of course. We are ready," Ahmed replied proudly, "for whatever plans you have." Obviously they had heard the same news and knew it would change their lives. Like Jabari, these exceptional men were true Egyptians, loyal to their roots and heritage. And they would not let the state of their homeland's sorry politics get in the way.

Leopold and Jonathan sensed that their own roller-coaster ride with the eminent Egyptologist was drawing to an end. They, too, were anxious to get on with their search for Naunet, and promised Jabari to try and salvage the Saqqara tablets. If they could locate the elusive Edward and the Turk on Crete, there was no doubt in their mind that those two were at the root of the theft.

"What will you do with the others," Leopold asked, assuming that the ton of gold in the tail section of the jet was not destined to buy these extraordinary men a cushy life in exile in some benign foreign country.

"I shall bury them." Jabari said without hesitation.

"On Crete?"

"No, no, in the sands of el-Kharga where they belong."

"Then they'll be lost again. Perhaps forever," Jonathan protested. He had not admitted to himself that he had become thoroughly intrigued with those tablets.

"Ah, my young friend," Jabari smiled indulgently. "There are such things as tracking devices."

"And then what? What will you do then?" Jonathan asked quickly, annoyed with himself for his stupid assumption that Jabari would leave his tablets to the whims of another Khamsin piling the dunes high over their new tomb.

"Well," Jabari winked, "after that, I might just have to borrow this jet for another little trip across some welcoming border. Qatar perhaps. I know the Amir quite well. As the Commander in Chief of the Armed Forces and Minister of Defense there, he can smooth entry into their airspace, assuming the Saudis do not shoot us down along the way." From Jabari's raised eyebrows and accompanying grin, he did not seem too worried about the latter happening.

"There is a U.S. embassy in Doha. If I can outrun—or in my case out-fly—the news and the slow arm of my accusers, your ambassador will hopefully issue me a visa. Then I can go on to London by commercial jet. From there, I thought, it might be a good time to pay a visit to my old friend Bruno. We still need to discuss the exhibition of the Narmer pieces."

Leopold looked on, slightly confused.

"I'll explain later," Jonathan nodded to Naunet's father. Turning back to Jabari, he put on his best boyish grin. "In that case, you are still on official Institute business. So we better keep that credit card authorization current a little while longer."

Jabari thanked Jonathan. What a thoughtful gesture. There was no need to deflate the well-meaning boy and tell him that he had already cleared this with Bruno. He had placed the call from Cyprus, after the power to their hotel had been restored. At that time, it was a precaution. Now, it had become a reality.

"Thank you, my friends. And mark my words. I shall not rest until I have my Saqqara tablets again. For right now, though, I cannot stay on Crete with you. You understand. Or I might lose the ones I have. Please, keep in touch."

"Of course," Jonathan said and grabbed Jabari's hand. "I'll see you back in Boston, Sir." Jabari nodded. He was still a force to command respect. Just then, being addressed again as 'Sir' did his nicked ego a world of good.

By 'we' Jabari assumed that Jonathan meant he and Bill. To Jonathan, the 'we' not only was meant for himself and Bill. It definitely included Naunet. If that were not to be, he did not want to dwell on that possibility just now. He felt it in his bones—or was it just the insane hope he nurtured in his heart—that he would find his answer, and her, and with it his love, in a little isolated village called Loutro.

Back at the main terminal of Nikos Kazantzakis Airport, Leopold and Jonathan put in a call to Josef McPeal in Kommos. Bill, of course, was still there waiting anxiously for news of their search on Cyprus. They quickly brought him up to speed until he told them that Bruno had already made arrangements for Dr. Jabari El-Masri's visit to the States.

"That sly fox," Jonathan grinned. He had to give the man credit for his foresight.

"I wonder when it was that he realized to make alternate plans.

Apparently, he is all set up to meet *Hobo* in California. Now, that's a smart move." They also told Bill and Josef that they were renting a car and planned to drive the coast route down to Sfakion. From there, they would take the ferry to Loutro.

"Be very careful," Josef told them. "That road—if you can call it that—is really treacherous. It curves atop the ridge of a steep cliff. The winds up there are fierce enough to blow a small car right off its wheels." They promised they would rent a sturdy vehicle with a four-wheel drive.

Josef knew what he was talking about when he had warned them to be careful. Even Leopold, who had explored many caves and sacred sites high up in these mountains, had a difficult time to stave off vertigo. Apart from a few wildly swerving trucks, they encountered no one. "Loose linkage," Jonathan commented and was sure to give the rattling vehicles plenty of room; which in itself was a feat.

After a last harrowing descent to sea level, Sfakia welcomed them late that afternoon. It meant, no more ferries that evening. Jonathan tried to talk several locals into motoring them over to Loutro. Normally, they said, no problem. It is not too far. However, there was a storm brewing. Not a time to be out on the water. And if they did not make it back home they were stuck in Loutro. Their wives would not like that.

"The storm has long passed Crete," Jonathan pleaded. "Look, the sea is calm again."

The men shook their heads. We do not mean this last one, they said. "That one came from the east. This next one is coming from the south. A *Sirocco*. We can feel it in our bones. And we heard it on the forecast. This late in the year, very bad." They shuddered.

Jonathan realized that his offer to pay them plenty for their trouble could not compete with a fisherman's instinct.

Another day spent. Another night lost. Jonathan felt like shaking his fist at a sea that spawned such late-season winds just to spite him.

Dawn had barely broken the next morning when Jonathan roused Leopold. They went to explore Sfakia's two small harbors in search of transportation to Loutro. The only boat docked at the eastern quay showed no sign of life. With nothing to accomplish, the two Americans went in search of coffee at the harbor-front. There was not much to choose from as Sfakia was a village of only about three hundred souls. It took another hour for a sleepy *Taverna* owner to scratch and yawn himself into action for his early customers. They asked about the ferry tied up at the dock. The man shook his head. "To Agia Roumeli," he said.

"Ferry to Loutro," Jonathan tried again.

More yawning and stubble-scratching. "Not today. Not tomorrow. Perhaps not until next week," the man said and then added the one hated, feared, and cursed word. "*Sirocco.*"

Jonathan jumped up nearly upsetting their coffees. "For God's sake, man. How do I get to Loutro?"

A few more customers, mostly the old men of Sfakia, had come to get some breakfast and the customary sharing of local news. They watched the agitated foreigner with interest. It was much better than yesterday's lukewarm gossip. There were also a few tourists. Judging from the binoculars around their necks, they were out early for good reason. Crete harbored many kinds of birds, and had become a haven for avid bird watchers.

In a last ditch effort, Jonathan stood and addressed his gaping audience. "Loutro. I have to get to Loutro." He turned toward the water with his outstretched arm. "Any of you..."

His arm stopped in mid-air. "Leopold! You don't suppose..."

Dr. Klein's eyesight was no longer what it had been. He fumbled for his glasses.

The nearest bird watcher thought she was being attacked and strangled with the straps of her own binoculars. Jonathan had practically pounced on the poor woman and pulled her glasses off with nary an 'I'm sorry.'

It fell to Leopold to calm her down. With his mature good looks and continental charm, it was not too difficult.

"That thing's a monster." Jonathan watched as the mega-yacht motored past majestically. "Damn. She's going full steam. But why is she turning further out? Wait! Now I can see the stern."

Leopold, hoping his soothing maneuver had worked on the woman, was about to reach for the glasses himself when Jonathan cried "*Bucanero*. I can read it! It's the *Bucanero*!"

For an instant, Leopold actually feared that the young man would tear down to the quay and dive into the water to catch the yacht. He laid a calming hand on Jonathan's shoulder. The sighting could mean only one thing—at least in their minds—the South American was looking for his illicit supplier.

Jonathan turned back to the *Taverna's* customers. "How do I get to Loutro?" Every last person there felt addressed.

A man with a stomach as round as a basketball had watched the two men since he idled into the cafe. Now he stood up slowly. He was almost as short as he was wide. As he made his way over to where Leopold and Jonathan stood, the locals seemed to scoot their chairs out of his way.

He introduced himself. "I am the mayor of Sfakia." Then, with a measured non-aggressive gesture, he took the binoculars from Jonathan's cramped hands. A quick nod of his head to a nearby listener made that man jump up and take the glasses from the mayor to be given back to their rightful owner.

The woman coquettishly tried to catch Leopold's attention, to no avail. She sighed, picked up her satchel, pulled the leather straps of her glasses back over her head, and tugged her creeping shorts back down over her fleshy thighs. She paid quickly for her breakfast and left with a shrug, pitying herself for another missed opportunity.

The mayor crooked his finger at Jonathan and pointed to a path that led west.

"If you are in such a hurry, you can walk to Loutro in little more than an hour. However, it is only a narrow path." He looked at Leopold. "I cannot recommend it to everyone. It is steep. We pull exhausted tourists off there all the time."

"Just tell me how I get there," Jonathan urged and then listened carefully as the mayor explained the way.

"I'll take the ferry later on," Leopold said to Jonathan, "and join you there."

"Not today." The mayor shook his head and pointed out to sea. "That storm is coming in fast."

It was all Jonathan needed to hear. "Join me when you can," he called back over his shoulder, already halfway up the narrow street to look for the path along the cliff. All he had to do was to follow it westward. It would drop him right into Loutro, the mayor had said.

"Could I join you for a moment, Mr. Mayor?" Leopold decided it was time to enlist the help of a local authority and the police, if there was such a thing in this small village. It could not hurt at least to talk to the mayor about most of it.

"Of course. Please, have coffee with me."

Sfakia's mayor was curious what these two men were up to. Neither of them looked like a tourist. The older one appeared downright distinguished, he thought. He wondered if they were scouting for new excavation sites. It would bring his little town some income, for sure, and he was willing to grant the necessary permissions. Except, of course, if they dug around the cemetery or near their little church.

"This may sound rather strange to you, and it is a long story," Leopold began after the *Taverna* owner had served him a reviving cup of coffee. After the flight and the drive from Heraklion, he needed it.

"I have plenty of time," the mayor said graciously and settled himself comfortably into his chair. As he stretched his legs under the table, he glanced out over the water.

The morning had been clear and crisp. Now an ugly brown haze was building way out. It stretched the length of the horizon. They had been told about it, but this late in the season, had not wanted to believe the television's weatherman droning on inside the smoke-filled *Taverna*. It was their only television set in town and there was always at least one person watching. That way, the others could go about their business and still, the news could be spread through the village like a wildfire.

"For sure, there'll be a *Sirocco*," the mayor said. "We better move inside."

* * *

Chapter Twenty-Two

The *Motor Yacht Bucanero* ran at full speed. On the main deck and above, the pumping from a pair of 1875-horsepower Caterpillar engines was barely discernible. If it had not been for the huge wake the yacht plowed up with its sharp bow, her one passenger—Lorenzo counted only himself as the three girls were merely decoration rather than guests—and the six crew hardly noticed as they cut through the cold waters along the southern coast of Crete at a steady twenty knots.

"Senior Dominguez, Sir." The captain briefly left the surveillance of the high tech instruments to the first mate.

"Yes, Captain Max, what is it?"

"We will have to anchor out. The Loutro harbor is deep enough. However, it is small. They have ferries going in and out all day."

"What? Oh, that's fine." The man in white slacks and cream alpaca sweater was deep in thought. He was looking at the coast gliding by. "I certainly do not plan to stay there long," he said.

South American billionaire Lorenzo Dominguez, sole proprietor of software development companies in Uruguay, Panama, and Sri Lanka, was born in Caracas, Venezuela, fifty-six years ago. That is to say, he was not born in the vibrant city proper.

Until he was four, he believed his mother's story that she had found him one morning in their hovel which clung to one of those rain-rutted hills looming over Caracas like festering cankers. On that fourth birthday, his mother told him that she had given life to him during a thunderstorm. Not shielded under their rusty washboard of a roof, but—because he was in such a hurry to come into the world—under the fronds of a precious banana tree outside. She claimed ownership to two of those trees, struggling tenaciously close to one wall of their lean-to. How fortunate they had been, for those bananas were their main staple morning and night. There was no noontime meal. From the time his brother and he could walk, they had to take turns leaning against those scaly stems all night to guard the growing bunches from thieves, neighbors and rooting pigs. Not their own of course, but wild and vicious ones. Later, he was told that his mother's family at one time had owned a small plot of land way out in the country where they did raise pigs. Most likely, that's how the family had come by its surname: Suarez. Swineherd.

He met his father the day his mother died. She was not old, nor had she been sick. She just wore out and gave up, the stranger claiming to be his father said. Lorenzo hated the pitiless man but being only six at the time, there was little he could do. Alonso, his then five-year old brother, and he were dumped into the back of an old pick-up truck and driven to the coast. All he remembered from that trip was that the truck was blue. Then suddenly, darkness enveloped him and he had screamed that the sun was slipping off the sky. After the long tunnel spewed them out, an expanse of deep blue stretched before the open-mouthed boys. Its surface moved and foamed, and spoke to him. He picked up a pure white shell and stuffed it in his pocket. From that moment on, he loved the sea. That new, overwhelming feeling lasted until he and his screaming brother were dragged onto a foul-smelling tug bound for one of the islands off the northern Venezuelan coast.

Margarita Island represented different things to different people. To the tourist, it was a pleasure haven with self-contained resorts that offered every luxury and diversion the sun and fun-seeking tourist could ask for. Including child prostitution.

To drug traffickers, it was the jumping-off point to reap their ill-begotten profits from North America, Europe, and many of the Caribbean islands. Sometimes, there was a raid and the drug dealers were caught and prosecuted. Thus, it was most expedient for the Venezuelan government to have a prison built right on Margarita Island.

San Antonio Prison was something else, to say the least. Viewed from the outside there were the walls topped by barbed wire. There were also the towers with guards, their rifles trained on imaginary escapees. As a matter of fact, loosely guarded prisoners came and went to cool off in the ocean, buy trinkets, and share a drink with the locals. The inside was a different story altogether. One could think it was a resort in itself—a sort of Hugh Hefner knock-off where prisoners swapped guns, girls and gonorrhea with their conjugal visitors. There were also the young boys. During the day they scurried about like sewer rats and performed menial tasks. They took messages to and from the prisoners, and scrounged leftovers dropped by amused inmates and their guests. At night, no one took heed of their whimpers. And every so often, one of them died.

Lorenzo and Alonso had been too scrawny, and too dirty, and too unruly to be hawked at the up-scale resorts. So they were taken to the prison where benefactors were less discerning, but a lot more demanding. The boys survived only because of the street-smarts that are instilled in outcast children.

When he was twelve and they were scrubbing pots in the huge prison kitchen, Lorenzo pushed his brother into a stinking fish tank that had come off a trawler with fish heads for the next day's soup. Then he crawled in himself. If one of the crew back on the trawler had not thought that he had lost his silver cross as he scooped the offal out of that tank, they surely would have suffocated.

For the following three months, Lorenzo hated the sea and could not run away fast enough when the trawler spilled them onto land in Montevideo, Uruguay.

It had taken him forty years of scrimping, saving, clawing, taking chances and outfoxing everyone he dealt with later on. But he had finally made it. And he had learned to love the sea again. His boat was another thing he loved. Designed by British super yacht expert Tim Heywood and built at the German shipyard Blohm and Voss, she was over one hundred feet long, with a capacity for ten guests and a complement of fourteen crew, although Lorenzo preferred to sail with a minimum of people underfoot. Lately, he spent most of his time on the *Bucanero* rather than back home in his very posh hacienda in an even posher enclave of Montevideo, where his wife could make life unbearable when she was in one of her moods. To think that she had told him the problem with their crumbling marriage lay with him! Was it not she who had not given him an heir! She was still young, and exquisite, and his fourth, each subsequent wife having been younger than the last. And still, there were no sons while his brother Alonso was slavishly dedicated to the plump mother of his lively two daughters and strapping three sons. It just wasn't fair. He had worked so hard to succeed. He had even changed their family name to Dominguez.

Lorenzo went to gaze at his latest acquisition hanging in his private office. He wondered if Karakurt really would come through this time. Imagine, having to chase after him. A stopover on Crete had not been in his plans.

He had met the sly Turk several years back when the man had come to Alexandria to deliver a small sample of the Cairo Museum's overflow, as Lorenzo's Egyptian contact had put it. When he had sworn that none of the items would ever see the light of day or be resold, the artifacts became more interesting—and a lot more expensive.

Then, a couple of years ago Karakurt's story was that he had supposedly asked for a holiday to visit his family in Turkey. In reality, he had captained the South American's previous boat for two weeks off that treacherous but incredibly beautiful coast. The older yacht had not been quite as large as the *Bucanero*, but Karakurt had loved the feel of it. He was actually quite a good skipper. It turned out that he was an even better thief. He told Lorenzo that on his way back from Alexandria that time, he had stopped off at the Giza excavation site to do something or other for his boss at the Cairo Museum. That was in August 2010.

Before driving back to Cairo, Karakurt had wandered into the Mohammed Mahmoud Khalil Museum close to the Giza excavations. Just to have a look around. He was astounded when one of the galleries had no guards and no visible surveillance cameras. Nothing! In addition, it was empty of tourists.

A *galabya* is a practical garment for hot climates; and it is just as convenient for an art heist. The opportunistic man simply took the smallest painting off its hooks, discarded the gilded frame and stuck it under his long shirt. However, the canvas was still nailed to its backing board. Having a twenty or so inch-long board stuffed behind one's belt made him walk like someone in a full body cast. Despite this little hindrance, he walked out the main entrance as stiffly as the sacred Ibis. No one seemed to notice or care. Getting back and sitting down in the Cairo museum van was a bit of a problem, Karakurt admitted, as the whole thing pushed itself high under his chin; he barely reached the ignition and then drove with extended arms out of the area.

Karakurt had asked Lorenzo if he was interested in the rather ordinary, he almost apologized, little painting of some red and yellow poppies in a vase. Since it had been hanging in a museum he thought it should be worth something to Lorenzo, and consequently to him.

"Considering that you stole it and cannot sell it on the open market," Lorenzo had grinned, "I tell you what I will pay for it." The sum had satisfied the Turk. It was a pittance according to the painting's worth listed in one of Lorenzo's art catalogues.

Poppy Flowers by Vincent van Gogh was described as being worth an estimated fifty million dollars. The interesting thing was, Lorenzo read in a footnote, that this painting had been stolen once before from the very same museum. That was in June of seventy-seven. Luckily, it had been recovered ten years later in Kuwait. Damn those Kuwaitis, Lorenzo fumed. They made it really tough these days to get one's hands on genuine artifacts and paintings.

"Well, the Egyptians are not going to get it back this time." He poured himself half a tumbler of Courvoisier. "That I promise you, old Vincent," he grinned.

Lorenzo walked pensively through to his master suite—calling it a cabin would have been insulting—and stepped into his equally luxurious bathroom.

There, the pinnacle of his acquisitions floated between two layers of sandalwood. When he had guests, or more frequently a guest of the female persuasion, the outer skin closed over the painting. He never tired of looking at his prize, talking to it, touching it. He ran his fingers reverently over the raised oils caressing the superb brush-strokes, and he allowed his pleasure to mount into its almost agonizing hot release.

Lorenzo swore that he was never going to part with this one, no matter what. He would commit murder for that painting. Well, actually, he already had. But that was twenty-two years ago when he could ill afford to pay the outrageous prices of the big auction houses.

Rembrandt's *The Storm on the Sea of Galilee*, painted in 1633, had fallen into his hands utterly by chance. A man had approached him as he was leaving a fundraiser at the Guggenheim in New York City. The scruffy thief wanted fifty thousand dollars for 'a large priceless painting.' Lorenzo offered him ten. They settled on twenty-five—sight unseen—and Lorenzo told him to come to the yacht he had leased for that week, his charters always made on a bare-boat basis. For good reason, he preferred to bring his own crew.

The next evening, the man rowed up to the boat in a kayak, and a long tube was handed up and passed on to Lorenzo by one of his crew. The man didn't say where he stole it—which was obvious with a canvas cut out of its frame—and Lorenzo didn't care, and hadn't asked. Once he was reasonably sure that it was an original canvas, he invited the man on board, gave him a drink, and slapped him on the shoulder for a job well done. His bodyguard handed the thief a sealed plastic bag with twenty-five thousand dollars.

Then Lorenzo's mood changed. He ordered the man to get off the boat at once. Two more bodyguards stood by, bulging arms crossed, feet spread apart. The suddenly very frightened man rushed over to the boarding ladder to jump back down into his kayak. Unfortunately for him the little boat was no longer there. He made quite a splash followed by two muffled sounds. Lorenzo's crew fished the plastic bag from the murky water and took care of any telltale flotsam. They also carefully cleaned their guns that night.

Later on, Lorenzo learned that there had been a theft at the Isabella Stewart Gardner Museum in Boston and it was not difficult to recognize the Rembrandt as one of several art works taken during the audacious heist.

A priceless painting without its original frame is like a beautiful woman without her hair, at least as far as Lorenzo was concerned. He loved to bury his face in the long dark silky hair of young women. Sometimes, that was all he wanted from a female guest. The fact that he had three of them on board at the same time meant peace of mind and body. They kept each other company and the favorite flavor of the day could be counted on jealously preventing the other two from making too many demands on him. That suited him just fine. There were times when all he wanted was to look at a flawless naked girl, then dress her in fifteenth century period clothes, of which he had a closet-full on board, and make believe that she was the Mona Lisa. Ah, if only he could get his hands on that one. *Maybe one day.* It had been done before, in 1911. Perhaps it could be done again.

Lorenzo knew a fantastic forger in Paris. Many of the rich and famous used him to copy their original artwork kept in their strong-rooms or walk-in safes while showing off the copy to unsuspecting guests.

When times got hard, it was often lucrative to have a copy stolen and then later claim it as having been the original. If insurance companies were suspicious, they nevertheless had to pay up. What they did not know was that Pierre, the Younger, often changed out the frame of an original painting for his own excellent copy as well. Sometimes, if there was a bidder rich enough, he returned two beautifully rendered copies to the owner claiming one to be the original. It was lucrative to have a good reputation with the rich and greedy.

When Lorenzo went to choose a new but period-authentic frame, he never left the Rembrandt out of his sight. He thought about the van Gogh. He hadn't been that smart then. *Damn, I might never know for sure.*

Lorenzo Dominguez was more than annoyed. Why he had let himself be duped into chasing after the Turk's supposed tablets, was beyond him. Not really, though. He was pretty much prepared to go to any lengths for those golden tablets, assuming Karakurt came through with his tantalizing promises. A month ago, the lowly museum employee had literally screamed into the Iridium telephone supplied by Lorenzo for that very purpose. Not to scream, of course, but to let Lorenzo know when he had something else to sell. That's when the Turk had screamed about dozens, yes dozens, of slabs of gold. Later on, Karakurt told him that more had been excavated in Upper Egypt and that he planned to somehow get his hands on them and truck them to Alexandria where they could be loaded onto the *Bucanero*.

Their last communication had not been as promising. Karakurt did not exactly tell him how many tablets he really had, but it no longer sounded that he had been able to steal dozens and dozens.

Lorenzo walked into his office and closed the door. *Just imagine: an entire wall adorned with golden pre-dynastic tablets. With me, the only person in the world, to know their meaning.*

He went through to his bathroom and looked pensively again at *The Storm on the Sea of Galilee*. If the Egyptian tablets were as magnificent and contained true curses, revelations and predictions— as Karakurt had sworn they did—those ancient tablets just might edge out the Rembrandt while he pleasured himself.

For the time being, however, it was still the Dutch master's evocative painting that took him from sweet ecstasy to hot relief. Newly gratified, he was pleased with how much he had accomplished in his life. If only there was a son.

Lorenzo took a leisurely shower after which he felt renewed and reborn. Toweling himself dry, he realized how hungry he was. They would arrive at Loutro shortly. He had plenty of time to have some lunch while his crew found suitable anchorage for the yacht. Then it would be time for him to find out what the Turk was really up to. With the instinct of a scenting predator, Lorenzo somehow felt that all was not right with this particular deal.

On his way out, the recently gratified billionaire gently touched the frame of the van Gogh hanging in his office. He smiled. What a pleasant life he led. Lately, though he had taken too many chances. It would be a shame to have his treasures besmirched by loose tongues. Perhaps it was time for him to stop dealing with the likes of the Turk's ilk.

Lorenzo breathed in the scent of the sandalwood paneling. It was good to be a billionaire. And that was in U.S. Dollars, not Uruguayan Pesos. He could afford to buy the help of a lot of people. Especially those who could make others disappear.

* * *

Chapter Twenty-Three

Naunet was furious with herself. What did she care! How ridiculous of him to sidle up to a plump local, with the black gap of a missing front tooth no less.

"Stop being so female," she said out loud and fell onto the bed. "He no longer means anything to me!"

How could Edward's newest conquest evoke such outrage in her? She hated to admit it to herself. But could there be just a tiny bit of jealousy? It was absurd. She certainly was no longer smitten by this... this... Naunet could not even think of a name vile enough for him. What confounded her was that she still felt something.

Love really is just a step away from hate. She breathed herself into regaining some semblance of calm. Then she settled on hate. Still, the thought of that exquisite strand of pearls on such a mediocre neck made her see red. Why would he do that? She was hard pressed to believe that his motivation was to get into the woman's native bloomers. *I bet he wants her to help him with something. Could he be planning to trick the Turk out of his share?*

The thought reminded her that Karakurt had not shown his ugly face since he and Edward dragged the tablet up to her room. *My room! By God, have I lost my mind? This is not my hotel room! They kidnapped me. They hold me prisoner. And once I finish the translation, then what?* Fear struck her as hot as lightening. *Yes, then what?* They were going to get rid of her. How, hardly mattered.

She remembered from her previous visit that the island was full of deep craggy gorges. Most likely though, Karakurt would row her back out to the disabled boat and wrap an anchor chain around her neck. Involuntarily, her hand went to her throat so recently encircled by something much more beautiful—and much less lethal.

These gloomy thoughts were getting her nowhere and she decided to take a crack at the last few lines of the tablet. She had done the first third, and would do the second third later. Right now, she had to know how the story of these unknown people ended, if indeed the fiftieth tablet was the end of Ramose's translation. She wiped more of the unguent away and noticed a curious seal in the middle and at the very end. It was the winged scarab again. Just like the ones stamped onto the rims of the tablet. Could they really be the ancient High Priest's seal?

Naunet forgot her dilemma and bent over the tablet. Too fascinated to put her translation onto paper just yet she wanted to do a quick overview and finalize the text afterward. Following the cursive writing between the scarab signs with her index finger, she read out aloud:

I, Ramose, High Priest of Ptah, under Hor-Aha, the Falcon King of the Two Lands, tell you this. The squares on these golden tablets were copied under Rahetep, Chief Priest of the Temple of Horus in Nekhen. They had been woven into the ancient mats, found at Badari by the Venerable Badar, the one who preceded me, and my great mentor. The Goddess Isis, through her Oracle, handed me the key so I could read them. It is the story of an ancient unknown people. Their homeland was destroyed by fire spewing from their mountains and a great upheaval of the sea. After much suffering, they were washed up on the shores of our Great Desert. Back then, they say, it was green and fertile with a great river. They called it Sahari. After many years, the Great Wind of Fifty Days drove them toward the rising sun where they found our own Great River Hapi. They lived along its shores for many good years, prospered, and had many children.

Their first account is one of sorrow caused by the fiery cataclysm that drove them from their homeland. In the last story, the elders warn of such a terrifying future for their children's children, that I dare not share these dire predictions with my own people. For I fear panic, strife and unrest might destroy us as well.

So I will consign these fifty Golden Tablets back to the sand where the Great Wind shall bury them forever. But to those, who may one day find them, I say: Take great heed, I beseech you. Let not avarice consume you. Give them back to the Khamsin—or you will be the cause of another great cataclysm on this earth.

But should it happen I, Ramose, have beseeched Ptah, and Isis and Ma'at, to save this earth. For I believe that the end is but a new beginning for the eternal soul.

⟷

"Wow," Naunet breathed, borrowing Jonathan's expression. She squinted at the text again and ran her fingers slowly over it. "Imagine! An ancient footnote."

Unable to sit still any longer, she got up and paced back and forth in the small room which had become more stifling by the minute. It was imperceptible at first, but then the uneasy feeling crept up her spine and the tips of her fingers tingled. Her arms were suddenly covered in goose bumps. She shook herself like a dog after an unwanted bath.

"Good grief," she said out loud. "After all the curses and supposed hauntings I have translated in my lifetime, I am spooked by this?" Was the sudden malaise caused by what she had been through lately? It could unnerve anyone. Still, reassuring herself did nothing to alleviate the gnawing dread deep in her soul. Or was it some sixth-sense premonition? She stomped her feet and shook herself once again.

"Oh," she laughed half-heartedly, "and let's not forget that this is, after all, 2012." To free herself from the trance Ramose's last words had brought on she re-read his words. After all, had not the high priest added hope for the world by beseeching his gods to save the world from another cataclysm? "Destruction and renewal," she mused, "that's the earth's own way." Still, she could not shake the clammy feeling of impending doom. Had she been chosen to avert the next wave of destruction by destroying the tablets? Naunet fled the stifling workspace and ran through the bathroom into the adjoining bedroom. Craving clean air, she headed for the open veranda.

Before she got outside, her bedroom door was unlocked. It creaked halfway open until Cassandra gave it a good shove with her ample bottom, stepping inside with a tray in her hands. Naunet sensed a change in the woman's demeanor: Part sheepish, part embarrassed; with the rest of her attitude steeped in defiance. At least, she no longer wore the pearls.

"Edward says you must eat. The other one wants you to finish your project."

"Cassandra…"

"You need to behave yourself. I don't want any trouble. I must go now."

Before Naunet could say anything else, the woman had set down the tray and left the room. The key turned again in the old-fashioned lock. Through Edward, a hoped-for ally had become an enemy.

The new spot in the lee of the island where he had been told to drop *Tumbleweed's* anchor looked still good to Karakurt. The only problem with it was that the small island obscured his view of the open water outside the harbor. He would not see the *Bucanero's* approach into Loutro. If it ever came, that was. Lorenzo had left strict instructions for him not to place any more calls from the Iridium phone to the yacht. He was to wait like a sitting duck. Rich people knew no gratitude. A knock on the hull brought him on deck.

Odysseus stood in his small boat clinging to one of the few undamaged stanchions. He grinned up at Karakurt, "You said I can take the wires."

"Take all you want. Take the stump of the mast as well, if you can cut off what's left of it. As a matter of fact, when I leave, you can have to whole damn boat."

The leathery face broadened into a grin. "When will you leave?"

"Not yet." Karakurt was aware that his reply was curt and dismissive. He noticed that the old man glanced at him sideways with calculating eyes. It was a look worthy of caution, especially among thieves. Karakurt wanted to check on the woman and her progress before Lorenzo showed up. Yet he did not want to leave Odysseus alone in the vicinity of the crippled sailboat. There was still the damaged tablet hidden in the now half empty chain locker.

"Hey, Odysseus! How would you like to have a bigger outboard for your boat?" He called out, a trifle too jovial. "If you can fix it, you can have it too after I leave. It'll be a lot faster than that crummy one you have now."

The old man eyed the Mercury bolted to the stern of the rubber tender and then looked back at his dull-looking two-stroke Seagull. True, it was old, and slow. But it had never let him down. He nodded just to show he appreciated the offer. If the Turk thought that this was an additional bargaining chip for him, he was mistaken. He would have to leave that motor behind anyway. Still, Odysseus figured the gesture made the man feel better, so he nodded. "I have to take it ashore to fix it."

They placed the Mercury on the bottom of Odysseus' boat, fastened the dinghy's painter to its stern and, with Karakurt sitting impatiently in *Thistle*, Odysseus pulled the dinghy toward the village. The water outside the harbor was getting choppy and it took half an hour before they got to the quay and found a tight spot that accommodated both their small boats as the landing was crammed with all sorts of small fishing vessels, more or less dilapidated. Even the space for the ferry had been taken up.

Karakurt wondered if it was a holiday on Crete for it was unusual for a fishing village to have most of its boats idled. "Why are all these boats in the harbor?"

"Storm brewing."

"Not another one!" That meant no ferry due to the forecast storm. Karakurt spat with such disgust that the old man turned up his palms and shrugged his shoulders. It was not his fault that there was a *Sirocco* this late in the season. It was supposed to be a bad one at that.

The moment Karakurt clambered onto the quay, he saw Edward sitting on the outdoor veranda of the *Kri-Kri Taverna* with his feet propped up on the waist-high wall. In his hand was a tall glass. He seemed to be holding court amidst a knot of locals.

It took Karakurt only half a minute to reach the insouciant scoundrel. "Get up!" Karakurt swiped Edward's feet off the wall and practically pulled the chair out from under the surprised man. "Where is she?"

"Hello, Karakurt. Sit down, old man. Have something cool. Cassandra makes the best concoctions. Can't tell you what's in it. But it's delicious."

"Where is she?"

"Cassandra?"

"No, you idiot! You know damn well who! Let's go. Now!"

If Edward had not been as tall, Karakurt would have taken him by the scruff of the neck to lead him off. As it was, he gripped the man's arm in a vice and yanked him along the short distance to the last entryway of the row houses. It was at that moment that he made up his mind. He had to rid himself of the useless dandy. Lorenzo certainly would have no use for him. Should have done it long before this, he seethed inside his black soul. Just for good measure, he jabbed the fumbling Brit in the ribs, and also to show him who was boss now.

"You are hurting me." Edward whined like a schoolboy being brought to task.

"Shut up!" Karakurt pushed his unresisting accomplice up the narrow stairs. The key was still in the lock. With a sigh of relief, he turned it to unlock the door. At least someone still had some sense around here. He assumed it was the owner of the small *Taverna*. What was her name? Cassandra. He glanced at the tall man next to him and wondered if he had something going on there. Best give the woman and her nosy uncle something to bring them over to his side.

They found Naunet back in the small workshop. Her hands were covered with black gunk and the room reeked of turpentine and gasoline.

"What is this?" Karakurt asked without preamble and pointed to a glass jar. Its contents looked like fine white sand, or sugar.

"Salt," Naunet said. "It was the combination of the gasoline, the motor oil, and the seawater dripping on the tablet that softened the pitch."

"Well, fancy that," Edward said, trying to regain some semblance of control over the situation. "And you and your fine scientist-friends could not discover this sooner?"

Naunet simply shrugged. Ignoring both men, she wiped her hands on a rag and bent over the tablet again.

The sharp slap on her neck stunned her. It hurt enough for her eyes to fill with tears.

"Stop that!" Edward slapped the Turk on the arm with a weak wrist. His intervention surprised the other two, but with different reactions. Naunet let her tears roll down her cheeks. At first, rage filled her. Then came the fear again. The trembling in her knees returned, and she felt the vein in her neck pulse so hard against her skin that it made her light-headed.

Karakurt had turned deadly white. He slowly turned to face Edward and was about to pounce on the impertinent Brit when

Naunet, forcing herself to appear much calmer than she was, said quietly, "Would you like to hear what I could decipher so far?" Both men turned toward her, their quarrel forgotten, greed quickly replacing anger.

Edward sniffed, "I can't stand the smell in here. Tell us out there." For once, the Turk did not contradict him and the three stepped into the bedroom. When Karakurt did not see a piece of paper in Naunet's hand, he brusquely asked, "Don't you have it written out?"

She had to think fast. No way was she going to reveal the notes she had just made in the logbook.

"I memorized it."

And she had. Except that she would tell them the saying from the first tablet she assumed Karakurt still had on the sailboat, unless these guys had sold it off for cash. She had long suspected that this was precisely what Karakurt had done in Cairo with the missing corner.

In addition, she was sure that he had used the Jenkins's stolen credit cards wherever he could. And he seemed to have plenty of American dollars to throw around, undoubtedly from poor Harry's wallet. Edward, on the other hand, appeared to be out of funds unless he still had a stash on the *Tumbleweed*.

"What I think," she began, "is that these tablets tell the story of a people who lived in the very distant past, when the Sahara was green and fertile. Then they apparently migrated east, to the Nile. All this happened long before the Egyptians came along. If I had the missing corner from the first tablet," she shot Karakurt the withering look of a disgruntled archaeologist, "I believe it would have told us where they came from originally." Again, she looked pointedly at Karakurt.

He glared back. "Well, you don't have it. So get on with it. What else does it say?"

"It says, 'These mats tell our story. But those who come after us must take great heed'."

"That's it?"

"That's all I have so far. It's difficult without my software. I need more time."

"You don't have more time. I need a translation by tomorrow morning. If you can't do it, make something up. Something good and scary, like an awful curse about the end of the world." Karakurt sneered. "Yes! That's it. Like the one the Mayas have," he nodded, hoping that Lorenzo's fascination with ancient riddles, curses and predictions would override his mistrust. "And you have to certify, as an archaeologist, that this tablet and your translation are the real deal."

"But you warned me not to make anything up, remember? And what about the other tablet? I assume you still have it?"

Karakurt did not deign to answer.

"Yes, why by tomorrow," Edward wanted to know. Karakurt was up to something. Some plan he had not shared. Were they not partners in this thing? Perhaps the sly Turk had enlisted Odysseus' help to take the tablets out of Loutro before the South American arrived. There was no way he could sail or even motor the *Tumbleweed* anywhere. That boat had had it. He would need help. The public ferry was too obvious. Besides, he hadn't seen one yet.

"Why do you need something scary tomorrow?" he asked again.

"Yes, why something scary?" Naunet asked as well. "I didn't think you'd be superstitious."

With fumes drifting slowly through from the workshop, her room had become stifling as well. Karakurt opened the door to the veranda and stepped outside for a breath of fresh air.

He saw the blunt bow as soon as it nosed around an outcropping of foaming rock. It was quickly followed by two round portholes. Then a huge elongated salon window glinted in the sun. To Karakurt, it always looked like an evil eye. The *M/Y Bucanero* had arrived.

"You stay here." Karakurt stabbed his finger into Edward's chest. "Don't you let her out of your sight. You understand!" He slammed the door so hard on his way out that it cracked back open. In his haste to rush down to the quay, he forgot to lock it.

"We need to get out of here. Now!"

"Excuse me?"

"You and I—the two of us. We have to stick together."

Naunet could not believe her ears. *This guy is like a chameleon. He changes his color to whatever shade suits him.* If she played along, she wondered what he would do with her as soon as he thought himself safe. She was not sure she wanted to find out.

"What about Karakurt? Aren't you in on this with him?"

"Are you kidding? He'll rid himself of both of us the first chance he gets." Edward leaned on the door jam of the French doors. "I wonder what made him run off like that?" He glanced out beyond the harbor.

"There's your answer."

Naunet too stepped out to the veranda. She shaded her eyes against the sun. It seemed hotter, more glaring, than it had been the day before. A yellowish band laced the horizon but her mind did not register it as something threatening. Beyond the harbor, whitecaps danced and swirled. The *Tumbleweed* strained at her tether.

Naunet looked further out where a rather substantial yacht had its bow trained on the little mound in the middle. She could just make out the big globe on top of its multiple-story cabin roof. Satellite navigation system! She straightened up as if a bee had just had its way with her. If they came in here to tie up, surely they would come ashore to explore the little village. That's what bored yacht people did, didn't they.

"Do you think they'll help us?" she said, already thinking of a way to get a secret message to the people on board.

"No, you stupid woman! That's Karkurt's buddy. More likely, they'll dump us at sea. Listen to me, Naunet." Edward's voice became urgent. He stepped closer to her and held her by her arms. His grip was firm enough to hurt.

Naunet bent backward to escape his stale breath. It took all of her strength not to spit him in the face. If he had not held her arms down, she surely would have slapped him.

"We've got the one slate. There is a footpath leading over the cliff to another village. I think it's called Sfakia. Sounds almost obscene, doesn't it." He grinned, his mind veering off for a brief moment. "It is not too far. Maybe an hour. Cassandra told me."

"Ah, yes. How goes it with the fair Cassandra?"

"My lady jests," he chuckled with a slight bow. "I am afraid that particular fair lady has withdrawn her favors from your humble servant."

Did he really think that his affected quasi-Shakespearean jest was going to win her over? *What a buffoon. Oh, God. And I am falling right into it.*

"So, you are going to run along some dusty trail for an hour or more, carrying a forty-pound slab of gold under your arm? Is that your plan?"

There was no response. Apparently his gray matter needed time to digest her remark.

"Edward?" His name felt slimy on her tongue. She could not help that the corners of her mouth turned down.

If he had noticed, he ignored it. "Perhaps there is a bicycle in the village. I guess a motorbike would be hoping for too much. I noticed that there are no cars here. We could strap the tablet onto a bike and push it. You get ready while I see what I can find. Luckily, I still have our passports."

"*Our* passports? You mean the ones you took from them." She could not bring herself to speak their names.

"Don't be pedantic. You can use your own, if you still have it." With that, he let her go and was almost at the door when he turned back. "No need to lock you in. Karakurt left Odysseus in charge downstairs. By the way, what do you have that I can give the old man to keep him quiet?"

"Try a golden tablet." Naunet surprised herself by her sarcastic reply. She stared at the impertinent man smirking at her as if he did not have a care in the world. It was hopeless to rile against someone with such a non-aggressive style. She almost had to marvel. *He is also like an octopus. You can never quite get a good hold of it. However it gets trapped, it always manages to escape.* The octopus's only obstacle was its large eye. Edward's 'eye,' might well be his carelessness. He was neither smart enough, nor greedy enough, and neither young enough anymore, to survive like this forever. Easy living and easy getting seemed to be the mantra of his existence.

Edward patted the breast pocket of the grubby white linen jacket he wore. Satisfied that whatever he had in it was still there, he grinned. "I'll go and talk to the old man. Meantime, you better write something down for Karakurt. You never know. That fat-cat friend might get impatient and come ashore before we can get out of here."

Edward attempted a smart turn-about though it backfired wearing a dead husband's dusty sandals, way too small for his large feet. His toes hung over by at least an inch.

Naunet doubted he would last long scrambling over a rough path, carrying forty pounds on his back.

Undaunted by his temporary wardrobe setback, there was no doubt in Edward Guernsey-Crock's mind that he could talk his way past a simple fisherman from Loutro. He was not only getting out of there; he was getting out with a fortune. And, he reminded himself, alas also a useless woman. Well, he would take care of her as soon as she had carried the tablet far enough.

* * *

Chapter Twenty-Four

Karakurt rushed down the stairs and pushed Odysseus aside so hard that the old man standing watch almost fell over backward. At the quay the Turk jumped into his dinghy, nearly swamping the bouncing *Thistle*. He rowed as fast as he could. But with the incoming tide and a mounting swell driven by the freshening breeze the going was tough. He was still inside the harbor when the wind carried the clatter of heavy chains toward him. Outside the natural harbor barrier, the mega-yacht paid out the massive rode of her bow anchors.

Damn. I'll never make it out there. He decided instead to wait for Lorenzo on the *Tumbleweed* hoping that the South American would realize that the dismasted hulk in the lee of the small island was the one Karakurt had described to him during their terse conversation on the Iridium, before his client had brusquely cut him off.

He did not have to wait long. As soon as the mega-yacht had set her anchors and tested her rock-strewn deep-water holding ground, a Chris Craft launch was lowered from the stern davits. Karakurt had found some intact binoculars and watched as two of Lorenzo's crew assisted their boss as he stepped gingerly from his yacht's comfortable boarding ladder into the bobbing launch. Revving up the overkill twin outboards, they cut through the heavy chop and soon entered the calmer waters of the harbor, kicking up a wake powerful enough to slam the well-secured fishing boats against their harbor docks.

Karakurt threaded his way through the tangle of *Tumbleweed's* downed wires and clambered onto the cabin roof. His frantic waving resembled that of a man spying his first vessel after being shipwrecked. The launch immediately swerved toward him. Bumpers were dropped over the side and, within a couple of minutes, the immaculate launch thumped gently against the sailboat's scratched-up hull.

Since the lifelines were gone and the stanchions promised only a tenuous hold, Karakurt was careful not to lean over too far. No need for him to endanger himself, he realized. The two deckhands had things well under control, steadying the launch against his hull. Before he could open his mouth to utter a greeting, Lorenzo had nimbly hauled himself up onto the *Tumbleweed*.

The South American grabbed onto the downed mast hanging a good ten feet out over the stern, and stepped into the cockpit. Splash! He looked down. To his dismay his fine shoes were soaked with pinkish water.

"Why in the hell don't you pull the scupper plugs and let this mess drain out," was the first thing that came out of Lorenzo's mouth.

The harsh rebuke not only deflated the anxious Turk but it immediately put him at a disadvantage. A sideways glance at the two burly characters in the launch confirmed that they would be watching his every move. A sudden knot in Karakurt's stomach told him to tread very carefully. If Lorenzo was in a bad mood, things could turn dicey in a flash. The fickle billionaire could simply take the remaining tablet off the boat by force and leave him stranded. Or he could take him and the tablet to his yacht, pull up anchor, and later throw him to the sharks.

The only leverage Karakurt had was the tablet in the village. He hoped the woman was finished with it, or at least had written up a suitable translation to entice his client into forking over a commensurate amount of cash. Of course, he would have preferred to keep both slates for himself. He would have them melted down into gobs of profitable gold. To hell with ancient curses; he was not the superstitious kind.

"Senior Dominguez." Karakurt stretched out his hand, but it was ignored. He awkwardly wiped his sweaty palms on his pants. Then he hooked his thumbs into his pockets and adjusted his stance for better self-assurance.

"It is good to see you. Sorry about Cyprus. Considering we almost sank, I am glad I can still offer you something rare and unknown to the art world." He hoped the South American's bodyguards were out of hearing range.

"I have it down below." As Karakurt motioned for Lorenzo to duck through the hatch, he glanced back and caught one of the goons tapping his mid-section. The gesture did nothing to sooth his nerves.

The cabin was unbearably hot and stank of rotting offal. For a second, Lorenzo was slammed back onto the reeking hillside of his childhood. It did not improve his mood. He sullenly waded through the sodden debris that littered the warped cabin sole. When he almost stepped into a hole he let out a guttural curse. He could see oily water sloshing around in the bilge, and there was a distasteful smell of sewage. Dirty boats disgusted him. It was unreasonable perhaps but he blamed the Turk for exposing him to such offending chaos.

They reached the forepeak where Karakurt forced the hatch open wider for more air. Then he sprawled on top of the gasoline-soaked triangular bunk mattress and yanked at the tiny swollen access door that led into the chain locker. Lorenzo saw that it held a fair amount of chain nestled atop a coil of rope.

"What!" It sounded like a pistol shot. Because of Karakurt's crouching position, the sharp retort bounced harmlessly off his wriggling bottom as he strained to pull his tablet off the chain and through the small opening.

"What!" Lorenzo shot at the Turk's stringy backside again. He hated small spaces, and smelly ones in particular. Despite the open hatch and his men outside, he felt trapped. It was unreasonable, he knew, and only the anticipation of the promised loot kept him where he was.

"This." Karakurt said. He shoved the heavy tablet across the bunk.

Lorenzo stared at the black slate. He could barely see the gleam from the few exposed inches of the corner break. "Is this a joke?" He glared at the Turk. Perhaps he should strangle the scoundrel right now and be done with it.

"Lorenzo, listen to me. Underneath all this, there is pure gold.

And ancient curses and omens are written on both sides." Given that the South American did not reprimand him for his informal address, Karakurt decided to stick to the first-name basis, hoping it would lessen the irritated man's suspicions.

"How do you know that, Turk?"

It occurred to Karakurt that this was a gamble for his life. There was nothing left but to admit that he had a second tablet. He just hoped that the woman had concocted a believable story in the meantime. If she really did need more time, he just thought of a way to provide it.

"Why don't we transfer this slab to the *Bucanero*. It will be much safer there. Then I'll take you to the other one in the village."

"To the other one? Are you telling me that two is all you have! What about the twenty or thirty you promised me?"

Karakurt did a mental quickstep. He might as well paint the moon since he had no intention of sticking around this snake pit for any longer than he had to.

"They were buried during a tunnel collapse in Upper Egypt. The dig is closed now. Only I know where they are," Karakurt babbled. He'd say anything to save his hide. "I'll go back there and get them for you."

"You know damn well that you can't go back." The Turk's nerve amused Lorenzo, though not enough to let him get away with such trickery. First, he had to get to the second slate, if it indeed existed. Then he would deal with Karakurt's frantic lies.

"Let's go then. I don't have all day. The weather is supposed to turn."

Karakurt wrapped the tablet in a blanket that had escaped the dripping gasoline. A bungee cord dangled from a hook. With it, he could secure the precious package. It took some effort for him to haul the forty-pound tablet back through the ruined salon toward the main hatch. He realized that he had not yet regained all of his strength. True enough, he could not make it up the few steps while holding onto the tablet with both hands. Unlike most women, it is not natural for a man to use his posterior to shimmy himself up through a chimney-like space. He ruefully thought about the dead woman's backpack. After grabbing the two passports, he had discarded it carelessly on the side of the road together with the bodies. At the time, it had seemed a good decision in case of a roadblock between Hurghada and Safaga. It would have come in handy now.

Lorenzo saw the other man's struggle and with a disgusted grunt took the tablet from Karakurt who then clambered up the steps and waited for Lorenzo to hand the tablet out to him.

Both men had to crouch low to avoid running into the felled mast, with the boom mashed underneath the massive spar. Fused together by the crash, they looked like the formidable battering ram on an ancient warship. Except that this contraption extended out over the damaged stern.

It took a while even for the launch to make its way back to the mega-yacht. As powerful as the two outboards were, their progress was slow because of the relentless rollers slamming into them from the open sea.

Looking back, Karakurt noticed that the stricken sailboat bucked and sea-sawed wildly around its anchor rode. He was sorry now that he had not let out more chain as Odysseus had told him to do. The more length was played out, the better the Danforth's flukes could bite into a sandy bottom. If he were anchored in mud, however, that could be a problem unless he'd used a Bruce.

Once he got back, Karakurt would check if those people even had such an anchor stashed somewhere. He would also retrieve the Jenkins's travelers checks hidden in a cubbyhole. It was stupid of him not to have taken the substantial blue packet before Lorenzo had come on board. Instinctively, he patted his back pocket. Good. At least he still had their wallet with the nice green dollars.

After they negotiated the boarding ladder together with the tablet, and the crew had winched the launch back up where it dangled safely from the davits, helping hands reached for the bundled-up slate. But Lorenzo told Karakurt to hang on to it and follow him. Then he called up to his captain who had watched the boarding. "This weather is not getting any better, Max. If there is a storm, I'd rather ride it out at sea."

Karakurt had never been on the *M/Y Bucanero*. Their clandestine dealings in Alexandria were always carried out in a hotel suite close to the marina. He lurched after Lorenzo who led the way into a large salon. Karakurt could fairly smell exotic oils oozing from the paneling. His eyes widened at the sumptuous furnishings; even more so when he spied three caftan-clad girls pouting decoratively in overstuffed white chairs. Suddenly, he felt bone-tired. He would have liked to sink into the deep leather with at least one of the girls. To his dismay, Lorenzo told them to go to their cabin and wait for him there. Their undulating exit made Karakurt aware of his own sorry state. He wanted to be clean again. And rich. And have three beautiful girls at his beck and call.

When he stumbled and almost fell, he was brought up sharply from his reverie. Startled, he looked down. His foot was caught in the gaping mouth of a panther, the sharp incisors barely missing his instep. Bad luck, he shuddered and tiptoed around the glistening black pelt. He had to hasten to catch up with Lorenzo who stepped into another cabin. Karakurt looked around in awe. Perhaps a study or Lorenzo's private office, he thought. The quiet sumptuousness of it was almost overwhelming. Only once had he seen such luxury, and that was when he had been called to Jabari El-Masri's inner sanctum at the Ministry in Cairo. His arms were getting numb from carrying the heavy slab and he looked around for a place to lay it down.

Lorenzo pointed to a tufted maroon leather couch. When Karakurt straightened up, he was eye-level with the little picture he had sold to Lorenzo a couple of years ago.

"You got a new frame," he said. "It looks good." When he saw the obvious pride on Lorenzo's face as the rich man gazed at his small van Gogh, Karakurt knew he had been a fool. By Allah, he should have asked more for his trouble to cut those silly flowers out of their original frame. Yes, much more; even though it had been an easy steal.

"Well, Karakurt," Lorenzo sighed. "You did not bring all the tablets you promised me. That is disappointing. But I must consider the ordeal you have endured. Sadly, it seems that I must now be content with only two."

It was the first time that Karakurt saw hope that things might still turn out all right. When he heard Lorenzo add an icy 'for now,' he knew that his ordeal was far from being over. He wished that the woman had hurried up with her translation. She should, if she knew what was good for her. If not? Well, now that he knew how to remove the stubborn pitch, he might just do so himself. Besides, there were other scientists out there anxious to be of assistance—for the right amount of Lorenzo's money.

The more he thought about it, he felt this might be the better way to go. Considering how much the woman knew, and how uncooperative she had been so far. For now, he needed to get back into Lorenzo's good graces. In his mind, the pesky Brit had already become expendable. He would talk to Odysseus. The fisherman knew the island well. Karakurt remembered that the old gnome had babbled something about cliffs and gorges while he was cutting some of the downed wires from the sailboat's twisted hardware.

Lorenzo stepped into his line of sight. "Ask one of my crew to help you change that bloody rag on your head. You look like a pirate," he grinned. He was holding up two crystal tumblers. "Here's to celebrate what we have so far."

Karakurt gratefully eyed the honey-colored liquid. It went down as smooth as oil, warming his insides. He eagerly accepted a refill and relaxed his fear-clenched sphincter.

Once again, Lorenzo lifted his glass. "And here's to what was promised me."

Lorenzo stepped closer to his couch. That's when he noticed the missing corner. He turned slowly back to Karakurt and then simply pointed at the tablet, his eyebrows raised.

"It came that way," Karakurt stuttered. "But all the others are complete."

"I thought you only had one other," Lorenzo said slowly and slithered closer to the Turk. "Or did I not hear correctly?"

Now there was a double-edged sword if Karakurt ever heard of one.

"Yes, here in Loutro. I only have the two. But I swear, Lorenzo, I know where the others are. And I can get them for you."

"Make sure you do, my friend. Make sure you do."

The silence in the small cabin deepened and this time around, Karakurt sipped the expensive Cognac much slower. He felt dizzy. Surely, he held his liquor better than that. His eyes narrowed into suspicious slits. Both drinks had been poured from the same decanter. Faint nausea swept over Karakurt. He began to sweat.

"Let's go on deck," he heard Lorenzo say. "It's getting rough. And you look like you could use some air." At the press of a button, an impeccably dressed steward slid in on quiet soles and began to secure the liquor cabinet.

Out on deck, they saw nothing but whitecaps. All around them, the sea was whipped into frenzy by the stiffening breeze. The *Bucanero* danced around her anchors, with her bow straining to point into the changing gusts. Overhead, low clouds scudded across a yellowish sky, and screeching gulls fled toward the cliffs that rose steeply above the village.

Cold spray made the two shiver and Lorenzo took Karakurt into the steering station. If one could call it that. It looked more like the glass-walled cockpit of a spaceship. Despite his experience with larger yachts, Karakurt was amazed at the display. Every imaginable—and to him hitherto unimaginable—piece of modern navigation blinked, beeped and squiggled from an array of large monitors. There was no wrestling with a contrary wheel in here. The temperature was a perfectly dry seventy-two degrees. Within the comfortable space, the worsening howl of the wind outside was reduced to a faint whistle. This captain's command post was a peaceful and deceptively safe oasis.

While Lorenzo conferred urgently with his intent skipper, Karakurt looked out to the forward deck below him. His nose began to twitch. He sensed trouble.

Two deckhands lay flat on their bellies on the forward deck. One leaned out over the port side, the other hung over the starboard gunnels. They shouted something into the chain pipes directly below them and Karakurt knew there had to be others in the large chain lockers. One look at the captain confirmed to a knowledgeable observer what every sailor dreaded: fouled anchors. Judging from the way the captain flipped the same switch and pressed the same button over and over again, they must have fried the electric windlasses with their repeated attempts to yank the massive anchors loose.

To raise a fouled anchor by hand was a difficult task even on a small boat. On this monster yacht, with the wind driving it backward, causing the flukes to dig in even deeper, it would be impossible. The way the chains fed out directly from their large lockers below-decks, the crew would have to haul the heavy anchors in manually cranking a large winch handle, a Herculean task.

Karakurt watched as the two guys got up on their knees and

shrugged up to the captain who then engaged the bow-thrusters, alternately applying power. This shook the yacht from side to side like a buffalo trying to rid itself of pesky flies. It had about the same effect. Then he drove the yacht slowly over the anchors hoping to loosen the fouled flukes in a last-ditch effort.

Wedged into a rocky crevasse, Karakurt guessed. *Serves this fat-cat right.* No longer nauseated and pleasantly tipsy, he enjoyed the little drama. Until he realized that he himself was stuck on the *Bucanero*. Well, if things got really, really bad, they all could take the launch to shore. He counted off the crewmembers on his fingers. So far, he had seen six. Adding Lorenzo and the captain made eight, with him, nine. There should be just enough room for them on the Chris Craft. *Oh, I forgot about the girls.* Never mind. Women didn't count with him. Not in an emergency. He figured that they would not with Lorenzo either.

The swells increased to a good six feet and as the chains alternately slackened and went taught, they threatened to chafe right through the metal lining of the chain pipes. Things became uncomfortable even in the steering station.

Lorenzo lost his cool. "Bolt cutters!" he shouted. "Somebody get some bolt cutters!"

The captain began to sweat. One of the crew rushed from the bridge ostensibly to find those cutters, but more so to escape his skipper's wrath as he knew full well that the simple tool was nowhere to be found on this sophisticated yacht.

"Give it another try, Max," Lorenzo urged. "If we can't get free, we'll have to cut those chains." Intent on their problem, they forgot about the Turk.

Karakurt tried to melt into the background. *Allah save me. If this goes badly, Lorenzo will surely blame me for his bad luck.* He glanced longingly toward the harbor where the water was still relatively calm.

Suddenly, out of the corner of his eye, he caught a glimpse of something moving. There it was again. It came up on a wave from behind the mound in the middle of the small bay. He recognized the small *Thistle*. Had the dinghy broken free? He squinted harder and saw that the rubber dinghy was jammed up against the white hull of the sailboat, straining at its thin painter. The boats seemed to drift backward. *Impossible!* If the sailboat was dragging anchor it could not move that fast. Then, as the two boats cleared the protective lee of the small island, they gathered speed. *It's that damn current*, Karakurt realized with a jolt.

He saw the sailboat's anchor chain paying out fast. Within thirty seconds, its metal glint was gone. The one-hundred and fifty feet of chain had changed to rope. Then there was nothing as the anchor rode's bitter end slipped into the waves. A wave swamped the light rubber dinghy. Its painter snapped. The sailboat was free.

The wind howled into the bay. The upwelling current rushed out. *Tumbleweed* was caught within opposing forces. She began to spin. And like a child's top, she whirled toward the *Bucanero*. Karakurt's mouth went dry.

"She's going to hit," he croaked at last.

Lorenzo and Captain Max spun around. Following the Turk's pointing finger, they stared in utter disbelief at the dilapidated dervish bearing down on them. The now profusely sweating captain yanked a mike from his console and flipped a switch. His orders blared over the entire yacht.

"Gaffs and poles to starboard. I want those chains cut now!"

Four deckhands stood bunched together on the forward deck. They looked up, confused. They shrugged up to the bridge not yet having noticed the new threat. Lorenzo and his captain pointed frantically toward the whirling sailboat. When the men below them finally realized what the problem was, they rushed about to find long poles and grabbed handy fishing gaffs. Then they all lurched to the starboard side. Against all odds, everyone on board now hoped that the two deckhands still wrestling with the manual windlass handles in the chain lockers had found a pair of bolt cutters.

Lorenzo snarled at Karakurt. "Get that piece of shit of yours out of here!"

Was he to swim? Karakurt stumbled out on deck and grabbed at a passing crewmember to ask him for help with the launch. But the wind ripped the words right out of his mouth. The last thing he saw of the frantic man was a drawn gun as he scrambled down a narrow gangway.

As a drug smuggler, Lorenzo's newest hire—a young hothead— had more than once successfully shot the bolts off warehouse locks. Surely, his aim was still good enough to split the links of an anchor chain. He crawled into the port locker and told his desperate buddy to stand aside. It turned out to be a bad idea. The bullet ricocheted and hit him in the head. His buddy dragged the unfortunate man on deck and pushed the body overboard.

The impromptu burial-at-sea had taken the captain's eyes off the careening *Tumbleweed* for a moment too long. With a resounding thud, the overhanging contraption of the fused boom and mast impaled itself into a weak spot in the *Bucanero's* starboard hull, just above the waterline. The mega-yacht shuddered and shook as the crew jabbed at the low-riding sailboat from their ineffective angle above. The *Tumbleweed* remained nailed to the *M/S Bucanero* like the thief *Barabbas* to his cross.

Karakurt, stunned by the impact, and even more so by the repercussions for him, rushed back from the deck and almost collided with the South American who stormed about in a mad rush. Not knowing what to do next, Karakurt followed him into the salon. Nothing seemed out of place. Only when they came to the lower level and entered the owner's bedroom suite, did they notice a trickle of water that stained the white carpet. Lorenzo ripped open the door to his en-suite bathroom.

The chaos that confronted him at first seemed like an ironic optical illusion. Floating in mid-air was a painting of a storm at sea. It brought the grown man to his knees. Pierced to the core of his collector's soul, Lorenzo keened and wept.

Only when Karakurt looked closer did he realize that a canvas had been ripped from its frame and now hung obscenely skewered on the frayed mast-end from the *Tumbleweed*. He knew then that he had run out of luck. Furtive like the thief he was, he backed away from the distraught man and rushed up to the main deck from where he groped his way back into the study.

"Ah," he breathed. It was still there, his for the taking. With the heavy slab tucked under his arm, he fled to the stern where the wind ripped at him from all sides. Luckily, the crew was still busy on the starboard side trying to extricate the *Bucanero* from her would-be murderess.

As Karakurt was actually more familiar with large yachts than small sailboats, he pretty much knew where the power toggles for the electric davits would be located. Besides, the *Bucanero* was simply a larger version of Lorenzo's previous boat. Just as was his habit with his women, the billionaire did the same with his yachts. He replaced each one similar in type. They were simply newer, faster and ostentatiously more expensive.

With some effort not to drop the heavy slab, Karakurt flipped the power-on toggle and pressed the down-button on the sturdy frame. In order for the launch to clear the yacht's massive stern, the davits arched way out. His mistake was to lower the Chris Craft completely until it splashed into the water twelve feet below. With no time to swing the boarding ladder out, he would have to jump. A risky maneuver at best, but with forty pounds under his arm, he would hit the launch's deck like a stone, if at all. Karakurt heaved the tablet as far out as he could. It glanced off the closest outboard motor precisely at the right angle for most of the brittle unguent to splinter off before the golden tablet thudded onto the floorboards of the launch.

The greedy man was so mesmerized by the glint of gold that he did not jump after his prize at once. Behind him, footsteps thudded closer. With not another second to spare, Karakurt snapped from his avaricious trance and released the bobbing launch from its restraining shackles. Frantic to save himself and his treasure, he clambered onto the yacht's stern rail and took a deep breath. He jumped, windmilling his arms to breach the widening gap between the two vessels. Against all odds, he smashed onto the launch's deck. The fall broke both his ankles.

Karakurt clenched his teeth against the searing pain and managed to crawl back to the steering console. With fluttering hands, he flipped the two big outboards into position and pressed the starters. Only one of the motors rumbled to life. A lick of gasoline trickled from the dented housing of the other, exactly where the slab had hit it.

Despite his mounting nausea and dizziness, Karakurt could not stop himself. He looked up at the yacht and grinned at the *Bucanero's* looming stern from where a frantic Lorenzo screamed Spanish obscenities down at him.

"Up yours too," he shouted back in Turkish when he saw the man raise his arm as if to waive farewell to him.

With the yacht's anchors wedged into the rocks a hundred feet below her and no spare run-about, these dumb-asses had no means of pursuing him. Karakurt tested the lopsided pull of the starboard screw and turned the wheel hard to head east. He counted on hiding out in one of the deep gorges that spilled into the sea along the rugged coast. What he had not counted on was to be shot.

Despite being mortally wounded by the eccentric South American, revenge and avarice boiled up in him. With just enough strength left, the dying man pushed the throttle to full speed ahead. Red fog wafted before his eyes, and he slumped to the right, his cramped hand pulling the small wheel with him.

The launch bucked and turned sharply, drawing ever-narrowing circles around the *Bucanero*.

Pandemonium erupted on the high decks. Lorenzo screamed and emptied his gun at the circling launch. Extremely frustrated, he grabbed the nearest deep-sea fishing pole off its clamps. Realizing that it was of no use, he cursed and threw it overboard. Helpless to do anything to stop his run-away Chris Craft, he raced around the outside decks to keep the spiraling launch in sight.

A faint "Hurray" from the bow topped the howling wind. Lorenzo dashed forward and watched the port anchor chain disappear back into its chain pipe, link by link. The going was painfully slow. He hoped that the other deckhands were successful in hauling in the starboard chain as well.

Lorenzo rejoiced. His yacht was wounded, but she would be free. Then he remembered the sailboat.

Freed from the rocks, yet still shackled by the massive weight of her dangling anchors pulling at her from a hundred feet below, as well as the albatross impaled amidships, Captain Max tried in vain to drive the yacht out of the danger from her own errant launch.

During its tightest circle yet, the Chris Craft missed the *Bucanero*. Instead, it broadsided the *Tumbleweed*. The impact split the launch's damaged engine housing open.

The outboard's gasoline ignited. Within the blink of an eye, the flames spread to the sailboat and then leapt across to the mega-yacht's hull where the extreme heat shattered the fixed windowpanes.

Melted fiberglass dripped inside the large vessel, and smoldering burns erupted into fire all over her white decks.

The villagers had gathered along the quay at the first sign of trouble. When black smoke erupted from the stricken vessels, they knew that all would be lost by the time anyone could make it to the outer harbor. Usually quick to help another seafarer in distress, no one moved this time. With their boats well secured against the brewing storm they stood silent, curious what would happen next. They did not have to wait long. The multiple explosions were spectacular.

Suddenly, high above the black smoke, a yellow ray streaked across the burning vessels, held aloft for a few seconds by the terrific blast of a Propane tank.

Moments later, the sea welcomed its golden token from the Ancients who had fled these very shores millennia ago.

* * *

Chapter Twenty-Five

Despite her training, Naunet could not shake off the ominous predictions of the fiftieth tablet. The high priest's warning to let the golden tablets lie in peace or endure great upheaval, did nothing to ease her bewildered state of mind. She felt inexorably drawn back into the story of that unknown civilization as they apparently witnessed a great cataclysm that drove them from their homeland. Judging how their story began, it might have been a devastating earthquake or a horrendous volcanic eruption. There was also a sentence that led her to believe that those catastrophes could have been followed by a tidal wave.

Naunet had the feeling that these ancient words had come back to warn her; and this world of hers, as it was now: Full of petty avarice, unrelenting crime, as well as corporate and political greed. This wondrous earth, filled with natural abundance and man's technical innovations.

Had she been chosen to save this planet's diverse populace, so unlikely to heed an ancient warning?

Naunet shook the uncomfortable forbearing from her mind. She wished she had been able to go through all the tablets from the very start. From what little she had gleaned, she felt that the squares were a kind of code, an etched history of an ancient unknown people. She also now firmly believed that this First Dynasty high priest, this Ramose, had somehow been able to decipher this code; and it was his hieratic translation, together with the original squares, which had been stamped onto the tablets. That would explain the numbering.

And like an artist's signature, he had his scribes or artisans imprint his seal: The Winged Scarab.

Her head pounded from the combination of not having eaten anything all day, and from worrying about her own fate. But mostly, she suspected, from the fumes fouling the small room. To ponder about the fate of the world—with the abundant superstitions about the world's supposed end—was all too much for her right now. Still, way in the back of her mind, something warned her not to dismiss the warning of the golden tablets entirely.

Naunet went out onto the terrace to relieve the pain and her mounting stress. She gulped in fresh air until she became dizzy from it. To distract herself, she paced along the waist-high perimeter of the balcony. When she came to the end of the house she realized that she had been mistaken before.

Perhaps it was an optical illusion which had made her assume that the veranda ended at the villa's corner. Instead, it wrapped around to the entire outer wall. The strip was narrow around the corner, about two feet. She squeezed herself along the wall. Astonishingly, the house had been built right into the cliff where its earthen outcropping sloped toward the roughly cobbled street. Naunet leaned over the wall. One needed only to climb up on it and jump. No! It was too steep to scramble down the embankment. She was likely to slip and tumble all the way to the bottom, ending up badly scraped or injured. A groove had been smoothed out and ran down the packed soil like a slide. Most likely, nimble children had carved it, likely with an improvised sled. *It could work*, she thought.

Excited at the thought of escaping, she turned back inside to find something she could use. Perhaps a flat sofa cushion would do. Or the seat of a chair though she would have to watch her fingers as she clutched the rim. Bending over one of the side chairs, she tried to pry the seat loose. A shadow moved over her from behind.

Naunet nearly jumped out of her skin. "Cassandra!"

"Your friend is gone," the woman said as placidly as if she were discussing the ferry schedule.

"Cassandra," Naunet tried to sound normal. "I don't know who you mean. What friend?"

"See for yourself." Cassandra pulled Naunet out to the terrace where she pointed to the east.

A ways past the village, a narrow path wound steeply up the cliff where, eventually, it would join the road to Sfakia. Naunet noticed someone lurching up the steep trail. Dust devils swirled around the distant figure and at first she could not make out if the person was coming or going, or if it was a man or a woman. Then, with a jolt, she saw that it was Edward. Once her eyes had adjusted to the storm-darkening sky, there was no mistaking his height. It looked as if he was jumping from foot to foot. It puzzled her until she remembered his sorry footwear.

So, he had decided to split. But why? Could the jilted Cassandra have had a word with her uncle Odysseus? The two could have set the whole village against him, possibly for an imagined broken promise of betrothal. Nothing was beyond this trickster to save his own hide. What if he had run off with the first tablet she had assumed was still in Karakurt's possession on the sailboat? Was that why the Turk had run off in such haste? In that case, Karakurt would certainly be after him.

Naunet turned back to Cassandra. "You mean Edward simply walked out the door, past the busy terrace of your *Taverna*, along the quay, until he reached the path?"

"He took the alley, I am sure."

That was news to Naunet—and music to her ears. She tried to sound casual. "How can there be an alley. The houses are built right into the cliff."

Cassandra shook her head. "There is an alley from the next house over. It goes behind all the houses until it meets the path."

"But what about your house? I saw that it abuts the cliff."

"Abuts?" Cassandra looked confused.

"The back wall of your house is built into the cliff," Naunet explained impatiently.

"Oh," Cassandra brightened and then explained, "My backdoor goes out the side."

Naunet now desperately wanted to go back inside but Cassandra held on to her sleeve. The wind increased and tore at the two women, toying with their hair. When it ballooned Cassandra's voluminous skirts around her stocky legs, the woman finally stepped back inside.

Why did he leave? She could think of no other reason than that he had stolen the other Saqqara tablet off the sailboat. It was irrational, but as long as Edward had been around, she had hoped the men would let her go once she had finished her translation of both tablets. That happening, she chided herself now, was about as great a chance as she and Edward getting together. What was she thinking? They had never even been close to having been what one could call 'together.'

"Thieves is what you are," Cassandra spat out, suddenly no longer placid. Color rose in her cheeks and Naunet saw that her work-roughened hands were balled into fists.

"I am sorry if he stole..." Naunet almost said 'your heart,' but then finished with a safer "stole something from you."

"From me?" The jilted woman's laughter was derisive. "I do not allow anyone to steal from me. You! All of you! You are the thieves. That supposed glass plate of yours. Well, Odysseus saw another one just like it. And the way those people gawked at it he knew right away that it was made of gold. They dig up all sorts of things over there." Cassandra crossed her arms in front of her buxom chest with the satisfying smirk of someone who had just caught a liar.

"Over there? Where? What other people? Tell me!" Naunet shook the woman by her shoulders. She weighed probably half of the wholesome Cretan, but she was a head taller than Cassandra. It gave her the advantage of intimidation. If only she managed to stay calm. Her heart pounded a mile a minute and she started to get dizzy again. Could her father have been this close all this time?

Her ploy must have worked because the woman shrank slightly into herself, although her voice was still defiant. "The diggers. Over at Kommos."

Naunet hardly dared to breathe and was about to shake more information out of Cassandra when the sullen woman shook herself free.

"We telephoned the mayor in Sfakia half an hour ago. He'll send someone when the next ferry can run again. After this storm."

"What do you mean, you telephoned. Are you telling me you have a phone in this god-forsaken hamlet!"

"Of course, we do. We are not backward simpletons. Our tourists have to make reservations, no? We also have the Internet."

It was all too much. Naunet sank onto the bed and put her hands over her face. She needed to stay in control but the tears flowed through her fingers.

"You are my prisoner now!" Cassandra stomped out of the room.

When the key turned in the lock, Naunet knew that she would have to take matters into her own hands or perish ignobly on this isolated piece of real estate. Filled with the hope of a dangerous escape, yet emotionally utterly exhausted, she wept. When she had cried her fears, her doubts and the anger from her soul, she felt better.

Once again, her thoughts strayed to all the doomsday warnings that had swept the world of late. Most had been discredited, ridiculed, and dismissed. Though there were still those who clung morbidly to the belief that the Mayans just might be right.

As a scientist, she was insane to even think about all the nonsense people believed in. Many had completely changed their lives out of fear and were stockpiling beans and rice. Some—those who could afford it—had commissioned concrete cylinder homes in an undisclosed location somewhere in Spain, sunk deep into the earth. Bomb-proof. Radioactive-repellant. Impregnable by frantic hordes howling above for admittance to assured survival. And what about the emotional toll constant fear over some predicted cataclysm might wreak? Ironically, apart from wild suppositions, no one had come forth to say what form this supposed end of the world was to take.

After taking a few deep breaths, her reasoning returned and she went through her options in a scientist's objective way.

First, she went back into the workshop and picked up the *Tumbleweed's* logbook. She tore out the page on which she had concocted spells and omens to satisfy Karakurt's collector.

With a grim smirk on her lips, she read them again:

I heap these spells upon you:
A vengeful death if you have transgressed against Ma'at.
A barren marriage if you mistreated your mother,
And a stillborn son if you laid a hand on your wife's neck.
A casting out upon the river, naked, bound and cursed,
if you have stolen from the graves.
And never shall you find the Field of Rushes
if you have kicked Bastet.

The last sentence, she had thrown in for good measure. She liked cats and could not stand people who mistreated them. Of course, none of this nonsense was inscribed on the tablet. Who was to contradict her? As an illicit buyer, the South American might never have it verified. If he wanted to possess a few good spells to give him the willies, well, then she hoped she'd given them to him. *May he rot in hell*, she thought uncharitably. Satisfied with her made-up words, she placed the sheet of paper on her bed.

To walk off her nervousness, Naunet stepped out onto the terrace braving the freshening wind. The square below was empty now. All the picturesque blue shutters were closed up tight. Only the little boy's wagon stood below, abandoned by the child when his mother had called him to supper.

Suddenly, shouts raked over the empty square. Naunet crept further out. Below her, people ran toward the quay, calling for others to join them. The first spectators lined up on the seawall shading their eyes against the tearing wind. They watched as two boats drifted quickly toward each other.

By the broken mast, Naunet knew that one of them was the *Tumbleweed*. And the large yacht could well be Karakurt's illicit buyer.

When the two boats collided, a great hush fell over the crowd below.

Naunet squinted against the gritty wind just in time to see someone throw an object from the yacht into a tender. Then a man jumped after it. It had to be Karakurt. She could tell by the white bandage he still wore around his head. The object he had thrown off the yacht had to be the first Saqqara tablet. How could he possibly think he would get away with it? The yacht could simply run him down. Suddenly, she saw him slump to the bottom of the small boat; and she hoped that he was dead. For one vile man, this might have become the year of reckoning after all.

The villagers stood pressed against each other, mesmerized and silent now, their backsides turned toward her. No one moved, except for the little boy squeezing past the broad rumps to get to the front of the human wall.

This was her chance. Her hands shook as he rummaged through her carry-on. She pulled the sheath she had worn for the past few days over her head and threw it onto the bed. Then she stepped into her khakis. For a moment, she was surprised how loosely the lightweight pants hung on her. Had she lost that much weight? She shrugged and quickly finished dressing in more comfortable clothes and sneakers. On an impulse, she wrapped her chiffon scarf around her neck.

Then she remembered the log. She could not leave the book with her notes behind. Her passport! Her real one, this time. Frantic to be losing precious time, she rushed about and gathered what she could stuff into the large pockets of her cargo-pants.

The heavy tablet in her arms, she ran out to the terrace, rounded the corner and placed the tablet up on the wall, careful that it was well balanced. Then she clambered up and let herself slide down the other side, pulling the tablet after her. Carefully, she placed it pitch-side down into the grooved hillside and—just like the village children—sat down on it.

With the wind in her face, she careened down the precarious incline. If she had not been on a flight for her life, she would have enjoyed the rush toward the road. Luckily, her long legs made for good brakes and she landed safely. On tiptoes, she retrieved the boy's wagon and wrestled the tablet onto it. She crept toward the entryway hoping that Odysseus had abandoned his post as well to watch the spectacle beyond the harbor. But no matter how slowly she pulled the wagon behind her, the little wheels squealed and rumbled over the cobblestones.

The multiple explosions reverberated off the cliffs that towered above the houses. Naunet ducked into her doorway, went through a long hall and, pushing a backdoor open, found herself in the alley. She walked as fast as she could, pulling the rumbling little contraption behind her. Looking back over her shoulder, she made sure the tablet had not shifted. Even under the dull yellowish sky, it gleamed up at her. "Dumb," she mumbled and unwound the scarf from her neck. Hastily, she wrapped the thin material around her telltale hoard.

As the alley merged into the path she left the shielding row houses behind. The trail steepened. Because of the weight in the little wagon she had to slow down. How far along had Edward gone, she wondered, and hoped that his ill-fitting shoes had not forced him to stop. To catch up with him would not be good. As she followed the winding path along the cliff, she glanced down at the sea.

Suddenly, she noticed something detach itself from the burning hulks. It looked very small, and it was orange. A lifeboat! Now it turned toward the village. But Karakurt was dead. She had seen how he had slumped down. Shot, she had presumed. Who else then could this be? The South American! He would surely come after her! Or rather, the last of the golden tablets.

Had she been chosen to protect this world of hers from the ancient predictions? But how?

Naunet picked up her pace.

* * *

Chapter Twenty-Six

Jonathan had always believed that he was in reasonably good physical condition. Actually, he thought of himself as being in great shape. Sailing was hard work, and he had the stamina to show for it. It therefore surprised him that, within twenty minutes of his uphill sprint, he had to fight to catch his breath. *Pace yourself,* was always good advice. But with an over-anxious heart and his frantic desire to find Naunet, there could be no stopping now. He pressed on.

A short ways out of Sfakia, the path turned into more of a goat trail littered with scree. There was not room enough for two people to walk abreast. One of two passing each other would need to press against the high rock wall soaring toward the sky. On Jonathan's left, the trail snaked so closely along the cliff that anyone suffering from vertigo would surely be stricken by the affliction.

As if the sharp incline was not enough to slow him down, Jonathan had to fight against the rising wind. When he reached a level spot he could taste the salty air and, looking out over the sea, he noticed the yellow curtain building from the south. When the howling grew in his ears, and the turbulence lodged gritty sand between his teeth, he knew the Sirocco had arrived. With it, soon, all life on the island would struggle for survival.

The two men saw each other at the same instant. Both froze. Then Edward turned and, as quickly as he could in the ill-fitting shoes of a deceased husband, lurched headlong back on the uneven path he had just climbed, his strides lengthened by the instinctive fear that he might not survive this day.

Jonathan was a moment slower to realize what had just happened. He simply did not have the instinct of a predator. But he was younger, leaner; and he had someone to stay alive for. A ways further down, as the path widened again, he caught up with the panting man he had just barely recognized. He grabbed Edward by the scruff of his neck and at the same time delivered a hard punch into the small of his back.

On this barren cliff, Jonathan no longer needed to wish to have been born into the street fights of North Boston. He was there. The other man's knees buckled and both crashed to the ground. Amidst their grappling and hitting blindly at each other, Edward started to howl like a wounded animal.

Jonathan was struck in the face by a lucky punch. It incensed him even more. At that moment, gentle, caring, genteel Jonathan did not care. Through the red fog of his rage, he vaguely realized that he was about to kill the man who likely held the key to Naunet's whereabouts—if she was still alive.

"Where is she!"

"I don't know." Edward spit the blood from his swollen lips. "I swear."

"Where is she!" The pressure of Jonathan's knees against Edward's ribs became unbearable. The prone man gasped for air. He would not last much longer with this raging kid straddling him, strangling him, surely about to kill him.

A rustle in the dense shrubbery was followed by a high-pitched squeal. It startled both men long enough for Jonathan to release his hold. Edward wriggled out from under his attacker and, like a startled sand crab, he scampered sideways on all fours seeking refuge in the low bushes growing out over the cliff. Jonathan jumped after him. He hauled the despised man from the clinging branches by the collar. Maddened by Edward's cowardice, he spun the man around and, grabbing at whatever he could, he ripped Edward's breast pocket clear off his soiled jacket. The strand of Golden South Sea pearls arced high over them before it fell back onto the dusty trail.

Grunting and gnashing its sharp incisors, the wild boar broke from its hiding place and snatched up the lustrous orbs that had been so fortuitously strewn before it.

Edward Guernsey-Crock's last howl rivaled that of the wind; unearthly and inhuman. Spiked by the pain of his loss, the deprived man pounced upon Jonathan. They both lost their balance and again crashed into the bushes that clung to the rocky cliff. Entwined, the men tumbled until their fall ripped them apart.

Jonathan's flailing hands grabbed a tenuous hold on a creeping cedar's exposed roots. He hung there, trying to catch his breath. His heart beat in his ears. Below him, something large thudded savagely against rock after rock. He did not look down.

A mere kilometer out of Loutro, the path widened with a rock wall rising steeply up onto the inland plateau. To Naunet's right, the cliff tumbled straight down toward the foaming surf. The small area appeared well trodden. Perhaps it was a favorite lookout for the women of the village waiting for their fishermen to return from the sea. Or perhaps it was a place where lovers found some treasured privacy.

Naunet had to catch her breath again, partly from exertion by the steep climb, partly from pulling the rattling contraption behind her. But mostly from the deep-seated terror that had not left her since Port Said. Not during waking hours, not in her sleep. She glanced back. There was no one pursuing her—yet. She saw the lifeboat, now near the harbor entrance. She was still not safe. She needed to reach Sfakia. But what if she ran into Edward in Sfakia? If she gave him the stolen treasure, would he let her live then? Hardly, she thought bitterly. He was a thief, and a liar. And an accomplice to murder. The man had no scruples. No conscience. And, she was sure now, no heart.

The brittle leaves of a gnarled tree that hugged the cliff rustled into life. Naunet stepped out onto a ledge. The turbulence rushing up with its stinging spray caught her off-guard.

Sand laden air tortured the sparse shrubbery in earnest now, and the sea had changed from its brilliant mid-day green to a dull slate-gray. It had taken but a moment for the strengthening wind to turn the Mediterranean's capricious wavelets into crushing breakers. A reddening sun intensified the sea's pungent aroma, mixing it with the scent of wild sage. Within moments, everything on the cliff struggled for survival against the onslaught of the malevolent Sirocco.

The fierce wind tore at Naunet's sanity magnifying her inner turmoil. She strained toward the precipice. Bending over the child's little wagon, she pulled the scarf from the plundered tablet with great tenderness. At once, the rapacious air caught the feather-light material and whipped it out over the cliff where it floated for a moment: A banner carried toward illusionary victory by an invisible standard bearer.

Her fingers caressed the ancient writing. Lovingly, she brushed a few kernels of sand from the gleaming surface. Then, so contrary to her passion and professional training to preserve ancient discoveries, she wrestled the heavy tablet off the little wagon. With some effort, she cart-wheeled it toward the steep overhang. Tears streamed down her wind-reddened cheeks. Ah, mortal passion, she cried deep within her heart. It was always passion that led toward the abyss. Just one last push.

For a brief moment, an errand ray from the darkening sun caught a hold of Ramose's last golden tablet before the roiling waters below swallowed it.

*

Naunet stares down, and starts to recite the real ancient prophecies. Calling them out to the Sirocco, she implores the fierce wind to sweep her condemned world free of the predicted woe.

Once again, a day shall come
when an incessant storm rages
over land and sea.
When Ma'at is breached,
and usually calm tempers flare,
and violent crimes are committed.
Behold, for it is then that all peoples
will vanish without a trace.
Burned by fires that spew from the mountains.
Buried by hot ashes that rain from the sky.
It was our fate. It will be yours.
Beware, for that day has come
when your eyes rest upon these words.

Uncaring, the Sirocco howls its siren song. Her arms stretched toward the leaden sky, Naunet no longer resists the wind's maddening lure. She longs to be free again. To be forgiven. Her exotic features turn translucent. She can see Princess Nefret beckon from the surf below. Convinced that she saved humanity from a cataclysmic end, Naunet prepares to take her own leap of faith. At last, her *Ba* was to find eternal peace. She closes her eyes as the *Sirocco* sinks its teeth into her very soul. Just one more step.

*

"Noooo! Naunet! No!"

The cry drummed against her ears, jumbled around in her head until, at last, it reached her heart.

"Oh, Jon!" Her low cry held immeasurable pity rather than relief. Balancing on her toes, perilously close to the edge of the cliff, she seemed transfixed on the handle of the little wagon pointing the way down to the crashing waves.

"Naunet, don't move, my love." It took all of Jonathan's self-control not to rush toward her; to pull her from there; to take her into his arms. "Please, darling, I need you to come toward me. Slowly. No! Don't look down!"

She took a small step away from the gaping precipice. Just then, a latent gust snatched at the entranced woman. When she swayed backwards, Jonathan could not bear it any longer. Just like the *Sirocco* had done before him, he rushed at her and tore at her; and then he claimed her.

The two of them became one as Naunet wrapped her arms around his neck and buried her head in his shoulder. Jonathan could hear her mumble something but he was unable to make out the words. Knowing that he had rescued her from certain death, he was afraid that he had not yet saved her from the emotional abyss of her suffering.

"Talk to me, my love," he whispered and gently stroked her hair.

At last, she lifted her face to him and he brushed her cheek with his lips.

"Oh, Jon." She managed a wan smile. "I must look like hell."

The wind ceased tearing at the shrubbery, and the little bird took up its song again.

*

The villagers could not have been more helpful. Jonathan and Naunet found themselves fêted as heroes having survived the *Sirocco*; and on the dangerous cliff path, no less. What the good people of Sfakia did not know was that there had been a casualty on that trail; but it was not of the storm's making. Jonathan was sure that the rocks and the waves would never tell; nor would he. Only Naunet asked, her voice still laced with fear, if he had met anyone going toward the village, and he told her, "I can honestly say that no one passed me. Let's leave it at that for now. You are safe. Here. You'll always be safe with me."

When the major of Sfakia told Dr. Leopold Klein that the bridal suite at the *taverna* was free for the lucky couple to use, the older man thanked Zeus—the only god he revered and believed to be the true deity of Crete. Instinctively, he knew that his daughter was safe now, and that she had at last found her true love; whether or not she knew it yet.

Naunet did know. The moment the door of the humble, misnamed room closed behind them, she knew she had always loved Jonathan. Why it had taken her so long to admit it, she could not say. Perhaps their love needed to ripen, like a delicious fruit. Now, though, it was time for that fruit to be consumed; to be savored and, above all, treasured.

Without a word, and without hesitation, Jonathan carried her to the narrow bed. His mouth caressed her cheeks, her eyelids, her ears. When he very gently placed his love into her, she knew that he would be there for her, always. After years of denial, Naunet opened up like a rosebud kissed by the sun—immediate, eager, without a question. If her first union with him might be taken as one of desperation and need rather than bliss and want, of gratitude and relief, rather than sensual attraction, it suddenly became clear how much she had always cherished her boyish colleague; how much she would love her man from now on. At this instant, the years of emotional and sexual emptiness simply melted away.

"My Nefertiti! I love you. I have always loved you. Let's go home."

Among all the whispered endearments, these last words enveloped her more securely than did his arms.

"Yes. Home," she sighed, and knew that it meant: with him.

Epilogue

A hot-boiling and revenge-bent Jabari El-Masri stares at Princess Nefret's mask smiling up at him so serenely from the display case. He almost wills the royal heiress to whisper her secrets to him.

But more so, the two missing Saqqara tablets still haunt his waking hours. Jabari's strong chin juts out more than usual. It has been months since the thieving Turk disappeared with them. And still, the art world—usually awash with rumors about new acquisitions, legitimate or otherwise—has not breathed a whisper of his golden tablets. The year is coming to an end and he is glad for it; it has not been good to him.

Deep in his soul, Jabari senses that some calamities might still be in store for him and for his country. As an archaeologist, he scoffs at the media-driven frenzy about the world's approaching end. The drivel people will believe. All those would-be survivalists spouting fire and brimstone, promising salvation with dried beans and bottled water. He shakes his head. No doubt, they are making plenty of money off the fearful and the gullible.

Over a lifetime of excavating ancient sites, he had stumbled upon some of the most inscrutable mysteries. In the end though, science did unlock most of them; except for those written on the golden tablets. He was certain that their message would be deciphered as well one day. At least, on all those waiting patiently where they now lay reburied in the sand. He smiles to himself. Until that time, El-Kharga would keep her secrets well.

Jabari knows he has to lull Egypt's new Islamic government into complacency about his new loyalty. To gain face with the outside world, they forgave his misguided attempt to save Egypt's national treasures. It was of course unfortunate they had to admit—after listening to his impassioned testimony—that he had failed.

Jabari never meant to omit that the Turk had stolen only two slates. They simply never asked. It was assumed that the *Sirocco* had sent Karakurt Tiryaki to the bottom of the sea with all the missing ill-begotten tablets.

The new regime had magnanimously asked Jabari to remain in Cairo. Foolishly, naively even, he had agreed. What he had not agreed to—although the choice was never his—was to be assigned this lowly position in the dusty storage rooms of *his* museum. The mockery! The insult! The travesty, to be stripped of his former influence and power! Humiliated and embittered, Jabari grinds his teeth. Still, it was better than rotting in a dank Egyptian jail. There was one benefit to his situation, though. With Karakurt gone, he was the only one who knew the full extent of the crated treasures in the museum's basement. To prove himself grateful for the new regime's clemency, he had offered to compile new inventory lists.

Jabari laughs derisively. *Just be patient*, he reminds himself again. It was not an easy trait for him. Only the thought of loyal friends waiting at el-Kharga for their *Pharaoh* restored his zeal to persevere.

"Those fools," he whispers to the golden death mask. "They'll never know. What do you make of that, my beautiful Nefret? When the time is ripe, will you then come with me as well?"

All throughout the Christian world, children ask, "Today?"

And their parents tell them, "No, not today. Tomorrow." Even though tomorrow is still a few days away, the answer satisfies the little ones, for that long-awaited day is to bring them toys, and sweets, and perhaps a new puppy.

In bustling Mexico City, no one pays heed to the sigh that floats up from Popocatepetl as it rumbles its distant triplet cousins Thera,

Sakros and Cape Riva awake in their Aegean cradle. But on Santorini, the cats leap from whitewashed perches to hide under hollow steps; and the wolves of Yellowstone stop tearing at their kill.

On the island of Crete, everyone jumps out of bed as soon as the ground begins to tremble. They know their legends well; of mountains collapsing and the sea lifting up, and how an ancient civilization vanished in the fires that rained down from the sky thousands of years before another cataclysm annihilated the Minoans.

But then, for one more night, Earth holds her breath. And only the very young ask again, "Is it tomorrow yet?"

At last, the tortured planet exhales. Tomorrow has become today.

About the Author

Ms. Borg lives in a diversified lake community in Arkansas, where she continues to write fiction.

* * *

If you enjoyed **SIROCCO**, you surely would enjoy Book 1 in the *Legends of the Winged Scarab* series, **KHAMSIN, The Devil Wind of The Nile**.

In the novella **Edward, Con Extraordinaire,** another connection with *SIROCCO* is evident as it tells of Edward's deceitful existence prior to his traveling to Cairo.

* * *

Khamsin, The Devil Wind of The Nile

(Book 1 – Legends of the Winged Scarab Series)

This is a sweeping saga of Ancient Egypt during Aha's reign, the Second King of the First Dynasty—3080 BC.

Ramose, The High Priest of Ptah, vies for control over his weak King as he exchanges mental lances with Ebu al-Saqqara, the vile Vizier.

In a sub-plot, it tells of ancient mats with a woven code found over five-thousand years ago. Ramose translated them and ordered that young falcon-eyed acolytes chisel them onto golden tablets.

*

Khamsin was selected **Editor's Choice** by the **Historical Novel Society** for its August 2012 Historical Novels Review:

> "Borg's narrative structure is as supple as it is strong.
> This is a big book in every way.
> Sprawling, ambitious and marvelously executed.
> It's enthusiastically recommended."

* * *

29289881R00143

Made in the USA
Lexington, KY
21 January 2014